# My Mother's
# SUMMER
# VACATIONS

## COLLEEN GAREAU

"Loved the truthful telling of family dynamics. So telling of the way many events are dealt with or not. reality at its best and worst."

"Great story."

"A beautifully written story of mothers, daughters, and sisters--the differences that cause questions and pain, and the similarities that let them endure and love each other."

"Heartwarming and sometimes heartbreaking, this was a wonderful story."

"… a really beautiful story and shows that while perhaps you can never go home, sometimes finding out the truth from the past, will indeed set you free."

"Well written and realistic. I enjoyed this book a lot!"

"I felt Angel's teenage mortification more than once and have to admit I did almost snort with laughter when reading some of her journal entries. Very well written story."

"A well crafted, excellent read."

"The characters were all very well crafted…"

"I totally did not see the ending coming and the ending was one of the best that I have read in quite a while."

"If I could give it more than five stars I definitely would do so."

To Heidi and Liam
with love

# CHAPTER ONE

I lay with my eyes closed waiting for Matt's breath to deepen and slow. When it did and he rolled away from me, I slid off the edge of the mattress, grabbing my glasses from the nightstand and my T-shirt from the floor.

Easing the bedroom door shut behind me. I slipped to the living room where I stood looking out into the city's almost-dark. The streetlights hid the stars and painted squares of light through the room's windows onto the dark wood floor. Wishing for a cigarette, I found a glass of stale water left on an end table and sipped it instead. I tried to think of nothing at all.

There was little to see from my walk-up apartment, located as it was among a neighbourhood of equally squat, ancient, brown, brick buildings. The painted trim and wrought-iron numbers on the front doors were the only things that differentiated one from another. Still, it was a good street lined with old maples and oaks, branches lopped at odd angles to accommodate electrical lines. Through the foliage, I glimpsed parked cars, their owners probably tucked away in bedrooms similar to mine. Across the street, paned windows reflected my emptiness back to me.

I felt sick with myself and shuddered as spit watered the back of my throat. Someone walked over my grave Gran would say. I steeled myself to endure another sleepless night, waiting for the daylight hour when he would leave and I would take my turn at sleep. Waiting took its toll on me yet I could neither kick him out nor sleep next to him or any of the hims I brought home for a few hours of fake intimacy.

My substantial library saw me through similar nights and I selected a volume on British history to occupy me. I settled myself on my favourite reading chair with a blanket to ward off the chill of the air conditioning, my feet raised on a hand-embroidered ottoman—an inheritance from a great-grandmother I'd never met. I must have fallen into a heavy sleep because when the phone shattered the quiet like a chain saw revving on a Sunday morning, it sent shock waves into my sluggish brain.

My head jerked and my glasses, askew on my face, fell to the floor. It was like my consciousness split in two: one half waking and trying its best to alert the slumbering half that it was needed on duty. Aching for rest, I pulled myself out of a gummy sleep while grasping at what thoughts I could to help me function.

Wake up.

It's the phone.

Answer the phone.

Yes, grab it.

Now push the talk button.

No, the other button.

Who is it?

Check call display.

Don't have my eyes in.

Doesn't matter.

Answer the damn phone!

I cleared my dry, gravelly throat. "Hello?"

"Kate? Are you awake?"

My mother.

"Of course I'm awake. You've woken me. What is it?"

"Jane called. Gran's dying; she wants us with her."

You'd think as a journalist my mother would be better equipped than most to provide a softer introduction to this cruel statement. But not my mother, at least not with me.

Antagonism and fear brought me to my feet and sparring with her became more important than her sad news.

"Celeste, you mean. Of course I'll go."

There was an icy pause as I knew there would be. I took advantage of her silence to get my thoughts in order.

Referring to my grandmother by her first name rankled Mother, although it pleased Gran to no end. Names were important in my family for reasons I'd never fully understood. Since locating and lobbing verbal grenades at each other was a long-standing tradition between my mother and me, however, I couldn't help but take aim. I pictured Mother's skinny, bloodless lips pinched tight, fine age lines radiating from them in a halo of disapproval. Her arms would be pulled in close to her soft, middle-aged body, her right hand playing with the collar of her invariable night-time uniform: white, or pale-blue, cotton pyjamas.

"We don't have time for this now," she said. "I'll be there in an hour."

"I'd rather take the train." Pick, pick, pick.

Exasperation crept into her voice. "The train doesn't leave till after supper and it's a twenty-three hour trip."

"Let's fly then."

"Are you insane? Ticket prices for last-minute flights are exorbitant. I don't have that kind of money. I'll drive. We'll be there in fourteen hours."

"It's not like you have to pay for me." I might be a waitress, a job she hated to see me in, but I'd been at it since I left home at 17 and earned more than she did, a fact she knew, though ignored, very well.

She didn't answer and, in the silence that followed, my desire to fight evaporated and I became too sad and ashamed with myself to argue. Why did I have to fight with her? I was glad she couldn't see my burning face and wondered what I would do without my Gran to smooth things between us.

"Nevermind. We can drive. I'll be ready when you get here."

I slumped back into the chair then began a hunt on the floor for my glasses so I could see the time. Three o'clock. I'd been sleeping for almost an hour.

In the bedroom, I turned on a lamp and Matt rolled onto his back, his long, dark lashes contrasting against the pale of his cheek.

He was such a sweet guy—but now the attraction was gone and I wanted him out of here. What was I going to do with him?

I'd leave him a note. Surely, he could be trusted to lock up.

I packed, then left a voicemail message for my boss. My shifts at the restaurant were prime; they'd be easy to fill.

There was plenty of time left for me to pick up a coffee from the all-night place at the corner of my street. I ordered a large black for me, one for Mother—skim milk, no sweetener—and half-a-dozen donuts. I wasn't sure if she'd need carbohydrates and caffeine to get through the morning. I knew I would.

Sitting on the curb outside my apartment, I blew on my too hot coffee and waited for her, listening to the quiet of an early city morning. If I leaned forward just so, I could see the outline of a corner column of the district court building a few steps away from city hall.

My eyes burned. My contact lenses were suction-gripped to my eyes and I wished I'd kept my glasses on—such vanity for a drive with my mother. At the least, I wished I had my saline drops, but they were packed away with my toiletries and it would take too much effort to dig for them.

Pigeons cooed, their sounds of comfort floating down from their resting places in the eaves. A few fluttered to the ground to march around in that funny, bobbing way of theirs, checking to see if I had brought breakfast. I broke a donut into small pieces and tossed them behind me onto the sidewalk. A male, uninterested in food, raced toward a smaller female. Hey. There you are! His neck stretched up then snapped down in amorous exhilaration, his chest swelled, dwarfing his head, and he spun around her, twirling in a manic waltz on tiny, red feet though she turned away in an attempt to ignore him. C'mon, baby. I'll make you happy, I promise. He continued his display until the smaller bird looked almost—could it be?—annoyed, the attention given her most unwelcome. Leave me alone, fool. Can't you see I'm eating? As his whirling closed in on her, she scurried away, deking in and out between other birds. Get away from me you lunatic. But her suitor pursued her down the street. Like the males of many species, he must have learned persistence is often required to win a female heart. I love you, baby. I'll always love you.

The pursuit of love. I had given this up long ago in favour of the pursuit of lust. Not so messy, much easier. By puberty, I had love figured as a fairytale. If the lessons of my parents were anything to judge by, life lived practically was less painful. My father flew the coop right after I was born. Maybe he could sense my future inadequacies and decided he wanted no part of them or of me. I'd never heard from him, not once in twenty-six years. And my mother? From early memory, she had been obsessed about her job like a sports fanatic to her team or an evangelical Christian to writing cheques. "Just a minute, Katie." "As soon as I'm finished, Katie." "Oh, for goodness sake, Katie, can't you find something to do until I get this done?" So, I stopped asking for the thing I couldn't have—her attention.

And, frankly, things turned out far better for me than they do for most women. I've never moped around waiting for some guy to call, getting confused between love and sex. I'd chosen the driver's seat and I liked it there.

The feathered vaudevillian couple were halfway down the block when Mother's green Camry pulled to a stop in front of me and dragged my attention to the wakening street. A delivery truck drove by, its tires loud on the damp pavement, the sound of packing tape peeling from a gun. Voices from the bakery a block away could be heard in the absence of Ottawa traffic.

When I stood, my backside was damp and cold from sitting on the curb, a contrast to the already warm air that promised another muggy day.

Mother was five minutes early, her surprise at my readiness apparent on her face still pale and puffy from sleep. Her appreciation for the coffee grated on my nerves. Like I couldn't be relied on for thoughtfulness or punctuality. I stowed my bag in the trunk and hunkered down into the passenger seat, slipped my headphones over my ears and closed my eyes. After receiving nothing more than my mumbled responses to her inane stabs at conversation, she gave up and we travelled in silence. In short order, I fell asleep to the sounds of Coldplay, waking as Mother came to a stop at a rest station just past Maisonneuve.

"Glad we got through Montreal before rush hour," she said with a satisfied smile as she unfastened her seatbelt. "Do you need to go?"

I'm not five, I wanted to snap. Instead, I nodded and followed her to the ladies' room.

With another coffee to sustain me, I pulled the next driving shift that saw us reach our halfway point by eight. Mother wouldn't sleep though; she couldn't when someone else was behind the wheel. Yet more evidence of her need to control.

We stopped for breakfast and she called to get an update on Gran's condition.

"Jane says she's rallied. Quite lucid. Talking up a storm and glad we're coming." After a pause, "Aunt Harmony's there already, of course." Displeasure oozed from every word as she turned the key in the ignition.

I couldn't stop the grin spreading over my face any more than my mother could help the grimace spreading over hers at the mention of her younger sister: Harmony, the free spirit, the dancer.

The screw-up, my mother would say.

When I was little, I dreamed Harmony was my mom. She'd had the tiniest apartment in New York City—three words that will forever excite me. It was one of those walk-ups in a rundown neighbourhood that I thought was the height of chic. I'd follow her everywhere, sitting backstage at night—plus afternoons for matinees—to watch her perform, thinking she was most beautiful human being I'd ever seen. After the show, we'd eat out with her friends from the chorus line, opting for dimly lit restaurants offering foods unfamiliar and foreign to me. The dancers would talk and drink and sparkle. Their ringed fingers fluttered around them, punctuating their speech, their voices tinkling in the warm air and rippling across my skin. Fairy people, I'd thought. I could barely eat for watching them, afraid they'd disappear before I'd had enough. When I got a little older, they'd pour me wine and I'd pretend to drink it, feeling the magic of inclusion.

Aunt Harmony would stroke my face with her long fingers and smile into me. We'd walk home, arm-in-arm, singing show songs and racing each other to the next corner. Then we'd cuddle up in a bed festooned with sarongs and she'd throw cushions that glittered with beads and pieces of cut mirror onto the floor to make room for me.

"Can I live with you?" I'd once whispered.

"I'm not your best bet, kiddo," she'd replied with a sardonic grin and I knew she would remain beyond my reach.

Had she let me stay in her world, I would have sat at her feet, a little lapdog for her to command. There must have been some mix-up with the stork, I'd often thought. I'd been sent to the wrong mother.

Before parting, she'd hug me and say, "Don't ever change, my sweet girl."

I'd try to stay the same for her, but, of course, couldn't and now was only able to grasp my younger self through the cloudy window of half-forgotten memories and old photographs.

Yes, I had changed.

My train of thought was interrupted when Mother stopped for gas. I got out of the car to stretch my legs.

"Can I drive now?" I asked her.

"Forget it. We'll never get there. You can pay for the fill-up though."

If it wasn't her, I would have laughed. Jesus. She was so anal about driving.

We finished our business and my thoughts turned to the landscape before me. I hated New Brunswick leg of the journey. An unending stretch of road that, with each travelling, seemed to stretch even farther than the trip before. On this journey, my lack of sleep had caught up with me making the afternoon a misery. The excess of coffee I'd been sipping throughout the day had set my nerves on edge and wrung the contents of my stomach into an acid drip. The highway offered little in terms of a view, the French blue-collar towns of the north giving way to the more affluent, English towns in the south. The one advantage to travel in this part of the country was the newly paved highway, a treat after the potholes of Ontario and Quebec. Mother used this to advantage as she barrelled down the TransCanada at one hundred and forty kilometres an hour while I prayed we wouldn't be picked up by police radar.

In the late afternoon, we crossed the border to Nova Scotia, the tiny province that strained against the narrow ribbon of land that bound it to Canada as it leaned into the Atlantic, much as I pulled away from my mother. She and I had been so long at odds and angles with each other it seemed our differences must have been foreordained during some ancient stone age, perhaps about the time the province was being formed. I felt a great kinship with this place.

We reached the tollbooth on Highway 104 and paid our four dollars for the privilege of travelling the bone-jarring, often-patched roads that were the source a many tall tales among the locals. We began watching for the sign that would point out the lone exit for Halifax. Having one turn-off for a capital city might be ill-considered to some, but roads and signage, I had long ago learned, weren't among Nova Scotia's strengths. Vigilance and a good map were vital to arriving at your desired destination successfully.

Just after eight o'clock, we came to in the little village at the top of St. Margaret's Bay. Minutes later, I spotted the pair of massive mugo pines standing sentry over Gran and Jane's driveway. My heart leaped at the sight of the century-old home. The cedar-shake, two-storey had aged to a deep grey and showed off the cream and blue trim to advantage. The tension eased from my shoulders as we rolled along under the ancient, arching branches of the maples. The yard was lush and spotted with perennials: bleeding heart, forsythia, dogwood, and euonymus shrubs. I rolled down the window to smell the salt from the bay, feeling the fog mist my skin as it reached me.

I hopped from the car before Mother brought it to a full stop.

"Kate, the bags," she called after me, but I ignored her. Invigorated by my returning blood circulation, I bounced up the front steps and crossed the sun porch, entering the house without knocking.

Inside, a small foyer was flanked by a living room to the left and an oversized country kitchen to the right. Straight ahead was the staircase to the second floor. I turned toward the living room.

My knees locked as my gaze hit the hospital bed and the medical paraphernalia set up there. Jane had been right, Gran wasn't doing well. She was hooked up to oxygen and had traded her ruddy complexion for one the shade of putty. Even her silver hair had fled, leaving her with colourless, chick-like down sprouting in soft tufts around her head. Still, she was sitting and she smiled when she saw me.

I ran to her. "Celeste!"

Holding out her arms for a hug, she whispered, "Kate, my dear Kate, you've come. Give me a hug. Where's your mother?"

I rolled my eyes. "She's bringing in the bags, insisting they come in right away."

"Oh, that's her all over." Gran started to laugh, but phlegm caught in her throat and she gagged. I handed her tissues to spit in.

"Kate. I didn't know you'd arrived," Jane said as she rushed to my side, hugging me to her with a ferocity she'd never shown. This has been hard on her, I realized and held on to the big-boned woman who had been Gran's lover and companion since before I was born. I inhaled, she smelled so good. Fresh linens and citrus soap and something spicy from the kitchen all mingled together in her copper skin.

"We've missed you, little girl."

Her words hung in the air as Mother entered, struggling with my bag and two of her own.

I felt guilty watching her labour. "Why didn't you wait? I would have gone back to get them."

"Because now they're in." Mother walked past Jane with a stiff nod and gave her mother an even stiffer hug. "How are you, Mom?"

"Oh, Mom, always Mom. You're so conventional, my girl, but I'm glad you're here." Gran's voice slipped to a near whisper. She was tired and the lines in Jane's forehead deepened with concern.

She turned to my mother and me. "Have you eaten? I've held off supper."

"Where's Harmony?" Mother asked.

"Gone for a walk along the shore. Don't imagine she'll be long. We didn't think you'd get here for at least another hour."

"You know Mother's driving," I said. "The one and only time she lets go is when it's most likely to kill us."

It was true. The woman drove with a heavy foot and we'd made the sixteen-hour trip in the fourteen she'd promised. With music playing in the background, she was silent and single-minded on the road, anticipating other drivers' moves with an elegant intuition. Whatever her demons, she wrestled and beat them over the gas pedal.

Mother shrugged. "I'm a good driver."

"That you are, Angel," Celeste said. "Now give me another hug then go get something to eat. You know Jane won't be satisfied till she feeds you and I need to rest."

At the mention of Gran's partner, Mother frowned. Her already-rigid posture drew in upon itself until she stood rocklike, a soldier coming to attention.

Long ago, she had told me, "You don't know what it was like to have your mother announce she was a lesbian. That last year of high school was the worst of my life. People didn't understand like they do now."

"It was so long ago. Can't you just get over it?"

But she couldn't. I had long wondered if there was more to the story than I knew for her to have held on to her discomfort with Jane for so long.

Harmony barged through the door from the side porch as we brought dishes filled with Jane's fishcakes and sweet potato fries to the table. My mouth watered as the smell of her food reached me.

"You're here!" Harmony squealed and held me at arm's length as was her habit, looking me over for signs of change or deterioration. "She looks like me, don't you think?" she asked for what must have been the hundredth time then gave me a kiss and whirled away to take her seat.

It was easy to bask in the spotlight of her attentions when they were on me. She could be vibrant and tonight was full of stories of her students at the dance academy she had opened following a career-ending injury. Even Mother was laughing as Aunt Harmony impersonated one of her stage mothers describing the custom-made dance shoes required by her daughter to protect her "artistically delicate feet."

"That's what she said. Can you imagine? Artistically delicate, my ass. Does that even mean anything? More money than brains, that one. But, what the hell, she pays on time and her little darling isn't too hard to handle."

Aunt Harmony's eyes twinkled in delight. She hiccuped then giggled, her eyes sliding to an already-emptied bottle of Chablis on the kitchen counter. Her tipsiness aside, I was as enchanted as I had forever been with her. Like a sponge, I sucked in her high spirits hoping her glow would be big enough to encircle me. I knew to grab it when I could, having felt the sting of her mercurial nature in times past.

We kept an eye on Gran through a wide passageway between the rooms, but she slept on, and the evening took on the patina of something special. The four of us sat in the large kitchen eating Jane's spectacular meal and sharing impersonal anecdotes, the only ones that are safe to tell given the landmines of family history. A breeze blew in from the bay, and the smell of sea and the dampness of fog hung in the air, a welcome change from the heavy heat we had escaped that morning. My bare skin drank in the wet.

Mother seemed to be enjoying herself and, as sometimes happens when rowing siblings merge for a moment or two, she and Aunt Harmony bridged to sharing reminisces, building on their legends and sharing the stories that only the two of them knew as they did.

How alone the survivor would be when the first died despite their years of locked horns and heavy silences. To lose the only witness to the events of one's life would be a loss unlike any other. The memory bond of siblings could recall the past with a single word or meaningful look.

The faintest whiff of sulphur slipped by, the smell of skunk tickling an old memory.

"Remember that time we went camping?" Mother asked and Aunt Harmony choked, nearly losing a mouthful of wine through her nose. Droplets splattered from her mouth onto her white shirt.

We chuckled as my aunt mopped at her chest with paper towel.

"That awful smell," Mother added.

"And Celeste with her we-must-honour-all-creatures shtick."

"Until the skunk got us."

"Oh my god, that was so bad. Kate, you should hear this."

So they told me the story I had heard at least once a year my whole life. They told their polished routine like it was new, and Jane and I laughed at them laughing.

"Celeste had some new scheme every summer," Harmony began.

"Oh, what do you know? You missed most of them."

"That's because I'm younger than you and always will be," she smiled, choosing this one time not to take offence. "Anyway, that summer, Celeste agreed with our dad that we could go camping and we were thrilled."

"I was beyond delighted having been dragged off to every cockamamie excuse for a summer vacation Mom could think up from the time I could walk." Mother raised her wineglass in a self-congratulatory toast.

"We figured it'd be great. We'd have a lake to swim in and we could explore the woods. See some cute little animals, that sort of thing."

"Something normal. Like other kids."

"And your grandfather Denham was so happy."

"Because Mom wasn't relegating him to staying home and watching you. Wonder why he ever agreed to that."

"Because he loved having me to himself."

"It was to keep her happy," Mother motioned with her chin toward the living room where Gran slept.

"Anyway, Miss Wet Blanket, we drove from our house in Ottawa to Harrington Lake in Quebec. I was so anxious to get there, the drive seemed to take forever."

"We took the ferry in Wakefield."

"Would you quit interrupting me?" Aunt Harmony wasn't angry, she was enjoying herself. "Neither Denham nor Celeste had much experience in the great outdoors."

"Everything was such a chore. Building a campfire, keeping the tent dry when it rained. Cooking. Remember when Dad tried to build a latrine?"

"And it rained and overflowed?"

"He'd dug a too-shallow hole away from the tent, but on sloping ground so when it rained there was a definite stream of sewage flowing down the hill," my mother frowned with mock exaggeration.

"Ewww," we chorused on cue, just like we'd done for years.

"So, as I was saying," Aunt Harmony looked at mother pointedly. "They didn't know anything about keeping food away from the sleeping area and in tightly-sealed containers. One night, we made popcorn over the fire."

"One of those Jiffy-Pop contraptions. Burned most of it."

"We'd thrown the mess into the trees and the smell must have attracted a skunk. Not long after we fell asleep, Celeste woke us up, jabbing at Denham. She sounded terrified. She could hear something in the tent with us, its claws scratching on the canvas wall that separated the sleeping compartment from the storage area. Sure enough, as soon as Denham opened the zipper to find out what or who was with us, the little bastard sprayed. Oh, god, it was awful. I thought I'd die."

"It burned like you wouldn't believe. It was quite frightening, actually."

"We were all screaming and trying to get out of our sleeping bags to get some air."

"I thought I was going blind. You have no idea what an awful experience getting sprayed by a skunk is. We washed and washed in the lake until we were raw and still we couldn't get rid of the stench. The brand new tent and our sleeping bags were ruined. Mom threw out everything. We even had to buy new clothes. We couldn't even sit in the car till we coated the interior with plastic garbage bags to make sure our smell didn't soak through the seats. We never went camping again, but we could smell sulphur in the car for months afterward."

The sisters were laughing, tears pouring down their faces. Aunt Harmony turned to me. "And on the drive home, after this horrible and expensive ordeal, this one," she said hooking her thumb in Mother's direction, "says: 'Celeste, are skunks one of the creatures we should love and honour?' And Denham, who's driving, says, 'Not now, Angel. Just not now' in that Jesus-don't-get-your-mother-started way of his."

It was great to see Mother laugh and carry on. Forgetting for a few minutes her self-inflicted role as family straight-guy.

Aunt Harmony reached for another bottle of wine.

Mother sobered instantly and grabbed the corkscrew. "Maybe this isn't the best time to overindulge."

"To enjoy myself, you mean?" Aunt Harmony's voice was sharp.

"This isn't a party."

"When is it ever a party when you're around?"

"Oh, right. Well, by all means, don't let Mom's condition make you act like an adult for once in your life." She tossed the opener onto the table. "Drink up."

"Mother –"

"Never mind," Aunt Harmony interrupted. She grabbed the corkscrew, the bottle, and her glass and stomped outside where we heard the clatter of a lawn chair and her curse as she stumbled into it.

We had managed to get along for a whole ninety minutes.

The three of us who remained, cleared the table and washed up in silence. Jane switched on the radio to cover the emptiness. I was angry with Mother, but too tired to say anything. Why couldn't she ever let things be? We'd been having such a good time until she decided to criticize.

As we finished our chores, the night-duty nurse arrived with a bag of knitting to keep her busy while she sat beside Gran till morning. It was then that exhaustion hit for real and Mother and I dragged our tired selves up the stairs to bed though it was still early—at least by my standards.

"Wall or window?" I asked as we undressed.

"Window," she said, pulling the top half of her crisp blue cotton pyjama set over her head. "Mind if I read?"

"I've brought a book too."

We completed our routines, plumping pillows and angling reading lights to our individual preferences. I pulled the covers to my chest and looked over at Mother. She was fast asleep, her novel resting on her chest, her mouth open ever so slightly. Slumber must have been instantaneous. I don't think she'd had time to read a single sentence. I slid out of bed and crept around to her side, placed her book on the nightstand and, before turning off her light, studied her. She was pretty and looked younger in this light. The severity of her features had softened; the worry lines across her forehead and at the corners of her mouth were hardly apparent. She looked serene, happy even.

I felt the urge to curl up beside her and rest my head on her shoulder. Something I hadn't felt in many years. I turned off both lights, returned to bed, and let my hand drift across the mattress until my little finger touched hers.

The wind had picked up outside and, like flipping a switch, rain fell hard against the house. When I was little, I had been terrified by thunderstorms. The booming sound and the evil jagged peaks of lightning filled me with fear. Caught alone when it struck, I would be paralyzed, screaming for rescue. Mother would come to me then, gathering me in her arms and telling me stories about animals bowling in heaven, eventually convincing me to cheer for a strike. If a storm began at night, I'd dash to her room and launch myself into her bed where she'd let me stay safe and warm beside her. Nothing wicked could happen with her there. Eventually, I looked forward to storms, having discovered my fear as the key to her affection.

# CHAPTER TWO

I admit I'm not the sunniest person when I wake up. About all I can muster before noon is coffee, a croissant, and a superficial look over the day's news, perhaps a little channel surfing. It's been difficult for me, as a night worker, to rise to an alarm or lift my head off the pillow at the same time as the nine-to-five set. Scintillating conversation does not roll from my lips before I've investigated my day and determined how it might play out.

One of the benefits of living alone is rarely having to engage with anyone before I'm ready. While I like to think of myself as quiet rather than tetchy, friends who have had the misfortune to cross my path in the early hours have informed me otherwise. To them, my attitude seems even worse now that I've quit smoking. In their minds, my need to lunge for a cigarette to accompany that first hit of caffeine gave me some leeway on the surliness scale that isn't allowed me as a newly confirmed non-smoker. Like not having a smoke means I don't have the craving. It's the curse of being surrounded by those who've never had the habit.

And so, it was with great relief that I found myself alone in bed when I woke.

I lay there, looking around the room, fighting the urge, just like I did every morning. The old bedside clock told me it was lunchtime as I breathed in the damp air from the open windows and listened as the gulls called out in their perpetual search for food. Waves rolled gently to the shore. The faint chugging of a fishing boat was carried to me on the breeze. I strained to hear sounds beyond the thick bedroom door to figure out who was doing what inside the house. It seemed unnaturally quiet and my curiosity got the best of me, propelling me downstairs.

Peeking into the front room, I saw Gran sleeping and Jane sitting next to the hospital bed, the sunlight from the front windows spilling over her quillwork laid out on a small wooden table. Piles of quills in crimson, robin-egg blue, yellow and ebony lay next to a piece of tanned deer hide. She smiled when she saw me and removed the barb-less quills from between her lips where they softened in her saliva.

"Where is everyone?"

"Your mom's at the beach. Harmony's gone to get groceries for supper," she said. "Coffee's made. I put on a fresh pot not too long ago."

"Mother's out?" She had been in such a rush to get here and now she was lounging at the beach.

"She relieved the nurse at seven. I could hear her talking to Celeste, but couldn't make out what they were saying. When I got down here, she looked pretty upset. Said she needed to be alone for a bit."

So, it had begun already. Great. Just great. Even her mother's poor health couldn't thaw Mother's unwavering heartlessness.

I closed my eyes, letting anger wash over me. "She's so selfish."

"You're too hard on her."

"Me?" Was she kidding? I gave Mother nothing she didn't deserve.

"Daughters and mothers. Never easy, eh? Go get yourself a coffee and come sit with me."

I did as I was told and scanned the current issue of Macleans, while I watched Jane's nimble fingers fly, stitching the coloured quills into place.

Gran stirred and opened her eyes.

"Thirsty?" Jane asked. She raised the head of the bed and held a tumbler half-filled with apple juice close to Gran.

After a moment, Gran pulled her mouth from the bendy straw and relaxed against her pillow.

"Morning." I kissed her soft skin.

"How's my girl?" She tried clearing her throat, but her voice was little more than a wisp of air and her breathing was laboured. Had she sounded this bad last night? Is it possible I wouldn't have noticed if she had?

"Just got up. How are you?"

Gran smiled then turned to watch Jane who had resumed her work. "Look at her go. She's something, isn't she?"

"Oh, Gr— Celeste, so are you." I wanted to weep seeing her lie there. She looked so much more fragile today.

"That's my girl," she said, patting my hand.

I bent at an awkward angle and rested my head near her chin, her scrawny collarbone hard against my ear. Where had her padding gone? She stroked my hair twice with quivering fingertips before her arm fell beside her.

"Are you hungry?" I asked.

"Some."

"There's broth in the fridge you can warm," Jane mumbled through occupied lips.

I heated the bouillon then spread a tea towel over Gran's chest to catch the dribbles and chatted about my work while I fed her. By the time the bowl was empty, my stomach was growling.

"You should have been a chef," I told Jane. "You'd be rich and famous with your own swanky restaurant where all the bigwigs would go to eat."

"I never wanted to be rich and famous," she said through the quills. "I'm content with this."

I knew she meant being with Gran. They were the happiest couple I'd ever met—Gran loud and disorganized, Jane supplying ballast with her serenity.

Jane was in her late fifties, two decades younger than Gran and only a few years older than my mother. She taught courses in Mi' kmaq history and culture at two high schools: one up the road in Tantallon, the other a half-hour away in Halifax, as well as a course in quill work at the Nova Scotia College of Art and Design.

"We have to keep our culture alive," she'd told me. "To stand strong in who we are."

Just then, the front door banged shut and Aunt Harmony walked in clutching bags of food. "You're up." Her tone was less jovial than it had been the previous night. Hung-over, I suspected.

"Here, I'll put those away," I said taking the load from her arms.

She nodded her thanks, and slumped into a chair, her sunglasses remained in place.

"What's for supper?" I asked.

"Salmon with Jane's chili rub."

At the mention of food, my stomach growled louder and I rummaged in the pantry, returning with onion bagels.

As I pulled one out of its bag, Aunt Harmony groaned. "Ugh, that smells. How can you eat something so gross this early in the day?"

A grin spread across my face. When I looked at her squinting eyes behind her shades, I couldn't keep from laughing. My aunt, another night person.

"You should eat," I told her.

"You could make her a milk shake," Jane said as she entered the room. "Best medicine for what ails her."

"Lovely carbohydrates," Aunt Harmony purred.

I munched my toasted bagel as I loaded ice cream and strawberries into the vintage blender.

"Duck!" I warned as I hit the speed button.

Aunt Harmony's hands flew to cover her ears at the roar of the machine and she escaped the noise to the sounds of our laughter. "You're evil," she mouthed as she retreated upstairs to her childhood bedroom.

In that moment, I felt such affection for her. I adored her frailties. To me, her warts were more like badges of honour than things to be ashamed of. Aunt Harmony had lived.

"C'mon down, ya big baby," I called from the foot of the stairs. "I'm finished making noise." On my way back to the kitchen, I peeked in at Gran. She was sleeping again. I heard the sound of a car pull into the driveway. Mother had returned.

I glared at her over my last bit of bagel. Where in the hell have you been?

She paid my scowl no mind and set about gathering the items for a sandwich.

"Getting warm out there," she said to no one in particular.

"Weather's been good this year," Jane said, assembling her spices for the chili rub. "There's coleslaw to go with that sandwich, if you want."

"Thanks," Mother's arms were piled with tomatoes, cheese, salad dressing, and fresh buns, but she managed to scoop up the container of slaw before nudging the fridge door closed with her hip.

"Want one?" she asked Jane.

"Sure. Thanks."

God, the woman had been home just minutes and we were all acting like we had broomsticks up our arses.

Aunt Harmony returned and sat at the kitchen table sucking on the shake that she held up to me in mock salute. "Thanks, kid. You're a life saver."

Jane slid two ibuprofen toward her as she took her seat at the head of the table. "Anyone have plans today?"

I shrugged. "I don't. How about you, Mother? Going to disappear again?"

"That's enough, Kate."

"No, it's not. What were you doing, taking off on Celeste? I thought we were here to be with her."

"I did spend time with her. While you were sleeping. And I don't have to justify myself to you."

"Oh, no. Of course not. Why would you have to explain anything to me? I'm just your daughter, right?" My outburst surprised even me. I was being childish, an emotion my mother evoked in me, and the words escaped before I could stop them.

"Don't think you know everything."

"Everything? How about anything? Why don't you tell me what's up your ass about Celeste before it's too late to make a difference."

"This is neither the time nor the place …"

"This is exactly the time and place. If not now, when?" My voice climbed an octave and though inwardly I cringed, I was unable to stop my tirade. "What is it between you and her?"

Jane reached over and patted my arm as Mother spun around to face me, her knife clattering onto the tile counter.

"That's enough! How dare you yell at me about things you know nothing about. She is my mother, not yours, and you can butt out."

We froze, staring at each other.

Aunt Harmony curled one long finger around the frame of her sunglasses and slid them halfway down her nose. "Would the two of you please shut up?" she deadpanned.

My face burned red and I stared down at my plate feeling every bit the fool I knew I was acting. Gran was sleeping in the next room and here I was bawling out my mother because she had been gone for all of a few hours. "I'll head outside for a while."

Aunt Harmony followed me out the door. "Do you ever think you could cut the woman some slack? I know she's a pain in the ass, but she means well even if you can't see it." She left me with her sharp rebuke, and returned inside as I stared at the place where she had been. This day wasn't going as I'd imagined. Even my aunt was angry with me now.

It seemed the only one who could get along with us was the one person in the house who was not a blood relative.

What was wrong with the women in our family?

# CHAPTER THREE

"I don't remember much about the Great Depression," Gran began, the wet gurgle in the back of her throat constricting and sucking at air. She spit into a tissue. "But I do remember the War—the one we thought was going to make the world a better place."

Mother, Aunt Harmony, and I took turns keeping Gran company each morning after the nurse left so Jane could have a few hours to do as she pleased and not be responsible for anyone's care but her own. It was my day to be up early—a difficult mission for me—and I was glad that nothing was required other than to sit and listen to one of Gran's tales.

She was sitting up and I could tell by the sparkle in her eyes that she was feeling feisty despite her difficulties breathing. The fatigue of the previous day had passed and she wasn't the type to let lack of oxygen get in the way of a story she wanted to tell. Still, her voice was low and I had to lean in to hear her though Jane seemed to have no trouble making her out and nodded as Gran spoke.

"I've never talked much about my family, but you should know where you've come from." She drew in as deep a breath as she was able. "My family had been luckier than most during the dark years before the War. Dad was a handyman. Carpentry, plumbing, electrical, you name it he could do it. When my parents became engaged, my grandfather gave Dad a piece of land and helped him build a house on it. All that sweat equity meant that my parents didn't owe anybody a thing for it. That's what saved them. Having no mortgage. Whatever Dad could bring in was enough for them to get by. Plus, they had the good sense to stop after one child—"

"That's because you were such a handful. They couldn't manage more," Jane teased.

"Oh, what do you know? I was a sweet-tempered girl."

Jane arched an eyebrow in disbelief and Gran cackled in delight.

"Maybe not so much as I got older. But whatever the reason, they had only me and managed to get by. A few years after the Second World War came, Daddy signed up. There was a shortage of soldiers and a call had gone out for men to enlist. I guess he couldn't stay out of it with all his friends going. That day, I remember clearly though I was only about five at the time. He came home and, over dinner, announced what he'd done. Mother was so upset that he would have done such a thing without talking to her first, she cried all through the meal.

"After I went to bed, I heard them argue. Really argue. It scared the bejezus out of me, I can tell you. I'd never heard them fight before. Mother was still crying when I fell asleep and the next morning she looked like hell, her face all bloated and pale like the blood had run right out of her.

"Turned out, she worried for nothing. The Army needed men with Dad's skills to build and maintain barracks and equipment for staff and recruits. He was stationed in Quebec and never actually left Canadian soil. Mother fretted all the while he was gone though, but she did it silently and alone. Other husbands were at war and dying after all, she had only to live with the threat that hers might be shipped off to be killed overseas. There was shame in that too. Like my parents hadn't sacrificed in the way other families had. Mother could never forgive him his betrayal of signing up without her approval or the shame of his safe posting—an oddly conflicting position for her to find herself in, I'm sure."

Gran's voice sounded like a rasp on metal and I handed her some juice. She looked up at me, "What I wouldn't give for a cigarette."

"Isn't that what got you here in the first place?"

"Lord, yes, they're sinful things. But I still want one."

"I know what you mean."

"I'm glad you quit, dear."

Gran closed her eyes and rested for a few minutes before resuming her story.

"I remember when Dad came home." She took a breath and a veil cloaked her eyes. "I wore my white sailor dress with red and blue piping along the collar and hem, and frilly, white socks inside my black patent shoes, the ones I wore to church and on special occasions. We waited at the train station for him along with hundreds of other wives and children. I was so scared, afraid that he wouldn't know me or that we'd get lost and not be able to find him. I was getting shoved around as the crowd moved and Mother held my hand so tightly it hurt. The train came in, but I couldn't see a thing over the heads of adults. I drove my mother crazy with all my jumping, trying to get a glimpse of my father. "Where is he? Can you see him?" I must have asked her that a hundred times. She kept hushing me, more out of habit than for any practical reason I could figure. Voices rose to the ceiling and filled in every pocket of air around us. Crying, laughing, nervous chatter. It was a riot of sound. Some kids had whistles that would pierce the madness every so often and babies were crying everywhere. There were a lot of Nova Scotian and Canadian flags in the crowd, stuck in hat brims and baby carriages or waved by children. The heat was something too. All those bodies in such a small space. I was sweating and thought I'd pass out from heat or excitement.

"And then there he was. When I picture that moment it's like seeing the parting of the Red Sea. There were masses of people all around us and then bingo! my dad was there and the mob and the noise just fell to the sidelines. I jumped into his arms and think I stayed there for about three days. He'd been gone for years and I wasn't about to let him out of my sight.

"Mother offered him her cheek to kiss, but she grabbed his arm for a second and I saw how frightened she'd been. Looking back, I think she had worried herself into old age. She had become this stern, old spinster woman unable to bend herself back into love.

"How I wanted her to hug him and cry like the other mothers were doing. But she had lost the ability. I was angry with her for that then, but I think I understand her more now. She had been so afraid, her emotions just got locked up inside her and they never found a way back out.

"How sad our house was after that." Gran paused and I wiped tears from her face. "I can see it so clearly, like it just happened."

While Jane and I waited for her to continue, we could hear the radio and the occasional swear word or bit of laughter coming from upstairs. Aunt Harmony and Mother had offered to tear down the old wallpaper from the main bathroom and update it with paint. Jane had jumped at the chance to shed the textured, beige ugliness from the room.

It could be that she had cooked this up to keep Mother and me apart; things definitely went better when we weren't in the same room. If it had been, I appreciated it. I loved sitting and listening to Gran.

"My parents were never like they had been before the war," she continued. "I know I was little, but it seemed there had been laughter and then there was none. Just duty, Every day a carbon copy of the one before. Dad went back to working for himself, odd jobs and renovations, that sort of thing. Mother ran the house. They were like two vice-presidents who met over supper to fill each other in on the details of the day before parting for an evening of reading or sewing or tinkering, depending on their responsibilities.

"Oh my, they were still so young. Not even thirty when the war was over yet acting like they were one step from the grave. All that life left to live and no heart to live it with."

She paused in her recollections. The shadow of memories long forgotten flitted across her lined face, and then her eyes lit up. "You know all the immigration to Canada came through Halifax during those years, right?"

I nodded.

"Ships would bring people in and trains would take them across the country, dropping them off wherever they'd chosen to settle. More than forty thousand war brides came through the port with something like twenty thousand children to make lives for themselves with their ex-servicemen husbands. And there were many hundreds of thousands of people from so many countries who came to live here.

"When I was in my teens, I'd go to the harbour and watch these folks as they'd board the train. The clothes they wore and languages they'd speak were like rainbows and music to me. I didn't understand them, but I liked to listen just the same. My favourite was Italian because it sounded like the sun, rich and warm, exuberant. Listening to everyone made me wonder about all those countries they'd come from and why they'd decided to make Canada their home. Halifax was all I knew and it seemed a pretty grey and uninteresting place. I suppose most kids think that way about wherever they're from.

"Watching them and seeing their meagre belongings made me recognize a bigger world beyond my small one, and I started reading everything I could find about other countries. It developed my need to get moving, to do things." Gran smiled and a thread of spittle danced beyond her lips as air rattled in her chest.

"History and English became my favourite subjects in high school. I loved reading about battles or reading the works of writers from outside Canada. I knew I wanted to go on to university, but Mother wasn't keen on that. She couldn't figure why a girl would need to get that much education. 'Don't set your sights beyond your reach,' she'd say to me.

"To this day, I've never been able to figure out her thinking on that. She'd had to run the house while Dad was away, you'd think she'd be keen for her daughter to be educated and able to take care of herself, but she didn't seem to see things that way. She thought I'd get married and that I should focus on mastering my domestic skills.

"And we know how well you did at that." I tweaked her arm and she grinned.

"Dad didn't say much about school one way or the other, but I knew he was more on my side than hers. He'd even put aside a bit of money for me although it wasn't as much as I'd need. After high school, I got a job working at the power company as a clerk. I stayed there for two years saving for school.

"The day I got my acceptance letter from the University of Toronto I celebrated and danced all night long. I had way too much to drink and two of my girlfriends had to help me home and into bed. My head was splitting the next day, and Mother made sure to be extra loud while she made breakfast, but I didn't care. I was getting away from that house—that mausoleum. Three weeks later, I packed my bags and took one of those trains I'd spent years watching others take west, and I landed in Union Station.

"That must have been something being in such a big city. Didn't you feel lost?"

"Not at all. I took a taxi to campus and got out right in the middle of a Civil Rights protest. It was tiny, no more than a handful of students, but it caught my attention. I don't know how it was that I knew so little of black history. I grew up minutes away from Africville and Dad had hired a black man to work with him when business was good. He'd eaten dinner at our house and we'd spoken often, but I'd never given any thought to equality before. All I knew was that they lived there and we lived here and that was that. I'd never thought about anything to do with blacks. Funny, really, when you consider how interested I was in other cultures..."

Her breathing was arduous and she came to a full stop, gasping.

"You better rest. This is too much all at once."

"There's no more time." She sucked at the air. "There are things you have to know."

"What things?"

She shook her head, unable to answer.

I pulled Gran upright, hoping to help her, and looked at Jane, but she had no answers for me and sat poised on the edge of her seat, focused on Gran's attempts to breathe. My grandmother was going to do this her way, even if it killed her. It took some minutes for her to have the breath to begin again.

"A few days later, classes started, and the protest left my mind. But then something important happened, Rosa Parks refused to give up her seat on the bus for some white man and the bus boycott in the States began for real. Well, didn't that just fire up my imagination!

"I started going to rallies and listening to speakers and my inner activist was born. Before long, I was leading petitions calling for human rights legislation to be drafted here in Canada. Oh, I was involved in all sorts of causes and I loved every second of it. What seemed so subversive then seems so innocent now."

Gran beamed and took my hand. "Can you imagine what all of this was like for a girl like me? A girl who came from where I came from? All that passion about new ideas? It was heady stuff and I couldn't get enough of it. It was like being drunk only better.

"That winter, I met Addie at one of the rallies. We became best friends, inseparable outside of class. We studied side-by-side and talked long into the night about saving the world while we smoked cigarettes and feasted on cheap dinners and the cheapest wine we could find. It wasn't long before I started having feelings I'd never experienced before and, well, they scared me—scared me to death. I thought there was something wrong with me. I didn't know what to do about them so I did the only think I thought I could do. I stopped seeing her.

"I mean, for heaven's sake, who'd ever heard of that sort of thing? Certainly not me. Not at that point in my life.

"Addie called me a couple of times and left messages with the house mother, but I never returned them. Eventually, she got mad and ambushed me after one of my afternoon classes. She was miserable. 'What have I done?' 'Why won't you speak to me?' It was horrible. She was crying and I felt so bad for her, but what could I say? I think I'm in love with you? She followed me back to my room jabbering on about being friends and how friends shouldn't treat friends like that. My head was spinning. What was I to do?

"So, I kissed her. Talk about an act of desperation. I mean it was about as definitive a thing as I could do. I thought she'd hate me, pull away, slap me even. And yet, merciful heavens, she kissed me back. It was the single most astounding thing that had happened to me to that point in my life. It simply took my breath clear away."

She stopped and closed her eyes, the corners of her mouth turned up slightly. Minutes ticked past. I thought she'd fallen asleep and was about to stand when she spoke, her first few words no more than a whisper.

"We were both embarrassed and started giggling over each other. Eventually, we talked and the awkwardness worked itself out and we had a lovely few months together before her parents caught wind that something was up. I think her older brother, who was also at the university at the time, may have had something to do with that. She was permitted to finish the school year, which was only weeks away, as long as she kept away from me. That hurt like the dickens. Then they withdrew her from school and carted her home. I never heard from her after that. Her brother wasn't coming back either. He had graduated. Not that he would have helped me."

"The day she left, I stood outside her dorm, watching as they piled her things into their car. I'll never forget the sound of the doors on their big Buick as they thunked closed, taking Addie from me forever. Thunk. The sound of no recourse. So final. I've preferred smaller cars ever since."

She closed her eyes again at the recollection and her jaw slackened as though she might cry. Her cheeks collapsed as the afternoon sun slid behind a cumulus cloud casting shadows from the sharp angles of her facial bones. I shuddered at her unhealthy pallor and envisioned her corpse lying before me. The sun re-emerged and mercifully pushed the image from my head.

"After her, I chased love full out. Addie had opened another door inside me and I needed to have that feeling back. Not that I was promiscuous. If that's what you're thinking you can get that idea out of your head."

Her voice dropped away.

"Celeste?" I was worried that this exertion would somehow harm her, but I was fascinated too at hearing about her youth and hoped she'd be able to continue. Though I'd heard some of her tales before, they took on new meaning as she set them before me with the purpose of passing down her life.

"She needs this," Jane said as though Gran wasn't there. "It's good for her."

I jumped at her voice. She'd been sitting in silence long enough that I'd forgotten she was in the room.

"Let me rest for a bit," Gran said. "How about getting me a cup of tea? With lemon and honey?"

I went to do her bidding and when I returned, her eyes were closed as though in sleep. She opened them when she heard me approach and took a sip of the steaming liquid. "Ah, that's better. The honey soothes my throat. Now, where was I?"

"I think you were explaining about being a lesbian."

Gran chortled, her delight wheezing from her chest like notes from a squeeze box. "Oh, I was not. I was telling you about school."

"Have it your way."

"Going away to university was the best thing I could have done. It was my watershed—getting out of Nova Scotia and seeing proof of something else, something bigger. After years of being stifled I was energized by everything around me. It was a time of such optimism! We thought we'd build a great new world." Gran's voice had risen in her excitement leaving her gasping for air once more. I raised the head of her bed a few degrees and waited till her breathing calmed before offering more tea. She sucked at the straw then waved the cup away, impatient to get back to her personal chronicle.

"I saw my first television at school, black and white. A big brown box that sat on the floor in the corner of the commons room. The first show I watched was an interview with Marilyn Bell. You know, the first one to swim across Lake Ontario—not the first woman mind you, but the first person. Well, if a sixteen-year-old girl could do that, it seemed that there wasn't anything I should be afraid to tackle either. The world was opening up at grand speed and I couldn't drink it in fast enough.

"It was a time, my girl. It was a time." Gran struggled to breathe, panting, trying to drag air into her lungs. She closed her eyes once more.

"Why don't you rest for a little bit?" I said, again concerned she was over-taxing herself.

"There'll be enough time for that later. I'll be fine in a minute."

I could hear the rattle deep in Gran's chest and tried to pretend it was my imagination that invented it, but knew it wasn't. Her time was running out as was mine with her.

I waited and listened to the sounds of the house. Voices, laughter, a roller spreading paint, even the slight rustle of Jane at her craftwork. The sounds of domesticity soothed me and I wanted to carry this moment with me forever.

Gran began to speak, keeping her eyes closed like she was watching a movie play out on the insides of her lids.

"I liked to consider myself a bit of a wild thing. Just thrilled to bits about the beat generation. We were the first hippies, you know. The drugs and whatnot weren't for me, but the idea of throwing out my parents' old ideas caught hold of me like a fever. I gobbled up everything, in the classroom and out." She stopped talking, inhaling and exhaling in short gasps and then continued. "I took general arts with a major in literature. Did I tell you that already?"

I nodded, but she wasn't paying attention to me.

"My parents thought I'd be a teacher, a job that was considered to be respectable for a girl, even by my mother. Bet you can't imagine that there were only five prescribed occupations for girls. Five. And teaching was one of them." She snorted. "Back in high school, I, along with all the other girls, were given a booklet from the guidance counsellor stating such.

"What were they? … Secretary, teacher, airline stewardess, domestic engineer or some such twaddle, and nurse. Yes, I think that was it. Makes me mad even after all these years."

Her voice drifted, her words exiting on puffs of strangled air. After another sip of tea, she carried on. "I never wanted to teach. Law, now that was for me. I decided I was going to finish my Bachelor of Arts and go on to graduate study. I sent a letter to my parents announcing my big plan. You should have read the one I got in return. The wrath of god was nothing compared to that. The anger in that letter could have scorched trees off a hill. You would have thought I'd suggested working in a bordello.

"Law was no place for a decent woman as far as they were concerned. Dad had been fine with me getting an education, but then complained about me leaving home. Surely, had I stayed put and gone to Dalhousie, I wouldn't have picked up strange ideas about a career. How he regretted supporting my further education. Oh, boy! Had they only known what else I was up to. They would've died of shame. No, I was to get my degree and get home like a respectable girl. None of that hanging about with those degenerates in Upper Canada.

"It took me a while to figure that my leaving meant they were having to interact with each other for the first time in years. I wasn't there to be the buffer. Of course, they were upset. What where they finding to talk about over dinner?"

She drifted out and then, "I met Denny during my second year, you know. A boy from home. How's that for coincidence?"

She said it without drama or introduction and I tried to hide my shock at the mention of his name. The only thing I really knew about my grandfather was the stark fact of his death in a car accident. Even the hows and whys of that incident were never shared with me. My mysterious grandfather was one person we never, ever talked about, yet for the second time in as many days, he had entered the conversation just as casually as if we were talking about drinking lemonade on a hot summer day.

"He was a good man and he tried like the dickens to please me." Gran lowered her already quiet voice. "He knew about the women, you know. Don't think otherwise."

"If he knew, why did you get married?"

"He thought he could change me. I thought he could too. And it worked for a while. We were happy in the beginning."

Jane stood to excuse herself and I worried that Gran, in her tactlessness, might have hurt her feelings.

"Don't worry about me," Jane said. "There are some things better shared between the two of you. Plus, I've got a pie to bake."

Jane leaned over to kiss Gran then left the room, and Gran carried on without a break in her train of thought.

"We met at another Civil Rights rally. I had been asked to speak, to tell the crowd from away about Africville. No one had ever heard about Halifax's city council refusing to provide electricity and water to the black community. The situation was shameful and I wanted people to know about it. Of course, I only found out myself after I'd left home.

"The way Denny used to tell it, he was on his way from study hall and stopped to listen to me. He was captivated by my passion." Gran's laughter set off a coughing fit, but she waved me away as if wanting to win this battle without my help. "He started hanging around the student union after that. Started coming to events for causes he had no real interest in, as it turned out. But he tried for my sake, I'll give him that. We got to know each other and, after a time, his gentleness and friendship convinced me we should be married.

"He was quite handsome, you know, that dark hair that curled over his forehead, made him look like James Dean.

"And what else was a girl to do back then? I had little desire to teach and moving back with my parents wasn't an option I wanted to consider. To be honest, I'd grown tired of school and wasn't keen on living in poverty as an activist either. So, I struck a bargain. We'd get married and I'd still get to be the bohemian I fancied myself." A pained look crossed her face and she whispered, "I was such a silly, selfish girl. Thinking myself so clever."

"Oh, Celeste, that isn't true. You've been wonderful. Way better than any cookie-baking granny I've ever met."

"No, no, my love. I should never have married him. It wasn't fair. I got everything I ever wanted—trips and kids. He couldn't refuse me anything."

Her voice faded and I leaned in to hear her. "I killed him."

"No, Celeste. It was an accident—"

"No. It was me. I pushed him too far ..." She closed her eyes and sighed.

After some seconds had passed, she tried to continue, but when she opened her mouth a coughing fit choked the words from her. She wheezed, too weak to carry on, and was soon asleep, her face haggard, her jaw sagging.

I ached to ask her the questions her statement begged, but would have to wait for the answers. In the meantime, I didn't know what to think. Could it be true? Had she been responsible for my grandfather's death?

Diseased phlegm rose angrily, clawing at her chest and she gagged in her sleep. From above, angry voices could be heard.

"You can't do it like that; it'll streak," my mother said, annoyance clipping her voice.

"I'm doing it, so I'll do it the way I want to or you can do it yourself," Aunt Harmony challenged in reply.

"Fine. I'll do it myself then. Like I always do."

Jane and I met in the front hall, listening to the sisters argue.

"You're such a martyr," Aunt Harmony snapped. "Did you ever think you could just let people alone—that you're not the only one who knows how to do everything?"

"Don't be an ass. When was the last time you ever finished anything you started? If it wasn't for me—"

"If it wasn't for you, what?"

It was the same fight they'd been having for years and I couldn't listen to it again. The weight of belonging to this family bore down on me and my need to escape was overwhelming.

Not for the first time, I was tormented by our dysfunction. Our discord had so often—like a spark bursting into flame—turned something pleasant into something bitter and unkind. We were so quick to take offence.

I glanced at Jane hating the sympathy I saw in her face and fought the unwanted sting of tears behind my eyes. "I need to get out of here."

"Don't be gone long. It's almost supper," Jane called over the thwack of the screen door that echoed in my ears.

I was too angry to answer and stomped along the old path through the alders and scrub grass down to the water's edge. The summer blue of a jay skimmed across the deep green skyline of stunted spruces that bordered the rocky shore.

Past the trees, rounded beach stones created a twenty-foot-wide border, running along along the water's edge and stretching far beyond the horizon. The rocks were difficult to navigate and I wobbled along their tops, trying to avoid a sprain. I picked up heavy stones with both hands and threw them at the water as viciously as their heft allowed. The sound they made was less than satisfying as they plopped pudding-like into the sea.

Nothing ever changed between my mother and aunt. They were contrary and stubborn to extremes. Neither willing to bend the slightest to accommodate the other.

Angel and Harmony, my ass. Gran came up with those before she had a clue as to the characters of her babies, obviously. I couldn't imagine any two people more unsuited to their names than those two. Gran should have gone for something more tribal like Cat Piss or Snake Venom, something to ward off the evil spirits that had found homes inside her daughters.

Wind played on the water and grew stronger, bringing in high tide and the advent of evening fog. I gave up my rock throwing and sat on a boulder out of sight of the house. I pulled my knees up to my chest and wrapped my arms around them then leaned my head against my legs and listened to the waves rushing the shore and filtering back through the rocks. Shushing in and clattering out. In and out. Gulls circled over the midnight-blue water and called out for food or company. In the distance, I could make out the white sails of boats as their skippers explored the islands and inlets of the bay.

It was a beautiful place and I dreamed, as I often did, about moving here. As usual, I vacillated, not sure who would be more trying to live beside, Aunt Harmony or Mother. In small doses, Aunt Harmony was great, but the reality of her day-after-day could be every bit as dreadful as life with Mother. At least Mother was reliable. That Aunt Harmony couldn't be counted on for anything was a truth that had been proven to me time and again despite my denials of such to my mother.

During the first few years of my independence following high school, I latched onto my fantastical aunt, hoping to be welcomed as a permanent fixture in her life. Each time we'd make plans, I was reminded of her inability to commit. I'd travel to visit her and she'd forget to pick me up at the airport, or she'd come to Ottawa and neglect to call me. There were other times too when she'd simply vanish, returning neither phone calls nor emails, and then reappearing as though she'd never been away.

For the longest while, I refused to believe the truth about what I came to identify—rightly or wrongly—as self-absorption. Instead, I created a mythical woman, a woman free from convention, a romantic gadabout. Even now, I had difficulty erasing the image I had made that excused her from the many hurts she inflicted on me.

But here we were: Mother being her usual sanctimonious self and Aunt Harmony ditching another commitment, even if it was only painting a room, and not because Mother was directing her, as would be the excuse, but because she had grown tired of the task.

A breeze carried a bass chime through the trees and over the rocks to me and I looked back toward the house. It was the brass ship's bell that hung on the porch, ringing me home, roping me in.

# CHAPTER FOUR

There was a time when I didn't think my mother completely heartless, a time when I thought her starched shirts, grey trousers and polished black oxfords, her tiny gold earrings and oversized man's watch were chic, a time when I would have done anything to please her.

I was looking through Gran's bedroom shelves and had found the family albums overflowing with photos that chronicled major holidays and family milestones. I grabbed one and flipped through it, loose photos fell to the floor. A picture of my five-year-old self on my first day of school brought back a flood of memories. I looked so hopeful standing there at the front door of our house in my new red plaid kilt with its gleaming brass thistle pin. Arnie the sheep dog, my favourite plush toy, was clutched to my chest. I'd been happy I'd been allowed to bring him with me.

My stomach knotted at the sight of my little self as I remembered how I'd scurry to get ready for class each morning. I'd pull on the clothes mother had laid out for me the night before as quickly as I could, so afraid of displeasing her or of keeping her waiting.

"I can't be late for work," she'd snap. "You're a big girl now. You've got to learn to be on time."

Being late was a cardinal sin according to her. It indicated any number of character flaws, arrogance, laziness, disorganization or, heaven forbid, mental distraction. I'd urge my chubby fingers to shovel down my breakfast and brush my teeth without spilling or dropping. I'd will my wobbly toes and baby legs into my leotards. I tried to remember the right accessories for whatever hairstyle she'd chosen. All I wanted was for her to be happy with me. To get some acknowledgement that I had done well.

Being good, however, was expected and, therefore, unremarkable. I suppose things in our house weren't that different from what went on in the homes of other single, working parents. Rush, rush, rush. Christ, I hated it. There was never enough time and no matter how I tried, something went wrong. Toothpaste on my top or stubborn knots in my hair or my last-minute pleadings for something I'd forgotten, but needed, for class.

By the time I got to school, my innards would be churning, and I would continue my day fretting about pleasing my teacher. From Sunday to Thursday, I fell asleep each night worried about the next morning. It was the beginning of a life-long stomach affliction that manifested at the hint of stress.

Fortunately, there was one day that provided me with some relief. In the era before round-the-clock shopping, Sunday was a day that forced my mother to be still.

I remember those mornings as being such fun. With nowhere to rush off to, we could take our time and do whatever we pleased. Mother would make me a hot breakfast and I'd get to watch cartoons, sometimes lounging in my pyjamas till noon. After lunch, we may have taken a trip to the park or loaded a picnic into the car for a drive to the country. On rainy days, we'd bake cookies. The kind we'd slice from a package then eat warm in front of a movie. To this day, I never make cookies any other way.

I closed the album and selected another from the bottom of the pile. It was an older, thicker volume with a worn brown cover, and was filled with black and white shots. This was a special one, I could tell. I turned to the first page and saw a young woman in various poses: holding a diploma, seated behind a desk, lying on a beach towel, in a fancy dress ready for a night out. They were all of Gran taken in the days before marriage and children. I was enthralled. How was it I'd never seen these before? I ate up the snapshots of my grandmother holding my mother and then my aunt at their births, photos of little girls in diapers and first steps, of cake making and fort building, of dance routines and swimming lessons.

Here were the childhoods of my mother and Aunt Harmony. I stopped at a black and white picture of them leaping about on a lawn, their arms stretched high above their heads, their hands holding the corners of fluttering, gauzy scarves. They were captured in mid-air, their mouths open in laughter, their blonde and copper curls almost white under the glare of the summer sun—enchanting silver butterflies.

I held the photo close, examining my mother. Her head was tilted back and she looked carefree and fearless flying beside her sister. What had she been like back then? What had happened in the intervening years to make her so humourless, so conscious of the opinions of others?

Feeling like a thief, I slipped the image from the neat, black, triangular corners that held it in place, noticing how painstakingly the album had been arranged. Surely, this wasn't Gran's work. She'd never been meticulous. There was devotion in the neatly aligned photographs placed four to a page. I turned the stolen picture over and read the neat printing on its back: Leaving for summer vacation, July, 1967. Could I be holding something created by my grandfather? It was a heady thought. I placed the photo beside me on the bed and continued through the pages, looking at the visual history of the Simone family. My family.

Christmases, school plays, birthdays. All taken by my invisible grandfather, absent from every picture. There was my mother at seven blowing out birthday candles, at eight weaving a basket, at nine holding a fishing rod, and as a young teen trying not to look embarrassed as she smiled into the camera. By sixteen, she had already begun to form the seriousness I considered her true nature. But maybe I was wrong about that. This old book showed me other things about her. She'd had a delicacy to her and a sense of fun. Where had this girl gone?

The neatly filed snapshots ended before the pages had been filled and loose photographs were sandwiched between the last page and the cover. Pictures of a cottage and of Mother's graduation from high school. She looked happy, but there was something else too—a look of relief. Had she been as anxious to escape her home as her own mother had been before her, and as I had been a generation later?

I lingered over the last photos and felt a chill run through me as I stared at the blank pages that were as telling as a broken watch at a crime scene. My grandfather had died before he could finish his project and here I held the tangible evidence of the summer of his passing. I had discovered a treasure, a piece of my unknown past. I pulled the old album close and inhaled its dusty musk.

"Kate!" My mother's voice called me to the present. "Time for weeding."

I groaned and replaced the picture of the dancing butterflies inside the album that I carried it to my duffle bag. No one would notice it missing.

Quickly, I finished dressing and waved as I passed Aunt Harmony seated in the front room on Gran-duty, then met Mother and Jane at the vegetable garden.

"Get the ripe tomatoes before they spoil," Mother ordered. "Then hoe the rows of corn."

Whatever good feelings had flickered in me toward my mother were doused in an instant. My lips tightened and my shoulders pulled back, but I caught Jane's smile in time to avoid letting go of one of my usual snide comments.

"You're a big help to me," she said and, with that, what could I do but lend a hand with whatever grace I could muster?

I admired Jane immensely. She did so much around the house to keep it running well, things that were beyond Gran, even when she'd been healthy. Take the garden. Despite the work involved, it was Jane's solo project. It would have required too much of Gran. Too much planning, too much care, too much long-term investment. Jane, however, loved harvesting her own vegetables for cooking and took pleasure in the full flavour of her fresh produce.

I pulled warm, red tomatoes from their vines, savouring their sharp tang. I used my T-shirt as a basket until it was overfull. There were still plenty of ripe ones to be picked, more than two women could ever need.

"We can't eat all these."

"I'll make sauce to freeze and bring some to the homeless shelter," Jane said.

I carried the first load of tomatoes to the kitchen and unloaded them into the sink. I was rooting inside the pantry for a plastic pail to carry the next batch when I heard the soft yet unmistakable sound of grief coming from the living room. I froze for an instant before finding my legs and scurrying toward the sound. Tears were streaming down Aunt Harmony's face as she sat holding one of Gran's hands.

"No!" I gasped. "Not yet."

Aunt Harmony looked at me and realizing what I must be thinking, whispered, "Oh, no. No, she's still here. She's asleep. I was just… thinking… about things." She wiped her eyes and shrugged, attempting a smile.

"What things? What's wrong?"

"Nothing really. Just me being silly. You know. Crazy Aunt Harmony. I'm sorry I frightened you. It's just me, nothing to worry about." She sniffed and wiped her face with the palms of her hands.

"But it must be something? Is it Gran… Celeste? Is she worse?"

Aunt Harmony shook her head.

"Did Mother do something? Is it work? You know if you need to get back to teaching, it'd be okay. There are enough of us here and—"

"No. Nothing like that. Really. You'll have to trust me. This is just something I do every now and again. Break down. It's how I am sometimes. I suppose this must sound bizarre…" Her voice trailed off.

I didn't know what to do with her information. Go to her? Force her to talk to me? Leave her to her own resources? I settled on the latter. Emotionally, I was poorly equipped to do much else.

"If you change your mind and want to talk…"

"I know."

I returned to the garden, saying nothing to my mother or Jane, and worried about what could be troubling my aunt. I gathered the rest of the tomatoes and left them in the bucket by the back door then started on the corn, breaking up the soil between the rows. The sun beat down and sweat trickled from my scalp, stinging my eyes. My clothes stuck to me and I craved a swim in the cold Atlantic. It was too late in the day for sane people to be doing yard work. What's that expression about mad dogs and Englishmen? We were neither and should have started earlier, but I knew better than to say so. Mother would have told me if I wanted to finish before the heat of mid-day, I'd have to get my backside out of bed while the sun was still low in the sky and the air cooler.

"Like this." Mother was at my side. She demonstrated how I was to hoe the corn, bringing the soil up around the roots to form neat hillocks, row by row. I worked away, using her technique until I heard Jane call the world's most welcome phrase: "Break time."

As if I needed encouragement to set down my hoe, Jane held up a pitcher of ice tea. If I'd had the energy, I'd have galloped to the cool shade of the porch. The three of us sat in the old chairs quietly sipping our drinks and fanning ourselves with our sunhats.

"Has anyone seen Harmony?" Jane asked.

I was startled. "Isn't she with Celeste?"

Jane shook her head in reply.

"Figures," Mother snorted. "You can't count on her for anything. Is her car here?"

I checked the front drive and reported that, indeed, the car was missing.

"Well, you better get washed up and go sit with your grandmother. It's too hot to keep at this today anyway. We can finish up tomorrow." I saw mother shift gears back to her sister. "That damn Harmony. Give her a simple job…"

I didn't stay to listen to the rest. It was an old tirade I'd heard many times in the past, but this time I knew something my mother didn't. Aunt Harmony was terribly unhappy and I had to find out why.

# CHAPTER FIVE

The next day Aunt Harmony was still missing and my worry grew. She hadn't called and hadn't answered any of the dozen times I dialled her apartment. As far as I knew, she didn't own a cell phone.

"I don't need to be that reachable." She enjoyed her counter-culture way of life, thinking herself some new-age version of a hippy chick who shunned gadgetry.

It was my turn to sit with Gran while Mother went about the yard work. Although Gran was sleeping, we didn't like to leave her alone when there was work to do out-of-doors. I watched her chest rise and fall, the sound of her breathing shallow and ragged like someone with the flu. I held my own, waiting for her to inhale or exhale. The tension was tiring.

She looked so old. So very, very old. Her face had paled even further since we'd arrived and she'd gone from grey to nearly translucent. She was disappearing.

Her hands were cool and dry and her nails needed clipping. I ran my thumb along their uneven edges, tracing their outlines so later I'd be able to remember how it felt to hold her hand.

I hummed the Irish lullaby she'd sung to me when I was little and into my pre-teens. I jerked to my feet, as Mother entered the room. I'd been so engrossed, I hadn't heard the kitchen door.

Our eyes locked in challenge. Could either of us find an ulterior motive in her entering the room or in my singing to my dying Gran with which we could chastise the other?

Weakening, I pulled my gaze from hers and began Gran's massage. "Hot out?"

She walked to Jane's table of quills. "Where's Jane?"

"She's gone to Millbrook to get some sweet grass. She says we need a cleansing."

Mother looked toward the heavens as though pleading for rescue or patience. She didn't believe in spiritual ceremonies of any sort, thinking them all forms of superstition and nonsense.

"And Harmony? Has she made her way back yet?"

I hated giving Mother more ammunition to use against her sister and she saw me hesitate. "No. She hasn't called either."

"Big surprise."

Sometime during our exchange, Gran had awoken and now spoke up. "I don't want to hear any nastiness today. I'm tired. Get me some tea, Angel. Kate, raise my bed a bit. I'd like to sit some.

I watched Gran's face, wondering if she was aware of her youngest daughter's abdication. She had said nothing about her absence. Tact, I decided. Or maybe she was less aware of time passing, hours blurring into other hours, all of them seeming the same.

I rubbed her arms with lotion, using as much care as I could then her legs and feet. She was little more than bones. My great big Gran was shrinking. My chin quivered and I bit the inside of my cheek to stop my tears.

"Enough now. That's enough fussing."

Mother returned with the tea and announced that she was going to do some laundry.

"That's fine," Gran shooed her away, "I want to talk with your daughter anyway."

That cup of tea was all she'd had since I didn't know when, but that didn't diminish her desire for conversation. She motioned toward the chair.

I heard the water in the laundry room run and turned my attention to Gran, but she'd fallen asleep. Talking was wearing on her, using up her finite energy stores.

I tried to get comfortable in the chair and spent the afternoon reading and napping and hoping Aunt Harmony would call.

The phone did ring after supper by which time I was so tense I leaped on it much like a tiger on its prey. My heart pounding, I grabbed the handset, but it was a business call for Mother. It was her boss asking her to fly home to cover a news conference. The paper was historically short-staffed over the summer months and relied on interns to fill the holes caused by staff vacations. A media advisory had just arrived over the wire, announcing a news conference on Parliament Hill the next morning. The editor needed a reporter with well-seasoned skills and solid contacts to handle the double-talk that would undoubtedly be used to gloss over the latest political scandal. The paper would pay for Mother's return flight from Halifax.

"You can't be serious about leaving," I said when she announced her intention to go. "Being here is more important than writing a stupid article."

"Writing a stupid article, as you put it, is my job—a job that kept a roof over our heads, and continues to keep one over mine. I'll be back within a day. Mom will be fine with you and Jane to watch over her."

"You've barely spent any time with her as it is and what about Aunt Harmony? Aren't you worried?"

Mother rolled her eyes. "If I stopped work every time your aunt took off, we'd have lived on the street. She'll be back. She always has been."

"How did you get to be so cold? How is it you don't care?"

She took a step toward me. "Don't care? Don't presume to know what I think or feel. Just because I don't dramatize my feelings for public consumption doesn't mean I don't care or don't worry or don't hurt. You've become a real self-righteous jerk, you know that? Think you know everything, don't you? Well, let me tell you, you don't know much." She turned to leave the room, but looked back over her shoulder at me. "You can be a very arrogant young woman and I wish you'd get over yourself."

Her words stung, as they were intended to, and I fought the urge to bolt. There was nothing, not even Gran's illness, to bridge the bitterness between my mother and me. I thought of Matt, the lovely waiter from work, and wished he were here to distract me as he had been doing so ably before I'd left for St. Margaret's Bay. Seeking diversion was a habit I'd developed to escape the anger and sense of failure that accompanied my interactions with my mother. I'd lob and she'd volley and then I'd want to run and hide in some physical entertainment. I wondered whom Matt might be amusing now.

With no place to go, I crawled into the chair at my still-sleeping Gran's side to lick my wounds and glare at my mother whenever she crossed into my sites in her preparations to leave. Within no time, she was ready and nodded a terse goodbye in my direction. I heard her say, "I'll be home in a day, two at the most" before the door banged shut behind her.

At the sound, Gran stirred and smiled when she saw me. "You're still here."

"Yeah. Who would have thought I'd turn out to be the reliable one?"

"What do you mean, dear?"

"Never mind. I'm being silly," I said, borrowing a phrase from Aunt Harmony. Gran didn't seem to be aware of my aunt's disappearance or Mother's defection and I wasn't about to tell her if I could avoid it. "Are you hungry? Jane grilled some veggies earlier. I could make you an omelette."

"No, dear. Not right now."

She had been eating so little, just an meal-supplement drink or tea. I wondered that she had the strength to speak, but after a quick sponge bath, she asked, "Where were we?" as though no time had passed between our talk of days ago and now.

"You were talking about Denham—about the accident," I prompted.

"Oh, Denny. Dear Denny. But, no. So much comes before that. Raise me up some more, won't you? I'd like to sit straighter."

I unlocked the bed's hydraulics by depressing the latch at the head of the mattress.

"That's it. I can see you so much better this way." Her attention drifted, as though she were searching for the right thread to pull from the knotted spool of her years. Alighting on something, she laughed, "Can you believe I married an accountant?"

"Not really," I admitted. "How did that happen?"

"He was craftier than I gave him credit for, that's how. That man followed me everywhere, but was never pushy, never tried to force me into a relationship with him. He stood by while I had my flings and was there to pick up the broken pieces. He came with me to all my underground meetings and got interested in the same issues I did. He told me years later he knew he wanted to marry me almost from the beginning. I still can't figure out why, but he did." She stopped and I could see her grapple with something. "Now, I'm going to tell you things that only Jane knows because you're old enough to handle them. Am I right? Are you?"

Her eyes burned into mine and I was caught off-guard. I knew Gran had a rich history, but I'd no idea this frail, old woman had those kinds of secrets. It wasn't something I thought of older people as having. I guess Mother was right, I didn't know as much as I thought I did. This trip was turning into something far darker than I'd expected and I wasn't sure I was ready to be witness to the unveiling of buried heartbreaks and other ancient tragedies.

"I'm old enough," I said, not at all sure I was.

"Then sit still and listen," she ordered. Her voice was gravely and she blurted her story in staccato bursts between long inhalations of oxygen. "The summer before my last year at school I had an abortion. It almost killed me."

"An abortion? You?"

Gran puckered her lips, "I thought you said you were ready."

"I'm sorry. It's just that I've never thought of people having those back then. Were they safe?" Images of back-alley abortionists wielding rusty coat hangers came to mind and I felt ill.

"Some, not all."

"But wait. I thought you were dating women then."

"Don't be so literal, dear. Men, women. In the end, it's all the same really." Her tone was both condescending and dismissive. Maybe she was trying to shock me.

If so, it had worked. My thoughts bumped against each other. This is my grandmother. Bi-sexual? Jesus, I thought I was sophisticated. And an abortion? Back then? Jesus.

"I was seeing someone older and I got pregnant. I'm not proud to say this, but I wasn't strong enough to face the shame of having an illegitimate child. The father wanted nothing to do with a baby, or me for that matter, so I arranged an abortion. All the girls knew where to get one, but we knew it wasn't completely safe either. I was scared so I asked Denny to come with me and he did. Afterward, he took me back to his apartment and it's a good thing too because I almost bled to death. I lay on his bed and he packed me with towels. When I passed out, he called an ambulance and they got me to a hospital in time and fixed me up. I pretended I'd fallen down a flight of stairs and they pretended to believe me.

"But I learned something about myself then. Something I didn't like much. No matter how I'd fought it, I was a product of my time after all. And I hated knowing that. I hated knowing I wasn't the independent wild woman I'd fancied myself. Being pregnant taught me that. Of course, I continued my façade, but my reality was that I clung to Denny and when he eventually asked, I agreed to marry him." Her voice shook with her unburdening and I held her hand.

"Of course, I told him I'd never submit to being a regular housewife and he'd have to let me pursue my passions, as it were, but deep down, I knew I wasn't the person I pretended to be. And he unwittingly paid for that knowledge of mine with every escapade I had, trying to find something to make me real." She paused, out of breath. "Get me some honey tea, won't you?"

I was very happy to have an excuse to leave the room and compose myself in private. Leaning on the countertop waiting for the kettle to boil, I stared out the window seeing only my reflection staring back at me. First, Aunt Harmony's breakdown and now Gran's confessions, if I could call them that. They both shocked me. What else had we women hidden from each other? It seemed we had secrets lodged in veiled recesses that forged the most important aspects of who we'd become and yet we were as unaware of each other's ghosts as a newborn is of the wider world around it. I was filling the teapot as Jane entered the kitchen from the backyard.

I jumped. "When did you get home?"

"A while ago. You were occupied so I took the opportunity to check my vegetables. It's warm out there. The wind has died down and the bugs are coming out. How's Celeste?"

I wanted to dump my newfound knowledge on her and have her soothe me, but I smiled acting as if all was well. "She's talking, but not eating. She's asked for tea."

"I'll make it, if you want."

"No, that's fine. I'm almost done."

"I'll pop in to see her then."

I needed time before heading back to more confidences. Taking a few minutes to think made me realize I was loath to return to her side. She could be too much sometimes.

When I returned to the living room, Gran was sleeping and I felt I'd been given a reprieve. Taking the book I'd been reading, I headed off for a nap as well. I'd been doing a lot of that since my arrival. A coping mechanism, I was sure. Lying in bed, I thought about our relationships with each other. What was it between us—Mother and Aunt Harmony, me and Mother, Mother and Gran—that kept us at odds? My mother was the only common denominator I could see. What was her story? And where the hell was my aunt?

I fell asleep to the imagined sounds of crying babies and chanting crowds.

# CHAPTER SIX

"You need to get out of here for a while," Jane said, interrupting my pacing. "You're going stir crazy."

"There's just the two of us left. I think I should stick around." The day after Mother had escaped to Ottawa, Aunt Harmony was still missing and my worry was making me irritable.

"White people," she sighed. "You worry about the wrong things. You need space and I need to be away from your snarling for a while. I promise not to charge you with desertion. Now scoot." She smiled, her teeth iridescent against caramel lips. "Oh, and you can cook for me tonight. It'll give you something to take your mind off of what you can't control."

"But I can't cook …"

"Then this will be learning experience for you, won't it? Now go." She shooed me away like she would a swarm of black flies.

I dragged my feet up the stairs to my bedroom, wondering what to do with myself. It was too chilly for the beach. A fog had blown in during the night and was still hovering around us. Water droplets hung heavy in the morning air making my skin cool and clammy. I folded the bed linens back to air them. they smelled faintly of mildew. The fog might burn off if the temperature climbed later in the day, but then again, it might not. Weather was a hard thing to predict in these parts.

Aunt Harmony.

Her image came to me unbidden and I felt the familiar twinge of anxiety in my stomach.

Where are you?

Three days seemed an ominously long time to be missing without a call or message.

I raced down the stairs and gave Jane a kiss on her cheek before reaching for her car keys and dashing out the door. I would hunt for my wayward aunt.

Halifax wasn't that big.

It took me half an hour to get to the south end of the city and another fifteen minutes to locate the weathered building where she rented an upstairs flat. It had been some time since I'd been there and I couldn't recall her address. Hers was an area of heritage buildings many of which had been converted to apartments for the large population of university students who flooded the city for three quarters of the year. Some were well maintained and sported the traditional maritime paint palate. Hues and combinations of purple, yellow, orange, red, blue, green, and black were on every block. After combing a dozen streets I found Aunt Harmony's home, a greying wooden structure mottled with flakes of white paint and surrounded by other decaying structures. From the curb, I could see the tipsy front steps and overflowing mailbox of my aunt's unit.

If she was home, she hadn't bothered with her mail.

I sat in the car without a plan, imagining how the conversation might go if I were to find her.

"Where have you been?"

"What have you been doing?"

"Why the hell didn't you call?"

"Why do you keep fucking up, Aunt Harmony?"

The fog was lifting and the warmth of the sun nudged the temperature in the car upwards, sinking into my bones. I sat for a moment in the heat then inhaled deeply before making my way toward the front door. It wasn't locked so I let myself inside. The air was musty in the way of some old homes and a cobweb shimmered in a sunbeam that shone through the oval glass pane in the door. Neither sweeping nor mopping had taken place in the foyer for some time and a layer of dirt covered the floors and yellowed wallpaper. The narrow staircase lay to my left and I gripped the loose, but anchored, walnut-stained banister as I tiptoed to the top floor. The steps creaked underfoot adding to my nervousness. I felt like a third-rate gumshoe about to be caught at some sleazy misdeed.

Aunt Harmony's flat took up the entire second storey and her door lay in front of the stairwell landing. I knocked, timidly at first, then louder as I called her name. There was no response so I dug out the extra key she kept hidden under a loose floorboard under the blue and green area rug that served as a doormat.

Boy, this'd really fool burglars.

I called her name again as I let myself in. For a moment, I wasn't sure that I wanted to find her.

All the rooms fed off a central hall that opened up to a spacious living room featuring an unusable fireplace that housed nothing more incendiary than a quintet of pillar candles, and a spectacular turret that provided two hundred and eighty degrees of light and was used as a reading nook. A worn, red rug covered the uneven floorboards, and paintings and photographs covered the walls.

The flat was neat, a fact that surprised me given my aunt's character. With the exception of wrinkled furniture-covers that lay askew, and a pile of magazines that littered the coffee table alongside an overflowing ashtray, the room seemed in good order. I wondered about the ashtray as I had been under the impression that my aunt no longer smoked.

The kitchen was another matter. Dirty dishes filled the small sink and a sharp odour spoke of days-old garbage that hadn't been taken out. Under the sink, the garbage was, indeed, rank and half-a-dozen empty wine bottles stood sentry beside it.

I closed the cupboard door and made my way to the bedroom. The curtains were drawn and clothes littered the floor and unmade bed. It was impossible to tell whether she had been here recently or not.

Now what was I to do? I poked around looking for an address book without success. She didn't even have a home computer. The one at her dance academy was ample, she'd said. Part of her off-the-radar philosophy. The indicator light on her phone wasn't flashing so she must have retrieved the few messages I'd left her. I was relieved knowing that she was at least safe enough to have listened to her messages. Then my stomach tensed.

She knew I'd called.

I retrieved her mail from downstairs and rifled through it looking for a clue to her whereabouts. In addition to a handful of store flyers there were bills and an overdue notice from the electric company. Those nasty reminders that arrived on salmon-coloured paper announced the state of one's financial affairs to the world. With dismay, I caught myself rolling my eyes at the predictability of Aunt Harmony's money sense. It was a response my mother would have had and I was immediately ashamed.

I left the mail on the front hall table of her apartment, relocked the door, and replaced the key where I'd found it before heading to the dance studio. Although I hoped differently, I supposed it wouldn't be too far-fetched to think she might be carrying on her daily activities without a care for Gran or my worry. After all, if Gran were to slip into further decline, she knew she could count on getting a call. My irritation with her resurfaced.

There was a dance class in session when I arrived and I stood in the hall until its conclusion before approaching the instructor.

"Sorry, no," she shook her head. "I haven't seen her. I thought she was with her mother."

"She was, but now she isn't and we're getting worried."

"Sorry, hon. All I know is Harmony asked me to take over for her till further notice. I haven't seen her in a week. Good for me though. I need the cash." She flashed a blinding, bleached-tooth grin at me.

I glared back in reply, wanting nothing more than to strike the smile from her face.

As though able to read my thoughts, alarm flashed into her eyes and she backed away while attempting to amends, "Oh, now, doncha worry. You know Harmony. She can take care of herself. I wish I were as good at that as she is."

After eliciting a promise from her to call if she heard anything about my aunt, I retraced my steps to the sidewalk, anger overflowing my lips in a string of curses. A startled old lady in a straw sunhat fled to the other side of the street with her dust mop of a dog in tow.

"I'm sorry," I called after her but she scuttled away looking over her shoulder to be sure I wasn't following. I waited till she rounded the corner before starting the car, not wanting to frighten her further.

"Way to go," I scolded myself. Poor old girl thinks I'm dangerous.

Drumming my fingers against the steering wheel, I wondered what to do next. I didn't know any of her friends and figured it was too early to start checking out bars. Or was it? She had to be somewhere.

A call to Jane informed me that my aunt's favourite haunt was an oyster and martini bar situated on the harbour front. It had been converted from an old theatre and sounded like the perfect spot for my dear aunt so I set out in search of the place.

I parked next to the boardwalk and travelled south on foot. Success greeted me as I neared the entrance to Pier 21—now an immigration museum of sorts.

Entering the dark lounge from the glare of a bright evening left me temporarily blinded. When my eyes adjusted to the light, there she was. Sitting at the end of the bar in a white dress with peacock feathers for earrings, my aunt was holding forth trying to claim the barkeep's attention.

"Well, look who's here," she said when she saw me, her voice husky from drink.

I could have smacked her.

"Where have you been? I've been looking for you. Why didn't you return my calls?" The words tumbled out of my mouth faster than I could stop them.

"Now, now, angel…"

"I'm not Angel, I'm Kate and you're coming home with me right now."

"Whoa, there. I didn't mean Angel. I meant angel. My guardian angel. And I'm not going anywhere, my angel-girl. Now have a drink with me." It sounded more like: "Whoa, zere. I dinna mean An-gel, I meant an-gel. My guardian an-gel. An I'm naw goin' anywhere, my an-gel-girrrl."

I looked at the bartender feeling helpless.

He raised his eyebrows. "What can I get you?"

"Ginger ale." I couldn't very well pull her off her stool and drag her out to the car.

"That's better," she purred. "Now, what's all the fuss?"

"All the fuss?" I was loud and the other patrons looked at me. "Celeste has been asking for you," I lied, dropping my voice. "Mother's taken off for work, you're gone and what if Celeste dies while you're both away? What am I supposed to do?"

She patted my hand. "There, there, my little cat-angel. Don't worry so much." It sounded like mush. She was really loaded.

"Stop calling me angel. That's Mother."

"Tsk, tsk. You're so angry. You've gotta learn to relax."

A barrel-chested man with tousled salt-and-pepper hair approached and touched Harmony's shoulder.

"Hey," he said.

"Oh, Petey! What a surprise! This is my niece, Katie-angel."

"Just Kate," I mumbled and withdrew to my soda while my aunt giggled and the two of them whispered into each other's faces. I'd never heard of Peter before now, but by the looks of things, he and my aunt were old friends.

This was not going well. How was I going to get her out of here now that Romeo had shown up?

I needn't have worried. Within minutes, Aunt Harmony's voice rose above the din of the happy hour crowd.

"I wanna stay and party. I don't wanna go home."

"C'mon babe, we can get a whole lot more comfortable at your place." Peter tried to put his arm around her and as he leaned over, I could see a pack of cigarettes in his shirt pocket. The same brand as had been in the ashtray at the apartment.

"It's too early. I'm stayin' here." She turned to face me. "Right, Katie-angel? And you're gonna stay here with me."

I smiled in a way that I hoped didn't provide her with too much encouragement. Staying wasn't on my agenda. Peter scowled at her obstinacy, his overgrown, greying eyebrows knitting together. This evening was not turning out as he had hoped. His feelings however were no concern of mine. I loved my aunt, but I couldn't imagine why anyone worth having would want to bed her in this condition. She was slurring and her hair was greasy. After a few more attempts at seduction, Peter stomped out of the bar growling something about "not needing this bullshit."

I smiled in earnest then. At least one problem had been removed. While her wish to drink hadn't done me any favours, it had helped to quash her lover's desires.

One-nothing for the good guys.

Then it occurred to me, if she wouldn't leave with Peter, how was I going to get her into the car?

The answer came quickly enough.

"Bartender, mix me another!" Aunt Harmony waved a ten-dollar bill in the air.

"Ma'am…"

"Ma'am?" she brayed. "I'm no ma'am. I'm a paying customer. Now make me another vodka martini, pronto!"

She grinned and I knew she imagined herself quite the comedian.

"I'm sorry, ma'am, but I can't serve you." The bartender looked to be about my age, his eyes filled with discomfort at having to tell an older woman that her drunkenness had bypassed legal serving limits. Now it was his turn to beg me silently for rescue.

"Whaddya mean?" Aunt Harmony pulled herself upright, opening her eyes from the half-closed position they'd been in since I'd arrived. It was her final display of dignity. "It's so early."

"C'mon, sweetie. It's time to head home," I said.

She looked around the room hoping, I supposed, to see someone familiar. Someone who might bail her out of this humiliating situation.

"It's okay." I wanted to keep her calm and get her outside before she found someone. "I've got the car. Want to go for a drive?"

"That sounds juss fine," she said. "Juss fine. Lemme go to the ladies' room firsht." She slid off the barstool and turned her ankle as she wobbled her way to the back of the room.

I avoided looking at the bartender or anyone else as I waited with growing impatience for her to make her re-appearance. Minutes ticked by and no Aunt Harmony. I collected our purses and went to find her. Perhaps she had fallen asleep in one of the bathroom stalls.

When I opened the ladies' room door, the only thing to greet me was empty space.

I pressed my fingers to my temples. "Damn it."

I tore out of the bathroom looking for a back exit and found one next to the kitchen. Stepping outside in the gathering dusk, I nearly tripped over her crouched on the ground having a pee with her dress hitched over her hips.

"For god's sake!" I couldn't believe it. "The toilet wasn't convenient enough for you?"

"Paper, I need some paper." She waved an arm in my face.

I fished around in my purse till I found some tissue and handed it to her. "This is against the law you know. Do you want to get arrested for public indecency or something?"

She stood up, threw her shoulders back, and straightened her dress. Her nose was pointed into the air and her hands were on her hips. "Stop yelling at me. I couldn't find the bathroom. Geez. You're as bad as your mother. Stuffy and mad all the time."

I was about to tell her exactly what I thought of her escapade when she hiccupped, triggering a fit of giggles. I couldn't help but laugh as well, shaking my head. She was a disaster. She'd probably spent all her money, she smelled like a distillery, and had, more than likely, peed on her feet. I'd hate to deal with the dagger-like headache she'd no doubt have in the morning. What was the point of getting cross? I led her to the car and buckled her inside.

She was asleep before I put the key into the ignition.

# CHAPTER SEVEN

When we arrived home, Gran was alert and ready to talk. After I dumped my aunt, fully clothed, into bed, and dealt with a phone call from my boss, I took a position on the hospital bed behind Gran, propping her into a sitting position with my shoulder. I rubbed the lotion I had already warmed between my hands onto her back.

"Ah," she gasped as I touched her.

Light massage helped with circulation and had to be done frequently throughout the day. After her back, I would proceed to her buttocks, legs and feet.

Her skin was dry, but doughy too and loose against her ribs, as though it was separating from the rest of her. Shedding. Too bad she couldn't cast off the sick parts and allow healthier ones to take their places. New lungs. That was all she'd need. A couple of beautiful pink balloons.

I moved from behind her and rolled her onto her side using gentle circular motions to rub more of the moisturizer into her skin. Jane had warned me not to rub too vigorously, just enough to get the blood flowing. I moved to a chair to work on her feet and then reached for her hands.

"That feels good." She smiled at me and for a moment, I imagined her as she had been years ago when we'd head to the beach and she'd be the one rubbing sunscreen onto me.

I leaned over and kissed her forearm. "I love you, Celeste."

"I know you do, honey. I love you too."

Tears sprang to my eyes and I turned away to hide them from her.

"None of that now. I'm not gone yet. I have more to tell you before I go."

I nodded dumbly.

"Where did I leave off?"

"Marriage. You married Denham."

"Yes, yes I did," Her eyes lost focus as she gazed back over her years.

"It was lovely," she said. "We had a multicultural ceremony officiated by a very open-minded minister, blending elements from Judaism, the Sikh dharma, and Shinto ceremonies."

"How did you manage all that?"

"Well, as the minister read our vows, we stood under a huppah to signify the new home we were making together. It was beautiful, all gauzy and white. Then we exchanged cups of sake to signify our life-long devotion to one another. My parents just stood there, tight-lipped, refusing to drink, thinking it was a heathen ceremony. That didn't bother me much though, I'd been expecting it.

"At the end, the minister wrapped a marriage cloth around us and both sets of your grandparents to join the families. Denny's mom and dad, Millie and Roy, cajoled my parents into playing along. 'What could it hurt?' Roy said. That was the kind of people they were and why I included a few verses from the Bible, to make them happy. I figure that must have been the only part that let them know it was legitimate." She crowed, her voice stretched thin then broke. "My parents hated every second of it, but at least I was married. That was a big deal to them. I bet they were happy we settled in Ottawa so their friends wouldn't know what I was up to."

"What was it like, when you were first married?"

"We pretended to be so grown-up. Kids in adults' clothing. Not that we were so young. I married later than most of my friends, but being married felt like a game of make-believe we were playing, trying out our new roles and acting however we thought smart, new marrieds should. Denny got a government job with the feds at the Department of Finance."

"What about getting your law degree?"

"I didn't go back. Got a job at the Legal Aid Society as a receptionist. It could have been dreadful—answering phones, filing—but I met so many people who needed help, I loved it.

"I wish you could have seen our flat. It was a one-bedroom in the east end of Ottawa." She stopped, searching for some memory. "I stayed there till after the girls left, moved back here … now what year was it?"

"Mother went to university in the late seventies so about '79?"

"Yes, that sounds right." She drifted away from me and then, like an arrow, was right back on target. "I used to drive Denny crazy dragging homeless men home for dinner and a shower. It wasn't that he minded me helping them; he'd even offer to cook food and help me hand it out. He just wasn't comfortable with strangers in the house. 'They could be dangerous,' he'd say. He used to do all the cooking, you know. That might not sound like a big deal, but he was a man ahead of his time. He'd get off work at four o'clock and when I'd get home after six, a meal would be waiting for me. He was a good guy, your grandfather was.

"Oh!" she said as though remembering something she'd long forgotten. "I used to volunteer at the library helping adults learn to read. I loved that too. Denny would get annoyed that I wasn't home more, but he adapted. As long as I was home for supper."

She was out of breath and labouring like a horse fighting to finish its last race.

"Has she eaten?" I asked Jane.

Jane clenched her lips together and shook her head.

"Not hungry," Gran said.

"Maybe something to drink?" I asked her.

She sighed, a gesture I chose to interpret as a positive sign. I went in search of a canned milkshake the nurse had recommended. It was full of nutrients.

Gran managed a few sips before she pushed the can away. "Never mind that now."

Her breathing calmed, her voice a whisper. "Life was good." She drew breath as deeply as she was able between each sentence. "We had a rhythm going that fit me fine. The only thing I didn't like were trips home to visit my folks. We used to alternate staying with his family and then mine. As much as I teased them about their devotion to their church, I loved his parents. They were good to me. Gentle and accepting people.

"I guess you don't remember your great uncles. You met them once when you were a wee one and you and your mom came to Nova Scotia to visit. They were quite a bit older than Denny, but they came for dinner one day to meet you. What a houseful that was, wives and kids. I had missed them all those years." Gran's voice grew distant; her eyelids drooped. "They're dead now, naturally. Nieces and nephews moved away. I lost touch with them years ago, of course."

"Why of course?"

Gran didn't answer. She was lost somewhere in another age. With her eyes still closed, she said, "Roy and Millie used to call Denny their Hail Mary baby, like he had been planned and hoped for in spite of their fading fertility, instead of the surprise he most likely was. They could be such characters."

"It was all great fun and then, snap!" Her eyelids flew open. "Angel came along and life did a one-eighty. I quit my job. Quit volunteering. Stopped bringing strange men home. That was okay though. Being pregnant and then being a mother was an experience beyond any I could have imagined. It was a change, but a good one. I know it sounds trite, but Angel was a wonder to me. So small, so dependent. I was caught up in her and motherhood. I truly believe it was the only time I was completely happy.

"Tell me about the day she was born."

"It was a little more than a year after we were married. I wanted a home birth. I figured what could be more natural than having a child? That was before labour began. Nothing prepares you for that. Woo wee. Twelve hours and a bottle of red wine later, she was born and was the most beautiful thing I had ever seen. Just beautiful. For three years, we got along just fine your mother and me. And then Harmony arrived." She paused.

"I thought life would just continue on as it had been going. It didn't though. From the beginning, Harmony was so different from your mother."

"Thank heavens for that." I slapped my thigh, mugging—joking but not joking.

"Oh, you tease, but it wasn't a welcome change. I had her at the hospital and they just knocked me right out. It was like being handed someone else's baby when I came to. And Harmony was demanding in a way Angel never had been. She cried all the time, didn't sleep through the night, wouldn't nurse. I was exhausted and my breasts were so sore I had to put her on the bottle. Boy! That added to my misery, being a failure at one thing women were supposed to do naturally. Harmony plain tired me out. Looking back, I think I had post-partum depression—nothing I'd heard about back then. Women called it the baby blues and expected it would simply vanish on its own. I guess for some it did, but not for me. I was overwhelmed. Life was not as easy as it had been with baby number one.

"I talked to my doctor about how I felt and he told me it was just a little anxiety so he prescribed a tranquilizer. Told me it was safe and would help me through the next few months until I could start getting some sleep on my own."

"I read an article about that. Weren't they called mothers' little helpers?"

"That's right and once I started, I kept taking them. Those few months turned into two years. He kept writing prescriptions and I kept popping those little pills. First, it was three times a day and then four and then five. By the time Harmony was two, I'm not sure how many I was taking.

"One morning, I was driving your mother to school. Harmony sat between her and me in the front. We had one of those bench seats like cars used to have. Most days we walked, but I had to get groceries that day so I took the car. We weren't wearing our seatbelts and when a cat ran out in front, my reflexes weren't fast enough to stop in time. I cranked the wheel to the side so hard I ran off the road and into the Wheeler's mailbox.

"That scared the hell out of me. The girls were crying. They'd both slid off the seat and bumped their heads on the dash. I could have killed them. We just sat there in the ditch for some time till my legs were steady enough for me to walk back home. I don't think the girls said boo all day. I'd look at them and start shaking all over, picturing what I could have done. Denham had to take care of getting the car towed and replacing the mailbox.

"That was it with those pills for me. It wasn't easy. I had the worst headaches and the nightmares, oh, they were bad. But I got off them." She shook her head, the recollection a difficult one for her.

"I'm never having kids. It amazes me that our species has carried on with all women go through. Were you okay after that?"

She shook her head again. "Something changed in me. Without the pills, I felt heavy, anchored in something that reminded me too much of my parents' space. I knew I needed a change and fast or those damn pills were going to come calling."

She had run out of breath again and when she exhaled, a tiny puddle of spit inflated at the corner of her mouth just like a cartoon dialogue bubble.

"Is that when you began to travel with Mother?"

"Don't rush me," she growled through tired lips. "I'll tell this my way." Then, she reached out to touch me. "I won't get another telling."

A lump caught in my throat and I fought it down. Gran didn't want my tears today.

"I need you to understand something." She spoke with effort. "I'm not proud of who I was. Even back then. I had a few years of being someone I liked after I got married. But since then? It's been all bluster, no substance. And I've made game of your mother and Denham, when he was here, so I could keep pretending to be the girl I had been, who I wanted to be. You see me as someone who lived a life, dancing to her own tune, even forcing others to dance along with her. And I see how you admire how I made them dance. But it isn't the truth. I want you to know the truth of me. And the truth of your mother."

A knot grew again in my chest. I didn't want to discuss my mother. Not now. I wanted to hear about Gran's exploits, so much different from mine.

"Don't do this, please. If you're trying to give me an unflattering picture of yourself to get me to appreciate my mother, forget it. We've got each other pegged pretty well."

"That's not true. You can be a mule and it's my fault. How can I make you see past the obvious?" Her tone switched; she was angry with me now. "Maybe you like it the way it is. Does it suit you to have her to blame for everything you don't like in your life?"

I crossed my arms over my chest and gritted my teeth. "I don't want to fight with you."

"Then don't. Just listen."

I became engrossed with an imaginary piece of lint on my T-shirt to avoid looking at her and chewed on the inside of my cheek, trying to hold back the self-pity that had been building inside me since arriving here.

"For you, just for you, I'll sit here and listen, but don't think I don't know you're conning me and if this situation were anything different than what it is, I'd be out of here."

"Well, I guess I can thank my failing health for small favours, can't I?" Her voice was low and swiped at me like a cat's claws. Her pale eyes crackled with anger and then faded, a flicker quickly extinguished.

I didn't know what to say or do. I had crossed a line that I didn't know existed and now faced my grandmother, angry with me for the first time in my life. Regardless of the situation, she had taken my side. Makeup, dating, clothes, music, even my decision to pass up university. She was my defender. I felt splinters spreading in the supports around me. It was like everyone had switched teams halfway through the series and I was left guarding the goal all by myself. I wanted to howl, I am right about her. I know her. You've always said I was right.

I lowered my head and choked down the bitterness of my own strong will. I closed my eyes yielding to the respect I had for Gran and prepared to listen to things I knew I wouldn't want to hear. When I looked up, for just one instant, there was a self-satisfied smirk on my grandmother's face that took my words away from me. An unbidden expression had been there for a second, but it was a second that told me something unpleasant. A warning perhaps? Of what?

I wouldn't pretend I hadn't noticed Gran's leer. Who was this person I saw just then? Perhaps the mother my mother had known?

Whatever the portent, the look was gone. Gran stroked my hand to quiet the thunder vibrating in the silence between us while I stretched my lips over my dry teeth to create the disguise of a smile, to pretend there was nothing wrong.

"I need you to listen to me, Kate." Her voice was urgent. Her breath came in gasps. "I don't want to go before I do the right thing. You cannot know how strongly this drives me."

Her breath caught and she began to cough, choking on the glue in her lungs. I reached behind to pull her upright, rubbing her back, trying to calm her. Her face turned red and then blue around her lips as she fought for air. I screamed for Jane who rushed into the room and adjusted the dial on the oxygen tank.

She thumped Gran's back and we waited, not breathing ourselves, to hear a regular inhalation. When we did, I laid her, exhausted and slipping into sleep, onto the pillow.

Gran's breathing was shallow, and Jane pushed me aside, talking to her unconscious lover, leaving me discarded and alone.

# CHAPTER EIGHT

"Wake up."

Strong fingers gripped my shoulder and shook me. I opened one eye, my lid etching the tracks of sleep over the soft surface of my cornea much as I've imagined the glaciers must have once done as they retreated and scraped slabs of rock across gentle meadows. The night nurse's face came into view, a look of concern showing in the pale morning light.

I jerked myself into a sitting position. "What is it?"

"You have a visitor." She was already at the doorway and flung over her shoulder, "He's waiting for you in the sun porch."

"Who is it?" My question went unanswered as she retreated to her patient in the living room.

I glanced at the clock and discovered it was shortly after four. Neither the soft chug of fishing boats or cacophony of seagulls broke the early morning silence. Who would visit me? And at this hour? I swung my legs over the side of the bed and turned on a light to check my face for tracks of drool or the crusty evidence of sleep. I hesitated before leaving the safety of my borrowed room, thinking back to the call I'd taken from my boss last night when I'd returned home with Aunt Harmony, hoping like anything this visitor had nothing to do with that.

My stomach curled into its usual knot at the thought that maybe I'd gone too far with him this time. But that was silly. He wouldn't have travelled here to fire me. Would he?

When a boss calls, it is either good news or bad news but it's never insignificant. That, in any event, has been my experience. Bosses don't call for something as trivial as, say, filling in for a sick waiter. They don't have to. If you're lying on your bathroom floor puking up the contents of your stomach and can't make it to work, you had better find the strength to crawl to the phone and find a colleague to cover your shift or else. Neither do managers pick up the phone to chat with you about the events of the day. When he has called, it has been either because I'm on the shit list for some impropriety (like last month when I told a customer who pinched my ass to fuck off) or about to receive a measure of his generosity. In the hospitality industry, the latter means either better hours, say regular shifts during Saturday supper hour instead of Monday lunch.

When Frankie Too called yesterday, he posed the socially expected questions of concern about my grandmother and then asked the question he'd really been calling about, "When will you be coming back to work?"

I knew him well enough to know that he didn't care about me or my grandmother, that the rest of his staff would love a chance at my shifts, and that he was calling to try to make me worry about my employment status. What class.

Screw you, Frankie Too, I wanted to say. She's not dead yet.

Instead, I used a tactic that I had learned from my mother, the reporter, one that had worked well for me in the past: silence.

As it hung there, heavy, dripping, reeking of his lack of compassion, a second of time stretching beyond his endurance, he stammered, "No rush, of course. I'm just making up next week's schedule. I didn't want you to be out—"

"Sure," I interrupted. "You're just looking out for me. Tell you what, Frankie Too, I'll let you know when Gran dies so you won't have to keep calling."

I could hear him grind his teeth at the mention of the nickname I'd given him. When I hung up, I smiled to myself. He wouldn't be phoning back anytime soon.

Could I have been more pleasant? Not for that bottom-feeding prick. And that was him on a good day.

As I dragged my reluctant feet toward whoever was waiting for me, I thought about how he treated the other girls at work—sleeping with new staff too young to know the score or giving bad shifts to those who wouldn't till they had to quit. Acting like a player with his loser friends and ordering the staff around like he was Napoleon and the restaurant was some country he'd just invaded. The only reason he had the place was because of the sweat and investment of his dad, Frank senior, a man I respected. I had started working there when old Frank ran the business so I'd avoided junior's lecherousness, but it still rankled to watch what he did to the female novices. I enjoyed sticking it to him when I could. It was great for my morale.

And I could get away with it. Like calling him Frankie Too, a nickname that drove him nuts. Frank senior was my ace in the hole. He loved me and his son knew it as well.

But yesterday's bravado didn't help to buoy my spirits as I slunk down the stairs toward my guest. My heart was pounding like a taiko drummer and I felt something horrible was about to happen.

My visitor turned to face me when I entered the room.

"Matt!"

There have been few definable points in time when I am quite honestly gobsmacked. Moments when my brain stands still, unable to sort out whatever is right in front of me. This was such a time. I watched as his face stretched to accommodate his wide, tooth-filled grin. As his arms reached out to pull me toward him, I stumbled into a hug that I returned with limp arms.

"What are you doing here?" It was the best I could manage under the circumstances as he rocked me from side-to-side as though he was an old friend giving me comfort instead of the one-night-stand I had intended him to be.

"I'm really sorry about your grandmother. I figured you might need some moral support so here I am." He took a step back, holding my shoulders, looking every bit like an optimistic pup about to wriggle his way onto my lap.

Crap.

In a vain attempt at graciousness, I asked him about his trip. He'd taken a flight after his shift and a cab from the airport.

"That must have cost you a small fortune," I said adding up prices in my head and wondering how I was going to extricate myself from this mess.

"Hey, you're worth it, even if you did take off without saying goodbye. At first, I was pissed, but then I figured maybe that was just your way of letting me know you trusted me in your place. I figured that was pretty cool."

I wish he'd stayed angry. My warm thoughts about him from only two days ago were so long gone, it was like I'd never had them. What a disaster this was turning into.

"Look, Matt. I think you've misinterpreted things between us."

It couldn't be possible, yet his ridiculous grin was growing wider. "Enough said. No pressure. I'm just here as a friend. I thought you could use one. I know you and your mom aren't exactly best girlfriends and I've got a couple of days off so here I am." He bowed low from the waist. "At your service."

What was I to do with that? Avoid it, that's what. I left to gather blankets and a pillow so Matt could make himself a bed on the porch sofa, then I returned to my room where I fell into a narcoleptic slumber—deep and stress induced.

Laughter from downstairs woke me later than I was becoming accustomed to rising. A deeper register disoriented me until I remembered Matt's arrival hours ago. I groaned and pulled a pillow over my face. This trip was becoming more bizarre by the day.

When I entered the kitchen after showering and dressing, I found Jane being charmed by Matt's tales of restaurant work.

"How come you never tell us this stuff?" Jane teased. "Serving sounds like so much fun."

"How's Gran this morning?" I asked, glaring at her in a way that I hoped would tell her I was not pleased at this turn of events.

"Sleeping."

"Morning, little Miss Sunshine," Matt beamed his irritatingly perky smile in my direction. Why hadn't I noticed his over-cheerfulness before? Surely I'd not have gotten involved—even briefly—with him if I had.

In stony silence, I poured myself a cup of coffee and Matt turned his attention to Jane asking about her work. I managed to stop myself from strangling him and caught her look of amusement.

"We're glad to have you join us," Jane said. "I'm sure Kate will be happy to have someone her own age around. The rest of us can be a handful."

She had either jumped to the wrong conclusion about the status of Matt and my relationship—which I doubted—or was trying to hide my lack of grace—which was more likely.

I was at a disadvantage. I had to either admit to Jane that, periodically, I did indeed sleep with men with whom I had no meaningful relationships, certainly not the kind that would include any expectation that one of them might fly to be at my side in a difficult hour, or I had to put up with Matt's presence, at least for a time.

I chose the second option. I didn't want to incur any more criticism than I'd already received. Jane was so well balanced, I often felt like an emotional misfit around her, although I knew she had had her share—more than her share—of troubles.

Perhaps I could play this out for a day or two. He'd have to leave eventually.

"Maybe after breakfast you could show Matt around," Jane said. "Have you ever been to Nova Scotia before?"

"Never," he replied. "I'd love to see the place though. Maybe check out a beach. See the Bluenose?"

By the time we were ready for a few hours of sightseeing, the day had become a hot one, at least by Maritime standards.

"I don't want to be out long," I cautioned him as we headed in the direction of Peggy's Cove. "I'm not here to party."

"Suits me. I'm just here to help."

"Frankie Too told you where to find me?"

"Like I would have asked that moron for the time of day. You might be surprised to find there aren't that many Simones in the Halifax phone directory."

"I still don't get why you're here." I could feel him staring at me, debating his response.

"I don't get you either," he said, his smile spreading once more across his face. "But that's okay with me. I like a challenge."

"Oh, for the love of god! We fucked, okay? That was it. One time. We're not engaged. I don't know what you think you're doing."

"Whoa. Relax a minute. Has it been so long since you've had a friend that you don't know one when you see one?" His smile disappeared.

"That's it! You show up in the middle of the night without so much as giving me advance warning and I'm supposed to be grateful? Maybe I've got things going on that have nothing to do with you and maybe I want to keep it that way." I was angry enough to forget about my decision to play nice for the sake of Jane's regard. I pulled the car onto the gravel shoulder and, once the road was clear of other traffic, turned around in the direction we had come. "Just leave. We can book you a flight back to Ottawa this afternoon."

We travelled in silence for ten minutes, my jaw clenched tight, my fingers holding the steering wheel in a death grip.

"Hey, I'm sorry," Matt said. "I thought we were just fooling around. I didn't mean to piss you off."

I ignored him.

"Really, I'm sorry. I shouldn't have come without calling. I had this stupid idea you might want me here. I didn't mean to cause you any more grief than you've already got. I know what it's like. I was only eight when my grandpa died and I was devastated."

Then I felt bad.

"If you want me to, I'll head home today. No hard feelings."

All I had to say was okay, but I knew I wouldn't do it. I wouldn't be able to bear being the cruel one, yet again.

"Never mind," I shook my head. "I'm just under a lot of pressure right now. I'm sorry I've been… Anyway, I'd be happy to have you here as long as we have an understanding. We aren't dating. We aren't in a relationship. We are just friends who work together. That's it."

"Fine with me. I promise." He grinned that big, stupid grin of his, the one that, at one time, I must have thought was charming, and gave me the three-fingered Boy Scout salute. I immediately regretted giving in.

"No funny stuff."

"You are one suspicious woman." He was laughing. "I think that's one of the things I like best about you."

I groaned and parked the car in the driveway.

"Why don't you go for a walk along the shore? I'm going to check on Gran. I'll catch up with you later."

Jane was sitting with my still-sleeping Gran, continuing with her quillwork when I walked in. "You're back early. You couldn't have gotten far."

She smiled at me, but I sensed her sadness and it weighed me down. My frustration grew in the face of my impotence in helping her or in dealing with Matt's naivety, Aunt Harmony's weakness and my mother's lack of caring.

As though reading my thoughts, Jane said, "Your mother called. She'll be on the late afternoon flight. Should be here about supper time."

"Great. She shouldn't have left in the first place."

"I know that's how you see it, but she's had to work very hard to make a good home for you. It's a hard habit to break."

"Why are you so nice to her? She barely gives you the time of day."

"Because I know it's not me she dislikes."

"Maybe you can explain it to me then because I don't get her at all."

"It's not my place to tell you. You should talk to her. And listen with an open heart."

"I've tried."

"Try again."

"C'mon Jane. We've been through this before. Could you just let it go?"

"First, let me tell you a story. You'll listen to me, won't you?"

I nodded. It seemed like everyone was telling me stories, but somehow I didn't seem to be learning a thing.

"You know my parents died in a car crash and I was sent to live with foster parents."

I nodded again.

"I was only six and the social workers decided I was better off with a white family than with my elderly grandmother. I was sent to live with the Tremblays, Edith and Jean-Guy."

"I know this already."

"Be patient." Her tone told me she was running out of the same for me. "My foster parents bought me toys and pretty dresses and sent me to a good public school. That you know too. Here's what you don't know: those toys and dresses were there to hide what I was. An Indian. They thought if they made me look like a white girl, I'd act like one and people would treat me like one. That I'd fit in."

"That's horrible."

"For a long time it was. To all those kids at school, I was the weird Indian kid and I was always going to be the weird Indian kid no matter how pretty my dresses were or how many new toys I had. It didn't matter how hard the Tremblays tried, I was miserable and lonely, and, in time, I began hating who I was too."

"I just don't understand what this has to do with me or my mother."

"Listen!" There was an edge to her voice and the words streamed from her with urgency. "I tried to do what they wanted me to do, but the colour of my skin and my accent got in the way. I was ridiculed. Although I did well in my schoolwork, I was so shy I couldn't speak when the teachers called upon me in class so everyone thought I was stupid.

"When I got older, I couldn't take the solitude anymore and you already know that I got into drugs and drinking."

I nodded.

"I needed help to deal with feeling like I was nothing. My crutch was drugs. What's yours?"

I opened my mouth to deny the accusation in her question, but changed my mind. I'd no idea what to say. I knew exactly what I did to help me through, but there was no way I'd share it with her.

"Whatever your drug, it will only help for so long. Like me, one day you're going to have to straighten out your emotions.

"Part of what helped me was relearning who I was. So many of us have had that taken away. That's why I teach what I teach. To help everyone know who my people are. If we don't know, how can we have pride in ourselves? And that's true for anyone who's lost. Even you.

"The thing of it is I could have hated the white government and the Tremblays for what I went through. I could have spent my whole life blaming them. But what would that have done for me?" Jane touched her chest with the tips of her fingers. "The government was wrong, but it was the thinking of the day. The Tremblays were wrong, but they had the best of intentions for me. They were kind people.

"I was angry for a long time, but then I found strength inside me and from the teaching of my people that allowed me to let all that hurt go. I found myself by myself and it feels good to have grown into the person I am. Not perfect, certainly. In charge of myself, definitely.

"That's what I wish for you, my girl. For you to be happy with who you are. I don't think that is ever going to happen if you can't make peace with your mother."

I was so frustrated, I couldn't respond. It's not my fault, I wanted to yell at her. My hands were shaking and I fought back tears. I'd been feeling that I'd fallen into a part that someone had created for me in a game I didn't understand. My role was built on petty resentments and childish rebellions that I was stuck carrying out with total self-justification. Blaming me for something I had no control over was so unfair.

I squirted moisturizer onto my open palm and warmed it before rubbing Gran's feet. When I drew the blankets back, I was horrified to see the sign we had been dreading. The tips of Gran's toes had turned black.

# CHAPTER NINE

I jangled car keys in front of Matt's nose. "Shall we try it again?"

"Is it safe?" His preternaturally wide grin spread across his face. "I knew you couldn't stay mad at me forever."

We drove the twists and turns to Queensland Beach. Despite its popularity, it wasn't much of a beach. It practically disappeared at high tide. There were many others far more expansive and beautiful, but it was close and, therefore, the one I chose.

I pulled off the main road to park in the sparse shade of the few trees standing opposite the water before I grabbed my sunhat from the backseat and walked to the ocean's edge.

I'd resolved to be pleasant today, to avoid all temptation to argue or harangue. Escaping the house and the conflicts resident there seemed a wise tactic to help me achieve this modest-sounding though difficult-to-achieve goal. The endless, verbal toing and froing was getting to me even though I seemed to be the cause of most of it.

I wiggled my toes, burying them in the wet sand as waves rushed over them. The icy water belied the season as was often the case along the south shore. The warm water of the Gulf Stream passed us by, by not passing by us, in its rush to get to Europe.

We left the water and kicked off our shoes, abandoning them in the dry, white sand and turned to walk the length of the beach. I stayed within reach of the icy tide that rode over my feet. Matt joined me, kicking at the waves as he walked.

The sheer gloriousness of the day, the warmth of the sun penetrating my skin and oiling my joints, the resonance of the peaceful surf, and the taste of salt carried by the gentle ocean breeze lightened my miserable spirit. Other visitors playing or lounging around us, didn't exist as I closed my eyes and willed them gone, my arms stretching up and out, expanding the tightness that habitually gripped my chest. A bubble of something like joy rose within me and I flung my arms wide. When I opened my eyes, Matt was staring and me.

Embarrassment replaced the happiness that had been so all-encompassing only a second before.

"Don't stop," Matt begged, his eyebrows crinkling in concern. "It was great to see you let go, to be happy."

"I like being here." The words piled against each other and caught in my teeth. I lowered my head and continued along the shore.

Matt slipped his hand into mine and anchored me. "Don't stop being happy just because I'm here." He released me and flailed his arms about, exasperated. "Don't be so worried about letting go. I'm not going to think less of you or tell anyone at work the big secret about Kate at the beach."

"I shouldn't be happy right now."

"Your grandmother wouldn't mind. I bet she'd be glad to see you like this."

I shrugged and then nodded. "Let's walk."

At the far end of the beach, ancient boulders had been stacked against a bluff, more likely by men in big machines than by Mother Nature although she too had taken a turn at hurling large rocks during the last hurricane. Two young boys scampered among them, hunting for some treasure.

I chose a seat away from the boys and stared out to sea, the horizon broad and empty. Matt shared my rocky perch.

With the exception of the kids, we were alone. A shadow cast each afternoon by the bluff kept sunbathers at the other end of the beach.

We spoke little and impersonally. Comments about sea and weather, about the quarry of the boys. Nothing that meant anything. It was a break from the goings-on at the house, and the tension that had crawled into my shoulders days ago eased a little.

"I love it here," I said.

"Favourite place?"

"No. There are far better beaches than this one. But the idea of this—the water, the wind, the sand—it's elemental and permanent. Gets to me somehow."

"Ever think of moving here?"

"Only all the time." I thought back to my recent self-questioning. Whether a move away from my mother to live nearer my dear loony aunt would be a good one. Something swirled within me and bubbles rose to my brain, tantalizing, teasing. A change was coming. A change that filled me with bigness and hope. But what was it? I'd no answer and I felt my conscious mind racing from one corner of my brain to another, trying, with growing desperation, to find one.

Stop. I wanted to hold on to the joy of anticipation without muddying it with fear.

One of the boys called out and the other ran to him. They were poking at something with a stick. Something under one of the boulders. I hoped whatever it was wasn't alive and I shaded my eyes with my hands, squinting, waiting to see if I should intervene.

The smaller of the two yelled in triumph. "Got it!" He held what looked like an empty crab shell over his head like he'd just won the World Cup of beach combing. He raced ahead of his companion to a man and woman sitting on folding chairs some distance away. In seconds, their voices were carried off by the breeze that had, in the minutes we'd been here, turned into a light wind.

Standing, I rubbed feeling back into my buttocks, cold and numb from the stone. "C'mon."

We ambled, retracing the steps we'd left in the sand not long ago, now undetectable under the incoming tide that had already swallowed inches of beach. Clouds scudded across the still sunny sky in the building wind and the glow of my anticipation faded under spots of shadow cast along the shore.

As earlier, I toyed with the waves, skimming my feet over their tips as they reached me. I stood still and closed my eyes feeling the power of wind and sea, the sheer enormity of nature, fill me as I inhaled deeply, trying to hold on to some of its peace.

Matt's hands again found me. They were warm against my neck as he worked my muscles. I slumped against him as his arms wrapped around me.

"This isn't so bad, is it?" he asked.

The spell shattered like so many shards of glass. I pulled away and shook my head. "So bad? No. But not what you want either."

"Christ, Kate. Relax."

"Why does this have to be something? Why can't you just be my friend without trying to make it something else? Isn't that why you came here? Because you're my friend?"

"You know that's why."

"Bullshit." I advanced toward him, the wind filled my shirt, and my shadow grew as large as the anger within me. "I don't want what you want. Can't we leave it at that? You shouldn't have come here." I turned from him and marched toward the car and my shoes. What a waste of a perfectly good afternoon.

Matt caught up beside me. "I'm sorry."

I ignored him.

"Really. I shouldn't have pushed you."

I stopped short and gave him what I hoped was a look that would make him flinch. "Two hours. That was all I wanted. A two-hour break from my family and obligations."

"I know. I'm—"

I turned away and continued stomping across the sand.

He caught up to me again, holding his hands up in surrender. "Just forget it, okay? Let's just forget this happened."

"Don't lie to me. Not about your motives. Not about anything."

"I won't. I shouldn't have pushed it."

I inhaled again and sank onto the warm ground. Matt sat beside. I drew my legs up in front of me and rested my chin on my knees, looking straight ahead.

The water was no longer in touching distance, but still nearby, still compelling, still omnipotent. I drank in the beauty that helped me regain some of my previous composure.

"I can't have a relationship with you." I didn't look at him. "There are too many other things going on. Can't you get that?"

"I really do want to be your friend. Even if there can't be anything else."

I laid back, the heat of the sand warming my back, the wind whipping my loose hair across my face.

Be in the moment. Don't think about anything else. Just be here.

I focused on the growing rumble of the sea and the heat that filled my pores and baked my pale skin. The salt was carried on every molecule of air until its taste coated my lips.

Just a few more minutes. Don't let anything spoil this for a few more minutes.

My eyes were closed and hearing the screech of gulls, I imagined them floating on air currents, their wings outstretched casting shadows on the water below them. The faint put-put of a boat further out to sea was barely audible.

I didn't know how long we laid there, my mind drifted. Unbidden memories of my childhood skipped into my head. My tenth birthday had been celebrated right here with a bonfire and ghost stories. I remembered Gran dancing with Aunt Harmony, a couple walking a large black dog and waving hello, I even remembered the Bruce Springsteen tape we listened to over and over.

What I couldn't remember was any evidence of my mother. She must have been with us. Why couldn't I remember her?

# CHAPTER TEN

Someone shook my arm. Matt's face came into focus. "I think we better get back."

I blinked and squinted into the afternoon glare. "What time is it?"

Matt shrugged. "I don't know, but you're turning red."

I looked down at my arms. After lying in the sun, they had a bleached, over-exposed look to them, but blood sprang to the surface when I pressed my skin with a finger. "Nothing like Irish skin for burning."

The day, though bright, had moved beyond noon and our shadows stretched before us as we brushed the sand from our clothes and slipped on our shoes. My stomach rumbled. We'd been out far too long. I'd had no intention of being away from Gran for more than an hour or two.

"God, I hope she's…"

"She's fine. She's fine. They would have called. Take your…" Matt's words were carried away on the wind as I sprinted away from him toward the car.

"Hurry up," I yelled as I fumbled with the door lock.

We sped home and I jumped out of the car as soon as it came to a full stop.

"You look like you've seen a ghost," Jane said as I ran into the living room.

"Celeste is okay?"

Jane nodded. "Still sleeping."

I was panting, adrenaline having fired my imagination to the terrible possibility of what might have been. "I'm sorry I was gone so long."

"Don't worry. We're all fine. Better than you from the looks of it. You are going to be in some pain tomorrow. Better get the aloe vera from the pantry."

Matt retreated to the porch while I attended to my skin.

It wasn't till late afternoon that Aunt Harmony slithered down the stairs to the kitchen where I'd been labouring over a crossword puzzle trying to get some distance from Matt. When I looked up, she held her shaking hand out before her to stop me from speaking. I watched as she poured herself a glass of ginger ale and bounced a couple of ibuprofen from their bottle onto her opened palm.

"You reek," I said without malice though, truth be told, alcohol and urine were an unpleasant combination.

She glared in return like a petulant child caught doing something she'd rather have gotten away with.

I sighed. "Why don't you go have a shower and I'll change your bed sheets?" They would most certainly be as rank as she was. I expected her to flip me off. Instead, she nodded and padded back up the stairs to the bathroom.

I changed her linens then decided to do the same for all the beds. Clean sheets felt so good and I needed something to be unsoiled that day.

The two of us finished at the same time and returned to the kitchen.

"Where is everyone?" she asked.

She said everyone, but was really asking about Mother. We could both see Jane in the next room watching over Celeste. I told her Mother was in Ottawa and due back that evening.

"Just as well."

I knew what she meant. She'd be able to get herself together before the onslaught of questions and indictments about her absence and her condition. Facing my mother while suffering from a hangover would inspire a saint to suicide.

I told her about Matt who was napping in the front porch.

"Ahh, the plot thickens." She poked and pushed at the scrambled eggs on the plate I'd placed before her before giving up on them and reaching for a piece of toast that she held to her mouth with both hands, like a raccoon or a large squirrel. She nibbled at it with rodent-sized bites until her hunger was piqued and then wolfed the eggs down in a minute flat before asking for jam for her toast.

When she was finished, she brushed the crumbs from her small chest onto the empty plate. "Let's go sit outside."

I poured two glasses of tomato juice, sprinkled liberally with pepper, and followed her to the side porch.

The cool wind that blew nearly without pause from the ocean had died down to nothing and the air was warm and close allowing black flies to exit the woods. The rapid change in temperature would bring in fog that evening. Aunt Harmony stretched out on a lounge chair. In spite of the heat of the day, she shivered from being over-tired and dehydrated. I fetched her a blanket from the house.

"I should keep you around all the time," she said as she reclined and adjusted the end of the cover over her feet.

"It's not like I never asked for just that."

Silence filled the space between us and I regretted what I'd said. The twins Remorse and Guilt had joined to become a motif of mine since I'd arrived and I didn't like it. I'd been pin-balling from Vesuvial anger to feeling terrible about my behaviour. There were too many unresolved issues among my family to make for a problem-free get-together and fuss was something that, in my day-to-day existence, I avoided. If I were to make an objective judgement about my recent behaviour, I'd have to admit that creating a scene was becoming a staple of my repertoire.

"So, what's the story with young Matthew?" Aunt Harmony watched me over the edge of her glass of juice.

I shrugged and refocused on my crossword puzzle. "Your guess is as good as mine."

"Somehow I imagine you have a few more details than I do."

"For heaven's sake, let it go. I don't know what got into his head to come here. I wish I could send him home. But I can't because I don't want Jane to think less of me than she already does."

"You're being a little overly dramatic, aren't you?"

"It was just supposed to be an insignificant fling. How was I supposed to know he'd think I needed him? And what do you think Mother is going to say when she gets here?"

"This could work. Might take the focus off me for a bit."

"I'm so glad this is a benefit to one of us." I wanted to ask about her drinking. Seconds ticked by as I screwed up my courage. "Aunt Harmony, are you all right? Mother thinks you need help and I'm wondering if she's right."

She made a face, puckering her lips in annoyance. "Really? The world's biggest tight-ass thinks someone isn't measuring up to her standards. Send out a news release. She needs to get a life and leave me alone." She swallowed a large mouthful of juice. "Actually. I take that back. I shouldn't say things like that in front of you. She's done a lot for me over the years."

My ears perked up. "Like what?"

"Like never mind, little Miss Butt-in-ski. There are things sisters don't talk about."

"Hey, all you've ever done is complain about her. Why the loyalty all of a sudden?"

"You know what Kate? I hate to say it, but your mother's right. You're turning into a real pain in the ass. Stay out of things that don't concern you."

Her words stung. I was beginning to feel like I'd walked into a family made up of people I only thought I knew. My aunt may have been unreliable in many ways, but I had been able to count on her to stand in solidarity with me regarding anything to do with my mother.

While I tried to think of something clever to say, Aunt Harmony rolled onto her side and after a few minutes began to snore. Far from being annoying, the sound was low and quite soothing. I let myself be lulled by it as I quelled my disquiet and wondered what favours my mother may have done for her little sister. Somehow I thought it was something more important than covering up a missed curfew. Otherwise why mention it? As I returned to my puzzle, a black fly flew into my ear and I swatted at it. I sipped my drink trying to think of a seven-letter word for "seltzer-making device" when I heard a car engine.

Mother was home.

Normally, I would have tried to keep her from berating my aunt, but Matt would be diversion enough, at least for the first evening. And it was a good thing too because I didn't have the strength to get between the sisters. It was enough that I'd have to explain the sack of testosterone sleeping on the couch.

I took another sip of my drink, and smacked one of the little vampires on my shin and another on my right arm while I waited for Mother to appear.

A black fly flew into Aunt Harmony's open mouth and she gagged. "What the—?" She ran her hands through her wet hair and over her face then looked around to get her bearings and yawned. "I'm going to bed."

"Mother's back."

She grimaced. "Well, I'm just going to have to take a pass at what I'm sure will be some terrific fireworks, but I'm beat. I can't deal with her right now." She pulled the blanket around her shoulders and walked inside, the screen door slapping gently against its frame behind her.

The bugs were becoming bothersome. I was bleeding from bites that circled my ankles like a tattoo completed by a shaky hand. Gathering my things, I waved my arms around my head to stop any of the bloodsuckers from entering the house with me.

Jane was still with Gran who was sleeping.

"Where's Mother?"

"Shower." Jane looked at me from her book.

"I'm sorry about Matt intruding," I began. "And I didn't mean to be rude earlier; I just don't want him here."

"He seems like a nice young man. It means something when someone goes out of their way to offer their friendship."

"I don't think friendship is what's really on his mind."

"You may be right. Or you may be wrong. Either way, he's here and I don't mind. It's nice to have someone to take our minds off each other."

Gran stirred and opened her eyes. She raised her arm, the slack skin drooping past her elbow. "Water."

I left to get some and when I returned, Jane was washing Gran's face. She ran the wet cloth across Gran's nearly bald head, flattening her wisps of down into a sad looking comb-over.

I grinned. "How are you feeling?"

Using her tongue to push out the straw I had placed between her lips, she mumbled something unintelligible then slipped back into sleep. She'd barely touched the water.

"What are we going to do?" I asked Jane as though she could have the answer to such a question.

"Wait and hope. Keep her company. Just keep on with what we're doing."

"She has to finish her story."

"She will if she can." The look on Jane's face wasn't hopeful.

We were intent on watching Gran, the blue veins at her temples pulsing, her mouth hanging open. When Matt entered the room, we both jumped.

"How is she?" He wiped the grit out of his eyes and Mother came in behind him.

"Who is this?" she asked, her left eyebrow arching.

Be pleasant. This will be difficult enough.

I made the required introductions, explaining Matt's presence as best I could.

"You're from Kate's work. How nice." I knew that she didn't think it was nice at all, but, she had seemingly decided that he might make himself useful asked. She turned to him and said: "Since you're here to help, perhaps you can lend me a hand me with dinner? Something simple, everyone? Toasted tomato sandwiches?"

Without waiting for an answer, she whisked my knight-errant into the kitchen and I exhaled, feeling for a brief moment like I'd dodged a bullet.

Over sandwiches and salted cucumbers from the garden, we made small talk. Matt seemed fascinated by my mother's job and grilled her about the day's news conference and subsequent story.

"It's not that interesting, really," she said, motioning toward me with her fork. "Just ask Kate. I'm sure she'd love to tell you just how unimportant my work is."

My eyes remained focused on my plate as tears pricked the backs of my eyes. I will not get into it with her. I will not.

"That can't be true," Matt said.

"Go ahead, ask her." The bitterness she had toward me was imprinted on every inch of her face.

"You want it, Mother? Fine, you got it. You know you should have put Celeste first. You should have taken care of your sister, but no. Work comes first. It always has. And I don't even get one bit of credit for taking care of things while you're away."

"See?" Mother looked at Matt, a triumphant smile on her lips.

"Kate's been taking great care of her grandmother while you've been gone." It was a valiant attempt to support me and I appreciated his effort although he was way out of his league. She could squash him like a bug if she so chose. Instead, she switched her sights to another target.

"Speaking of people needing care, has anyone heard from Harmony?"

"Upstairs. Sleeping," I said, defeated.

"Would that be sleeping or sleeping it off?"

"Does it matter?" Jane heaved a sigh. "Can't we get through one evening with you two in the same room without all the nattering?"

Silence. Horrible, anger-filled silence. My stomach clenched and acid rose to my throat.

"You're right and I'm sorry," my mother said, surprising me with her contrition. "This is your home and I've been behaving badly. I must be more tired than I thought. I have to call the paper to confirm the last details on the story then I think I'll curl up in bed and read. Get a good night's sleep."

She excused herself from the table as did Jane leaving Matt and me to handle clean up. I looked at him. "If any of this gets around at work, I'll know who it came from."

He shook his head. "I don't know who you're used to hanging out with, but you've got me all wrong. You know, at work, you're really funny and smart. When you started crapping on me after I got here, I put it down to this being a tough time for you. Since then, I've started to think you're just not that funny anymore."

He walked to the sink and fished in the cupboard underneath for dish soap. We cleared the table and washed the few dirty dishes in silence.

When we were done, he asked for the loan of a car. "I'd like to go for a drive. Are there any coffee shops around here?"

Jane loaned him her vehicle and gave him directions to the closest café about ten minutes away.

It was then I realized that Mother hadn't even been told about Gran's feet. Neither had Aunt Harmony. All this bickering. We had lost sight of our reason for being here.

# CHAPTER ELEVEN

My habit of going to bed after midnight had changed since arriving at Gran and Jane's and, as my bedtime inched its way counter-clockwise toward eleven and then ten or even nine, I found myself rising earlier and earlier each morning. By the end of the first week even when it wasn't my turn to be on Gran-detail, I rose to tend to the garden by seven. Mother was right. It was much more bearable to pull weeds before the sun's heat beat down and while the earth was still damp and amenable to releasing tiny roots.

With my iPod for company, I worked the rows of vegetables one-by-one. Sitting astride Jane's garden stool or bending on dirty knees, I crouched and plucked the unwanted sprouts. By day three, the muscles of my thighs and backside had stopped hurting.

I discovered that I enjoyed the solitude of early morning work. By breakfast, I had already accomplished something tangible. It was a great feeling and working a little bit each day meant that marathon gardening sessions were a thing of the past.

While I weeded, I mulled, trying to figure things out. My family's inability to connect with each other. My grandmother's role. My mother's thorniness. My aunt's sadness. And how Jane fit in to all of this. Though I tried, I couldn't get a handle on why things were the way they were.

To me, Gran was the best. Unconventionality was her trademark and I loved her for it. Why couldn't Mother feel as I did?

I stowed the gardening tools on the porch and headed indoors to shower. As the water ran over my skin, our family situation and my ineptitude at resolving it plagued me. I wrestled with ideas, hitting dead ends wherever my thoughts turned. My skin pruned as I stood brooding until Jane yelled that I would make the well run dry. While I dressed, I applied my happy mask, the smile that would hide my unhappiness from Gran.

The nurse had already left and Jane was in her chair between the window and the hospital bed, staring into space, her lips moving in what might have been prayer. It was unusual to find her empty-handed. I looked closely at her face. She'd been crying and looked tired. The lines on either side of her mouth were more pronounced and despite very few strands of grey in her hair, I could, for the first time, envision her as an old woman.

I kneeled on the floor in front of her and placed my head on her lap, stroking her hand. "I'm sorry about last night."

"I know."

The compressor in the fridge clicked on, the hum loud in our quiet.

"She's leaving me," Jane whispered.

I nodded though I didn't believe it. Not really or at least not yet. She had to come back and finish telling whatever had been so important that she would spend her last bit of energy to make sure I'd know.

My thoughts returned to Jane. How would she make out without Gran? They'd been together for nearly thirty years. More than my whole life and almost half of Jane's existence. I'd never known one of them without the other and the thought of that brought the old, black emptiness back to me.

It was the same feeling I'd had whenever something bleak or frightening had taken place. Aunt Harmony's rejections. My mother's distance. Family arguments. Loneliness. And here it was again. It was an unbearable thing that only experience had taught me to bear. I could wait it out, make it fade and then return to my land of nothingness, a place better suited to the daily burden of faking my own humanity.

Jane's hand trembled and her breast heaved as her sadness brought on more tears. I reached my arms around her waist and hugged her from my squatting position at her knees, my head burrowed into her belly. I wanted so much to run from the pain that was spreading through her and engulfing me. Run and cast off the feelings that threatened my practiced detachment. But how could I do that to my dear Jane? I loved her so much.

Instead, I stayed in place until my thigh muscles twitched and my knees screamed from the discomfort of the pad-less floor. I kept still so as to not disrupt Jane's grieving. It was a form of penitence for my poor behaviour.

I hated myself for my churlishness and self-indulgence. My inability to get things right. I so wanted to do better, to be of service, to give and receive love. Here I was with one of the two people on this earth who had loved me without condition and I was making a mess of things.

When Jane's tears had run their course, I drew my arms in and stood slowly. My back and legs were tight and unyielding.

"I will stay with you, if you want me. You don't have to be alone."

Her lips were dry and pale, and couldn't make the journey into a smile though she tried. "I'm not alone. I have family."

"But I can stay here for as long as you want me." With a startling urgency, I needed her to need me. Springing from a wound deep within me, I longed for her to tell me she wanted me to stay.

I needed to belong somewhere and to love someone. To know that my one-night stands, my arguments with my mother, my ongoing prickly, bitchy behaviour wasn't all there was to me. As these thoughts and emotions swarmed in my head, the black hole inside me was replaced with something far worse. Anxiety and neediness welled with the strength and fury of a gale-force wave washing over me. It was terrible and beyond any emotion I'd ever felt. I gasped and flung my arm toward Jane as a drowning woman would toward a potential saviour.

She grabbed my hand and I rushed at her, flinging my arms around her neck, grabbing handfuls of her clothes to anchor me to her. She stroked my hair and crooned something so softly that I could have been a baby being rocked to sleep. I couldn't understand the Mi'kmaw words yet they gave me comfort and we stood that way, rocking gently back and forth until she pulled away from me.

"It is time to stop the crying now. Her time is near and we will hold her spirit back."

Jane walked over to a candle and lit it with matches she had at the ready. "To light her way to the next world."

I held back my tears and swallowed the ache in my throat.

"I don't think she will come back to us now. We must stay with her so her spirit isn't alone."

I nodded and looked toward the doorway. My mother was there staring back, her tangled hair a cloud of blonde around a haggard, lonely face.

It wasn't often that I thought of how close in age these women were; my mother and Jane were only a handful of years apart.

Our eyes locked, mother's and mine, hers soft and unreadable, mine surely showing my confusion. Wanting yet missing something from me, she looked away and I studied her from the safety of Jane's shoulder.

Her lips were pursed as they often were, in distain or disapproval I'd usually thought. Could I be wrong? What if it was regret that drew her mouth so tight it wouldn't let words of sympathy or affection escape? What if it was her own personal pain that caused her to hold in her emotions? What if it was a secret as big as the one Gran wanted to tell that made her seem impervious to me?

These uncomfortable thoughts pulled at me. I wasn't wrong about her. Couldn't be. She'd virtually abandoned me for a job that gave her more satisfaction than being my mother. I'd created a life on this truth.

Her voice startled me into the present. "Has she awoken this morning?"

Jane shook her head. "It's time for us to be together now."

"I'll get dressed. Kate, perhaps you could rouse your aunt?"

Matt entered the room stretching his back and bending his neck from side to side. A second night on the old couch hadn't done his spine any favours. I had to admit that even tousled, he was a good-looking man. His thick, black hair darted out from his head at irregular angles, full brows framed hazel eyes that sparkled with gold and an angular jaw line led to an equally well-defined chin. His lean torso fanned outward toward square shoulders that he flexed under a blue T-shirt.

"Matt. Good morning. Why don't you make yourself useful and make us a pot of coffee?" Mother was smiling her most charming smile and Matt reciprocated.

"Happy to be of service, madam." He bowed low then scampered off to do her bidding.

I wanted to throw up.

The grand dame and her pet.

Jesus.

This was not how things were supposed to go. Mother wasn't flexible. She didn't like strange men popping up at any time let alone in the middle of a serious family event. What was going on?

My life had been going along just fine, thank you, until the moment Mother received Jane's call to come to Gran's side. Since then, I'd lost control. Of nearly everything. Gran's secrets I could take. Mind-blowing at times, yes, but manageable. Aunt Harmony's alcoholism I could tolerate. Knowing she had a problem made it even easier for me to accept how she'd sometimes treated me. But when Jane or my aunt criticized me and took my mother's side, or when my mother feigned delight in my supposed romantic interest, well, that was too much. There was no way she should be enjoying his company. She should be irritated at his presence. She should be critical and cutting. She should order me to tell him to leave.

That would be normal.

But everything was changing.

Life was rushing through my fingers like a wave ebbing from a rocky shore-line. I could hear the tide's tinkling laughter while I laboured to stop its retreat with every bit of determination I could muster.

How could I fight it?

Gran was dying and Aunt Harmony had become so sad. Even my mother was unreadable.

Maybe hell had finally frozen over. Maybe there was a rare confluence of celestial bodies creating havoc with my present. Maybe I'd died and gone to that place my friends had warned me I'd end up.

All I could be sure of was that I had all these stupid feelings racing around inside me and I hated them.

I listened to the chatter of new-found buddies, Mother and Matt, and felt ill. Wasn't dealing with Gran's death enough for one day?

"I'm going to get dressed," I announced to Jane. "I'll get Aunt Harmony up when I'm done."

I stood under the shower head, enjoying the warm water as it hit me with the softness of a summer's rain and delaying my exit as long as I could.

It was with sinking heart that I approached Aunt Harmony's bedroom door knowing that this day would place a strain on a healthy, functional family. What was going to happen with mine could not be anything good.

I shook Aunt Harmony awake, the smell of her breath hitting me like a hammer.

"Time to get up. Jane sent me to get you."

She brushed her curls out of her eyes and looked frightened. "Is Celeste gone?"

"No. But soon maybe. We should be with her."

"Let me get cleaned up. I'll be down in a few minutes." She paused, listening intently to the sounds coming from downstairs. "Is that Angel? Laughing?"

Only in my family would that noteworthy.

"Indeed it is. She's developed an instantaneous liking for Matt."

"Excellent." Aunt Harmony bounded out of bed. "This day might be do-able after all."

"Really?" I asked in a way that I hoped would cut her to her core. "Because your mother is dying so it's great that this day might be good for you."

Her eyes narrowed into angry slits. "Get. Out."

And I did.

If it wasn't for Jane, I'd have left then. Called a cab, fled to the airport and flown home. Back to sanity even if sanity meant having a boss like Frankie Too in it and, if I were to be honest, a rather solitary existence.

But that was better than this. Today needed the skills of a hostage negotiator or a seasoned improvisational actor and, while I was known for being a quick wit, I preferred my characters to stick to their established roles. Changing mid-way through the plot wasn't for me.

So, I clumped downstairs, my most optimistic hope was that I might escape having much attention paid me given the combination of Matt's novelty and Aunt Harmony's theatrics. The former being a fact and the latter being something I was pretty sure I could still count on despite the changeability of everything else.

"Matt's making cheese omelettes for us. They should be ready soon," Mother said turning toward me as I entered the room. "I've been talking to your guest. I must say, it took me aback when I arrived yesterday and found a stranger sleeping on the porch."

I shrugged, having no idea of what to say.

"Will he be staying?"

"Only for a couple of days.

"I don't like him being here."

"You could have fooled me. And him. You've likely got him thinking you're his best friend. How am I supposed to get rid of him now?"

"I was hardly going to be rude to your boyfriend. I don't think I've ever met one of those before."

"He's just a friend. He's here because he had some bizarre notion that this is what friends do for each other."

Mother had a disconcerting glint in her eyes. If it were anyone else I would have called it mischievous, but since it was her, I didn't know what to think.

"I'll buy if that's what you're selling." She turned toward Jane. "I think I'll go check on our food and leave you two time to talk. With everything that's been going on, you probably haven't had much time together."

It was a fraudulent pretext, naturally. Jane was the only one I had been speaking with. No one else had been around. Once more, I was infuriated by my mother. She never missed a chance to make her feelings toward Jane known. She couldn't stand spending more time with her than was necessary.

I sat next to Gran, resting my head on her bed. I inhaled her scent, hoping to trigger some past happy memory. She didn't smell like herself anymore, of course. Just a sick, old woman, sour and metallic from the medicines she took. I didn't know I was crying until I felt the sheets wet against my cheek and then Jane's warm hand rubbing my back.

"That's all right now, little one. Close your eyes and feel me with you. Remember some of the times we've had together."

"I don't want her to go."

"I know. I know. But we can be strong together. Do you remember when you were a little girl, about five or six, and we went to the Powwow? Remember how we danced? Toe to heel. Toe to heel. Around and around. And the beautiful ceremonial dresses the women wore? And the face paint of the warriors? You were frightened at first and cried when you saw a young man with black face paint. He was fierce and proud and his headdress of eagle feathers sprouted around his head like a sunburst. He chanted as he spun around the circle and I lifted you into my arms. You were so afraid. But we whispered as we walked and soon you forgot all about the scary man and you lifted your little girl arms to the sky to be nearer the Creator. It was a glorious day. That was the day you prayed in your first smudge. Do you remember what you prayed for?"

I shook my head.

"To be strong and brave like the warrior with the black face." Jane nodded as she spoke, a faraway look in her eyes. What else was she remembering from those good times past? Her attention returned to me. "You've turned into such a strong woman. Don't be afraid today. I love you and I'm still with you."

Tears exploded from my eyes in a waterfall of heartache. My body shook as I fought to hold on to my emotions.

"Let go," she said. "It's good to let it go. It makes you stronger in the end."

And so I did. Sobbing until my tears ran dry and my chest heaved, forcing sadness from me like a giant billows pumping air.

The remainder of the day crept by as we moved about the house like chess pieces, our antagonism driving each other from space to space. Perhaps we were too much the same, magnets pull together when they oppose, repel when they align.

We moved about the room, the house, sliding off at angles when another approached. Jane seated beside Gran, her queenly demeanour silent and deep. Aunt Harmony restless, hopping from chair to chair or from room to room, depending upon the direction of Mother's advance. For her part, Mother seemed to glide from her mother's bedside to a chair by the entranceway where she focused her formidable attentions on a tatty book, its corners frayed and its binding worn, a title stamped in gold that I couldn't make out. Whenever she broke from reading to stand over Gran, Aunt Harmony skittered to another corner of the room. When Mother returned to her seat, my aunt would take her turn standing vigil.

Dinner that night was gloomy. Matt was put to work at the barbeque with the steaks. I made a salad and boiled some corn. We played with our food or ate in silence. Matt attempted to lift our spirits by asking gentle questions about movies and books. Eventually, the weight of our mood bore down on him and he joined in our sorrow. We finished our meal, did the washing up, and spent the evening sitting around Gran's bed, hoping she might speak even if she could only muster a goodbye.

When the night nurse arrived at eleven, she noted Gran's vitals and looked at her feet. The purply-black had travelled up her now cold legs. "She may come around before the end. They sometimes do."

There was little for us to do other than sit and wait, hoping for a reprieve from the inevitable, if only for a few minutes. Our vigil lasted around the clock as we took turns sitting with the nurse during the long night and through the course of two bleak days.

I was anxious for Gran to finish the story of her life. Why had I argued with her? Now she might never have a chance to tell me whatever was so important for her to tell.

On that first night, when it was my turn to sit at Gran's side, Matt joined me. We played euchre and cribbage, occasionally forgetting why we were there and finding ourselves laughing at some joke or at our distress over a bad hand before we'd catch ourselves and lower our voices.

I shouldn't have been surprised to discover that Matt was a pleasant companion. His unexpected arrival had thrown me off and I had forgotten his good nature was what had attracted me to him in the first place.

That night, as we sat at Gran's bedside sharing in the most significant experience of my life, he played the good sport and fetched drinks and snacks that went mostly uneaten, but I could see he was trying to make my ordeal a little easier. I couldn't help but examine him in his display of compassion for me. What I couldn't figure out was why he'd bother. He only smiled when I asked him about his motivation for being there.

I was equally fascinated by Mother's reaction to him. Despite her assertion that she didn't want him here, she seemed to sparkle when he spoke to her and I wondered that she didn't, in fact like him.

On the second day, conversation among us dwindled to nothing, and Matt continued the fetch-and-carry role he'd carved out for himself, making coffee or tea and elegantly sliced tuna or cheese sandwiches. Otherwise, he kept out from underfoot, leaning against the doorjamb and bearing witness to our dysfunction which was highlighted ever more clearly by grief as we demonstrated our inability to console each other.

When deep dusk stole upon us, in the time just before dark set in, Jane lit a braid of sweet grass to cleanse the room of our negative energies. Waving the grass in small circular motions, she began the smudge in the doorway and made her way with great care around the room from corner to corner and then to the centre.

As she prayed, I joined her and drew the smoke over me. Aunt Harmony stood motionless beside Celeste. My mother pretended to ignore us though she had the good grace to wait till Jane was finished before turning on a light and returning to her reading.

Matt's face was in shadow as he looked on. I wondered, briefly, what he thought of our ritual before realizing that I really didn't care.

With the exception of Mother, we women now huddled at Gran's side, holding hands and watching the head of our family dwindle before us.

And then, with a soft exhalation, nothing more than a tiny puff of air, it was over. Gran was gone.

Jane cried for real then. I held her tightly, as close to me as I could hold her. My tears that had so recently run out, tore me apart once more.

When I looked up, I saw Mother clenching Aunt Harmony's hand. It was as much of a gesture as their volatile relationship would allow. They created a picture of such wretchedness that I saw them as the scared orphans they were, anchorless without their mother here to connect them.

# CHAPTER TWELVE

There are few ways to describe letting go of a person you love and none of them are adequate.

On the first day of life without my grandmother, we trekked to the funeral parlour, Matt acted as our chauffeur. We met the director who was dressed in the requisite black suit. It might have been dark blue. I cannot remember what this man looked like. What I do remember is his exceeding blandness and wondered what it would be like to travel through life having as your primary goal to not cause offence. That in itself, I found offensive and my innate prickliness rose against him.

He led us to a room in the back of the building where caskets filled every corner. Their surfaces were dust free and gleaming, spaces had been arranged between each row to allow for better examination of "your loved one's chariot to the afterlife."

I wanted to puke, but managed to swallow my gorge and took a spot on a sofa next to my aunt. I listened with growing rage as the pabulum-faced robot uttered reassurances about quality of wood and thickness of padding.

When I could no longer contain my indignation over the commercialism of our transaction, I leapt to my feet knocking the catalogue of caskets to the floor and fled outdoors.

Matt joined me as I paced the parking lot, my fists clenched and heat rising to my face.

"That son-of-a-bitch!" I roared. "What fucking difference does it make what kind of wood we bury her in? We're putting her in the ground. The ground! All he cares about is his fucking commission. I hate the mealy-faced little bastard."

Matt, wisely, said nothing, but walked beside me as I ranted and fumed. The pecuniary aspect of Gran's death was more than I could bear.

Within minutes, Aunt Harmony joined us. We sat on a bench staring into space as she lit a cigarette, a breeze carrying her first puff of smoke past us and into the trees lining the property.

There we stayed, leaving Mother and Jane to handle the dirty work. I winced in shame, feeling as I so often did that my behaviour was born of poor manners and immaturity. At some point in my life, I would have to begin to act like a responsible adult. I only wished I'd think of that before I followed my instincts into some rash action. This was too important a time to act badly. Leaving poor Jane with Mother to carry out what surely must have been a painful task was unforgivable.

I stamped my foot in aggravation. Aunt Harmony looked at me questioningly.

"Oh, never mind," I snapped. "I get so tired of myself sometimes."

"Join the club," she said then drew on her cigarette before leaning down to stub it out on the pavement. She flicked the butt across the parking lot then picked a speck of tobacco from her tongue. Her magenta fingernail polish was chipped and she focused on picking away at what remained.

She's really such a child. How had I not noticed this before now? I shook my head at myself then saw Mother and Jane walking toward us.

As it turned out, they had arranged a conventional funeral for tomorrow, two facts that took me aback. I'd thought perhaps a pagan ceremony—though I'd no idea what that would entail—followed by Buddhist chanting or some such thing, but no, there would some sort of non-denominational service at the funeral home followed by speeches from anyone wanting to make one. She was to be cremated, her ashes dealt with at a later date.

Although I wasn't happy with the arrangements, I was glad the obsequious mortician would have to make do with selling us a plain casket. Take that, sales-jerk. No big commission for you today.

We piled into the car and returned home whereupon Jane went to bed and the rest of us retired to our separate corners until the hour arrived when we too could find solace in sleep.

All I wanted was to survive the following day. As I lay next to my mother, I slept sporadically my thoughts uneasy, even suspended in disbelief. How could anything as mundane as cancer have taken Celeste away? Her presence had forever loomed over us, around us. It didn't seem possible.

By the time morning arrived, I was exhausted and joined the others as we proceeded through the actions necessary to prepare for the day. There were sandwiches to make, pickle trays to prepare, cupcakes to bake, alcohol to buy.

We were nearly soundless as we chopped and spread and stirred. Each of us looked like hell. With the exception of Matt, no one had slept well, it seemed.

Jane's family began to appear about ten thirty. Her brother and his daughters were the first and I ushered them to the back yard where Jane was reclining on a lawn chair. They spent the morning together talking and, by noon, her entire clan had arrived.

I knew some of them though not intimately. In my younger years, Mother's animosity toward Jane, and, as I got older, my geographical distance had precluded me from getting to know them. This state of affairs made me feel awkward. It seemed stupid that these people who should be part of my family were not.

Shortly after one, we left for the funeral home. The details of what followed remain foggy to me. I recall us going through the motions as decorum suggested we must. We were on our best behaviour—no arguing—though Aunt Harmony carried a flask in her purse that she sipped at regular intervals, her goal, I guessed, was to maintain enough of a buzz to get her through the day.

There was some sort of minister officiating. I'm still unsure who he was, but what did that matter in the end? Religious folk were the go-to people in these situations. They knew best how to handle these sorts of life events. Anyone who'd known my Gran would have to wonder at the choice though. She hadn't wanted a religious ceremony. I don't think she'd stepped inside a church since the day she'd left for university way back when. Over the years, whenever news would break about any religious scandal, particularly if it involved the Catholic Church, she'd launch into a tirade against the evils of organized faith.

"Keeping people dumb and poor, that's all they want to do," she'd lecture. "People too uneducated to know any better than what the Church tells them, and so poor they need their faith so they can believe in a better world after this one. Just look at what the Church did to Ireland or to Quebec. Tied women's fates to their ovaries. It should have been outlawed."

She'd as soon spit on a priest as say hello, yet here we were listening to reading after reading from the Bible.

I shut-up about the choice of service and closed my ears to the monotonous voice coming from the front of the chapel. I could feel Gran's wrath burning into the back of my bowed head. I could not imagine her wanting this. If there was an afterlife, you could be sure she was watching this as a betrayal.

When it was time to speak, I discovered I had nothing to say. My words had been used up inside my head, angry on Gran's behalf.

Mother pushed past my knees and took to the podium though. It would have been disgraceful not to have had family representation during the speeches.

"When my sister and I were young, we knew our mother was different from other mothers," she began.

I cringed, waiting for what might come next.

"Celeste didn't believe that women were less than men. She didn't believe that we couldn't do anything we set our minds to. She didn't believe that education was for men only. It would never have occurred to her to conform to the lives of others for anyone's sake. For that I am grateful. There were times when her unique way of thinking led to some not-so-funny results, but the ideas she instilled in us guaranteed that we'd follow whatever paths we chose and we knew she'd be there to cheer us on. I will remember also the wonderful relationship she created with my daughter, Kate. I know that they loved each other dearly and for that too, I am grateful."

Mother lifted her eyes to the ceiling, an anthropologically universal gesture whether one had a religious upbringing or not.

"Celeste, if I had a glass I'd raise it to you now. You were one amazing woman. We will miss you."

With that she returned to her seat beside me and pursed her lips while she played with a strand of pearls. Did anyone but my mother still wear pearls?

For my part, I was surprised. Surprised and moved. There had been so few, if any, kind words from Mother toward Gran. I had so little idea of the depth of her feelings for her mother. I reached over to hold Mother's hand, but she shook me off to blow her nose. Could it be that she was made self-conscious by my small display of compassion? How my repressed Mother grew from an emotive powerhouse like Gran, I'd no idea. I should have known that there would be no comfort for me from her or from me to her. We made a miserable pair.

We went directly home following the service to set out food and drink for the visitors who were sure to come. When we got there, I received an unwelcome surprise. Gran's hospital bed was gone. It was like she'd never been sick, never stayed there in the living room.

Mother had arranged to have it picked up while we were out.

"We needed the room for the reception," she explained when she saw the shock that must have been as evident as a red mark left from a slap to my face might have been.

How practical of her. For the second time that day, I bit my lips to stop from saying something ugly.

I retreated to the backyard and spent the rest of the day sitting with Jane and her family on the porch. Neither of us were interested in mingling. We left that to others.

I longed to ask her about Gran's religious ceremony, but had a feeling I knew who had been behind it. Mother and her need to keep up appearances, her need to do things that seemed right even if to do so wasn't the same as doing the right thing.

Matt had become chief assistant to Mother's role of hostess. They chatted with visitors and kept them all well oiled. I was happy to have him fill in as it meant I could indulge in keeping away from strangers for whom I cared nothing, though I'm sure his diligence served to highlight my lack of familial devotion. Throughout the day, I had a vague sense of his presence, his flitting about, but took little notice of him.

Strange though, that so many had come. Not a single visit from any of them since I'd arrived and now, a room full. Celeste had been well-known, I'm not sure she had been well-liked. I wondered if they were all neighbours showing up to see for themselves how this odd woman had lived.

Aunt Harmony held court within. By now she was a little tipsy and regaled her audience with stories of the theatre. At one point, when I went inside to fetch storybooks for Jane's nieces, I saw her in full animation, swinging her highball glass over her head as clear liquid sloshed onto the carpet. I ducked outside before she could see me and involve me in one of her tall tales.

The buzz of voices drifted out to us. All that talking, talking, incessant talking. Even keeping my distance wasn't enough to stop me from wanting to bolt. In time, I knew there would be a ceremony of a different sort in the Mi' kmaq community in Millbrook. I hoped I'd still be around when it happened.

The custom of inviting people to the home of the deceased was a morbid one. Gathering after a death to eat, to drink, to kid each other, to stoke our furnaces so we could carry on in defiance of the evidence of our own mortalities. It seemed a disrespectful thing to do.

In retrospect, however, I suppose this tradition served a more practical purpose for it gave us something other than "missing" to do. Set out the food, serve the food, mix drinks, prattle on.

There were even funny moments.

Like when a neighbour's dog got loose from its leash and raced through the house on the trail of something to eat. He crashed into Aunt Harmony who stumbled into a table though she did a valiant job of remaining upright—quite a feat given how tenuous her balance must have been by that time of day.

Overall, guests stayed far too long. Some had the good sense to leave after a respectable hour or so, the stragglers hung around till nightfall. What people won't do for free food and booze.

Jane's family remained till everyone else had gone in order to hold a smudge. It felt good to do something that felt genuine even though it wasn't part of my tradition. Maybe that was why it felt so real: I couldn't question or criticize symbolism I didn't know or words I didn't understand.

Throughout this final ceremony, Aunt Harmony was sprawled on the couch, her eyelids at half-mast, her lips spread in a garish imitation of a smile, her eyes unfocused. After some convincing, I managed to get her up the stairs and into bed and then returned to the kitchen to tackle the dishes. The warm water felt good on my hands, oddly cold on a warm evening.

Matt grabbed a dish towel from the oven door handle.

"Occupational hazard," I said.

"Just can't help myself."

"You'll make some lucky girl a great husband."

"That's what I've been trying to tell you." He flicked my bare legs with the towel.

"Look, Matt—"

"It's okay. I get it."

"No, listen. I'm sorry. I should have told you from the beginning that I wasn't looking for anything permanent. It was sweet of you to come here all white knight-ish."

"Kinda stupid, you mean." His eyes darted away from me.

"You were sweet and I wasn't. I hope, when I get back, we can be friends. You're a good one."

He hugged me. "I thought we had something, but I'm cool with this too."

Dishes done, we said our goodnights then headed in separate directions for sleep.

And that was that.

Just like any other day, night came and we washed and brushed and went to bed. A bit of routine during a singularly difficult time.

That was what happened, wasn't it? Slipping back into the mundane following a death. Yet death should matter. It should stir things up, unbalance us, make us reconsider everything we've ever believed. Instead, we were doing what humans did: forcing ourselves through the habits of life.

It seemed wrong.

I crawled into bed beside my mother, wanting only to sleep, to forget for at least a few hours that Gran was dead. Mother was staring out the window and remained as silent as she had been, with the exception of during the reception, for the past two days. She hadn't bawled out Aunt Harmony; she hadn't told me what to do or not do; she hadn't said a word about the smudging, though I knew she disapproved. Most of all, she'd not cried. Not a single tear.

"Good night," she said before rolling onto her side and away from me.

I balanced the novel I'd been trying to read for days on my stomach; my eyes traveled over lines of text without absorbing a word. Eventually, I gave up, placed the book on the nightstand, and turned off the lamp. When my eyes adjusted to the darkness, I noticed a crease of light under the door.

I crept out of bed and followed the beam. It came from Jane's room. Knocking gently on the door, I peaked inside. Jane sat on the edge of the bed that was now hers alone. She looked toward me with such sadness. "She hasn't slept here in weeks, but it's different now."

My heart broke for her. She was so old and so young at the same time.

I coaxed her to change out of her mourning clothes and to lie in bed. I curled up next to her, spooning against her back and wrapping my arms around her.

"You're not alone," I said. "I'll never let you be alone."

For a long time that night, she cried. Her body shook and I stroked her hair and sang to her. I told her things would be okay, upset with myself for my weak lie. Thankfully, as night lightened ever so slightly to day, she was released from her grief by sleep.

I lay awake for what seemed like hours. Someone used the washroom and, later, there were footsteps as someone crept downstairs for water. Eventually, I drifted off and as I did I wondered what life had in store for us without Gran.

# CHAPTER THIRTEEN

Matt was the first to leave, finally understanding that there was nothing be-tween us. He called a taxi to take him to the airport then kissed me goodbye.

"You're one strange girl." A grin spread across his face, in admiration I wanted to think. "But interesting too."

I felt more warmly toward him now that our relationship was truly over.

"Yes, interesting."

Before leaving, he promised to keep Frankie from bugging me for a few more days.

Aunt Harmony took off the day after that, heading back to the city and to her own life, one that I was much less enamoured of than I had been only weeks ago.

Then came time for my mother to depart. She promised to return in two weeks to help with whatever needed attention. Packing up Gran's old clothes, handling the requisite death paperwork. I wasn't sure why she'd bother with such a gesture. Hadn't her mother's death given her freedom from her mother's partner?

As for myself, I had decided to stay for an indefinite period and liked the idea of being without plans.

So, there we were—Jane and I—alone with each other within seventy-two hours of seeing Gran off.

I started thinking, really thinking, about moving east. What did I have to give up in Ottawa? A waitressing job? A repulsive boss? Hardly things one could not do without.

I did have a nice apartment, but I could find another one. Or stay with Jane. Was that an option for me? Did she want me to stay?

It was August and the fogs of July had finally retreated. The days were magnificent. Indolent. Sunny. Temperate. If there was a heaven, it would be filled with days just as those days were.

Jane and I were happy to exist in each other's company. We spoke rarely. There was little need. We gardened, cooked, ate, slept, read whenever we felt like it. She didn't ask me about leaving and I didn't offer that information.

The truth was, I was afraid to bring the subject up, worried she might ask me to go. I couldn't leave. Not then. I went for long walks and longer drives poking about beaches and inlets that were new to me. I gathered sand dollars from Carter's Beach and empty clam shells from Clam Harbour. I discovered the wildness of Rose Bay and spent an afternoon there lying on the damp shoreline as the wind howled around me filling my hair with sand.

Some days, Jane came with me. Other days, I travelled alone. Sometimes, I'd stay away overnight at one of the many bed and breakfasts or inns along the south shore. Wherever I found myself was fine with me.

I even managed to forget about my aunt who was back at her apartment living whatever kind of life she lived. Not that I wanted to know because I didn't. If she was doing herself harm with alcohol, I didn't have the strength or desire to deal with it. I didn't call her or drop in and she didn't call me. Was it even my job to look out for her? Stupid question. It was. Of course it was. She was family.

But not today.

I also managed to push aside the image of my mother. She'd dutifully promised to return even if she didn't want to. In her rulebook, that's the way it was done. Her mother had died and she would be expected to help. With what? Settle the will? Who knew what she thought. Jane was Gran's spouse. Everything would be left to her. I didn't want to think that anything else might occur. Mother wouldn't fight Jane, would she? It was too dreadful to think about. In doing so, she would get back at the woman whom her mother loved, but the cost would be so great. No, I wouldn't think about that yet either.

Still, Mother would come and end my idyllic few days. To compensate for this, I forced my thoughts to skip over her like a needle on a scratched LP.

No one existed for me unless I wanted them to exist. Mine became a small world, population two.

During those days, I felt free. Sad, but truly free. No one beaconed or expected. No one called or demanded. I was a child without childhood worries. A young woman without care. I felt for a short time that life was luxurious and I wanted to roll in the warmth of its bosom forever.

Of course, life loves twists. No sooner does one think a thought such as that, such as wanting a wonderful day to go on without end, when something or someone must come along intent upon ruining paradise. I should have been more attentive to superstition. I should have thrown more salt over my shoulder or touched wood or avoided black cats or done one of the many things that are supposed to avoid drawing the fates' attentions in one's direction.

First, my boss called. I delayed work for a few more days saying that I had to settle my grandmother's affairs, a bald lie as Jane would handle whatever needed handling. That call made me think again of work and of the possibility of moving and that made me worry about my apartment and how to get out of the lease and how I'd move my things and that led me back to thinking about my mother and whether she'd cause Jane more grief and that made me think about Gran.

Gran who hadn't finished telling me what she wanted me to know.

It was the thing that had been nagging deep within me that I'd been trying to ignore since she had slipped into a coma.

I'd waited and hoped that she'd have a final hurrah, a last lucid moment, before passing on. I knew that for as much as she'd told me there was so much more to tell. If only I had some inkling of what that might be.

The night that Frankie Too phoned was the night my freedom ended. In reality, nothing had changed—my life was exactly as it had been before his voice travelled the line—yet, in effect, everything was altered by that call. Decisions had to be made and I wasn't ready to make them.

I hung up from talking with him and curled into a foetal position next to Jane on the faded, plaid couch where she sat watching a black-and-white movie.

I had again become accustomed to seeing the room without Gran's oversized hospital bed in it. As they had in previous years, two occasional chairs sat in front of the large bay window, a long couch lay opposite and a fireplace stood at the head of the room that, when lit, gave a lovely, warm glow. The furniture was well-made and solid, though the fabrics were aged and worn. The carpet was new. Jane and Gran had it installed only a year ago, before Gran got really sick. It was a pale-grey Berber. A red throw rug was positioned over it, in front of the fireplace and, as in my apartment, bookshelves lined the walls. The one concession to modernity was the flat-panelled television that sat next to the fireplace with its ancient wood mantle that was laden with family photographs and candles.

Tonight, the candles were lit, the only other light in the room came from the kitchen.

Jane pulled a blanket over my bare legs and asked, "What's the matter?" so softly, I could barely hear her.

"Oh, Jane. Everything's coming to a head and I don't know what to do. But mostly, I've blown my one chance to figure things out. You know, our family stuff. Gran didn't get a chance to finish her story. I argued with her and she got mad and then it was the end and she didn't have time to tell me what she needed to tell me. I blew it and there's no do-over for that." I punched the back of the sofa.

"Well, well, my girl. I think I can help."

"Do you know what she was going to say?"

"I imagine I've got a pretty good idea. There are so many things you don't know about your own family, little one. Things I thought you should be told, but it wasn't my place to tell you. It would have broken some silly pact made so long ago. A pact that had nothing to do with me and everything to do with you."

"You're talking in riddles. What is it?" My stomach was in knots. I was afraid of what was to come.

"There are some papers in Celeste's chest at the foot of our bed. They are at the bottom. Tied with a purple ribbon. Find that first and read it, then we'll talk."

I leaped off the couch, tangling my legs in the blanket and falling to my knees. I yelped then scampered up the stairs. Tearing into Jane's room, I reached into the trunk like an archaeologist digging through the layers of Gran's life. The sharp edges of brittle paper cut my knuckles as my hand plucked through them, struggling to reach the bottom. My fingers prodded, feeling between sheets of paper, through bits of fabric, and around narrow boxes filled with unknown treasures as I sought the item I'd been directed to find. My hand skimmed over the smooth touch of a satin ribbon that identified my target. A hangnail caught on the torn corner of some unknown item and I winced.

Finally, there it was: a collection of papers, some three-hole punched, some on paper torn from a journal, and all bound with a piece of ravelled lavender-coloured ribbon.

I untied the bow and slid the unmatched papers onto my lap and read the top page.

## What I Did On My Summer Vacations:
### A collection of stories
### by
### Angel Simone
### 1966 to 1978
### gathered by Celeste Simone

This was typed by a typewriter whose lower-case "s" was missing its base, giving the impression of drunken c's floating mid-line. The paper was yellowed and the top corner was folded forward, bent sharply by the weight of other things.

I breathed deeply before untying the ribbon. An insight into my life had been promised me and I wanted to be sure I missed nothing, that some subtlety didn't slip by me unnoticed. I rifled through the pages and noted the passing of years. What I held was a series of stories and journal entries written by my mother annually right up to university. The stories of her summer vacations.

It seemed my mother had forever been a reporter and that my grandmother had made some effort to be sure these stories were kept.

There had to be something within this for me. I flipped to the second page, my heart pounding, my eyes racing across and down the page.

There was a hand-drawn picture in the familiar palette of the Crayola eight-pack. Two stick people, one bigger than the other. The larger one had scribbled brown hair, the smaller had swirls of yellow around an oblong head; they stood side-by-side. Green spikes with yellow ovals filled the background. A strip of blue represented the sky and another yellow orb, the sun. The smaller human held a white rectangle aloft with a black stick. There was a caption printed in an unfamiliar adult hand that read, "Angel and Celeste help farmers."

Smiling, I examined the picture. The green spikes were corn, the rectangle, a placard. This was my mother's view of a protest she attended with Gran.

How little she had been to be in the midst of a demonstration. Like the children in strollers or strapped to parents' chests and backs in video clips on the six o'clock news, so vulnerable to whatever might go wrong. I detested those images. What if? What if? Why was I asking that question instead of the parents? Was the presence of children a ploy to ensure police diplomacy or an indication of the demonstrators' absolute belief that peace would prevail? Sceptical me believed the former and marvelled at Gran's lack of judgement.

The next page was of another stick figure with a zigzagged line of brown hair running along the top of a large round head. Two half-moon ears framed a face made of blue eyes and a lopsided V-shaped nose. The mouth was a straight red line. A purple cocoon was attached to one of the stick arms. "Denham and Harmony" was printed beneath.

Evidence of the truth of Gran's tale. Denham stayed home during his summer vacations watching the baby while Gran tried to rid the world of its wrongs.

I found myself holding my breath and I exhaled slowly. My hands shook as I turned to the next page. In the capital letters of a novice, Mother had printed:

"I WENT TO AN ASHRAM WITH CELESTE. THE PEPL WERE NICE. I GOT TO WEAR A SARI. IT WAS PINK AND GOLD. WE TRIED TO FIND BLIS BUT I COULD NOT FIND HER. CELESTE SAYS I AM TOO YUNG AND NOT TO WORY. SHE DID NOT FIND BLIS ETHER. SHE SAID YOU CANNOT FIND BLIS IN A CROWD. DENHAM STAYED HOME WITH HARMONY BECAUSE HE IS A GOOD SPORT."

I bet he was a good sport. Like he had a choice. But maybe he didn't mind. He got the love of his life. So what if Gran got to do something for a couple of weeks a year? But, wow. How different that was for the times. No Father Knows Best in that house.

I wondered about my little mother and how she fared so far from home. What did she think of her excursions?

There were no pictures with this entry, but an Air Canada ticket to British Columbia was stapled to the bottom of the page.

I flipped to grade three. It was a letter addressed to someone I assumed was Mother's teacher.

Dear Miss Woodhouse:

This summer Harmony and I learned to weave baskets with real reeds just like Indians used to carry stuff in. Harmony didn't finish hers she just walked around and got in my way. I finished mine. It is beautiful even if it tilts to one side. Celeste put it in the den.

After basket weaving there was REALLY BIG NEWS! I

went to a KIBBUTZ in Israel with Celeste. It took a really long time to get there. The stewardess gave me extra snacks because I was so good.

Denham stayed home with Harmony. She is too little to travel.

We worked hard at the KIBBUTZ. I fed cows and cleared the table after we ate. There were a lot of tables and a lot of cows. I got poop on my new shoes. Celeste says it is called MANURE. I don't care what it is called. It was stinky. Celeste had to clean rooms. She got dry hands and a sore back. Celeste says we are never going to a KIBBUTZ again. First she said it was an adventure and we had to try new things then she said it was slave labour and who did those people think they were.

This is a picture of Celeste. She is TAKING A BREAK.

A photograph of Gran that had been held to the page with a dab of cracked glue fluttered to the ground. The photo was taken by an unnamed person and was of Gran's back. It showed her in a halter top sitting on a beach towel on a hill. Her hair was cropped short and her arms were tanned to mid-bicep outlining the boundaries of a shirt she must have worn often. The story continued:

When we got home it was time for school.

I would like to write more because writing is my favourite thing to do but I have to go now because Harmony is five and is starting kindergarten with Miss Pearl tomorrow and she wants me to help her pick the right dress to wear for her first day. I don't know why her dress matters but she says it matters a lot. Five year olds are weird that way. When Harmony gets an idea in her head Celeste says you can't knock it out with a hammer.

Summer vacation is hard work. I wonder what we will do next year. I told Celeste it would be easier to go to school all year long. She said I was being silly. She said travel is an experience.

Yours truly,
Angel Simone

I paused, thinking about the little girl who loved to write and probably just wanted to stay home during the summer and play with her friends. As usual, my feelings were not straightforward. As sad as I was for elements of this little girl's life, I was also enchanted by her and excited to have this treasure. I dove into the next page. The entry for grade four was another letter.

# CHAPTER FOURTEEN

Dear Miss Clarke:

Every July 1 we start the summer by doing a craft. Celeste says she wants to honour the Mohawk on Dominion Day by doing what they used to do. I'd like to see the fireworks, but Celeste says that Dominion Day is a time that honours how white people took the land away from the Indians. I say if you're that upset about it why don't we give them ours? She says that isn't a practical solution. So we do crafts instead. I think if we took our house from them they would appreciate if we gave it back a lot more than us making crafts but that's what we do.

It's not worth arguing with Celeste about some things. Harmony is like Celeste that way.

This year Celeste said that we were doing beadwork. I tried to make a headband but it's a lot more complicated than it looks so I made a bracelet instead. That was just putting beads on a piece of leather and tying the ends together. We got to pick out our own beads at the store. My bracelet is black red yellow and white. Those are SACRED colours. My bracelet is very pretty. I wear it all the time. You can see it in class anytime you want.

Harmony and I got some really good news after Dominion Day. Celeste and Denham said we could go CAMPING. So we did. Celeste said we could learn all about nature. It was fun! It was the BEST SUMMER EVER! I learned how to swim and how to pick blueberries. When we got back home Gran made a blueberry pie.

I got to go fishing with Denham. Celeste had to take care of

Harmony because Denham said she couldn't come on the boat. Celeste didn't like that. Denham said he took care of Harmony for two summers in a row so Celeste could take care of her for one fishing trip. GOD DAMN IT!

Harmony is still too little to do much except get in the way. She does that a lot like when she ate my yellow crayon. Then I couldn't draw a yellow sun. Celeste said I could use another colour but that's plain stupid. Everyone knows the sun is yellow. Except when it's red or orange. I guess I could have used another colour. Harmony still gets in my way though.

I almost forgot to tell you that I caught two fish. We threw them back in. I bet they were happy we didn't eat them.

Celeste says all animals are special creatures that have a place in the world and a job to do. She says that there are more insects than people and if people all died and insects lived the world would go on but if insects died and people lived the world as we know it would end. I guess insects are more important than people. Celeste says that we should honour all creatures.

That was before a skunk walked into our tent while we were sleeping and Celeste screamed and the skunk got scared and sprayed us and we all started yelling and it burned our noses and our eyes watered like crazy. We ran outside because we couldn't breathe. There is nothing on this earth that smells as bad as a skunk. Denham says that even skunks hate their own smell. They just can't help it. They spray when they get scared.

We jumped in the lake and washed and washed but it didn't stop the smell. Maybe just a little but not enough for me to notice. We smelled NASTY.

Then I asked Celeste what purpose skunks served and if we should honour them. Celeste said she couldn't think straight right then and Denham said that maybe I should ask her in a day or two.

Then he covered the seats in the car in green garbage bags so the car wouldn't get stinky too and he drove to town and bought two cases of tomato juice. You'll never believe what came next. We took a bath in it! It's supposed to get rid of the skunk smell but I think it's going to take a lot more washing before the smell is really gone.

We had to throw out the brand new tent and our sleeping bags and most of our clothes and Celeste said that we will never go camping again.

After we washed about a hundred times we went home and washed some more. I think I lost a layer of skin but we're back to normal.

When we got home from camping Celeste said I had to improve my mind and I couldn't spend the summer watching T.V. like other kids. I think she was just mad because her plan to get us to worship nature fell through. Making me improve my mind was her way of feeling better about things.

I don't think that other kids spend their whole summers watching television. They just get to do more kid things than I do. Like they go swimming and play baseball or visit their grandparents or go on a trip to somewhere fun like Niagara Falls not to ashrams or kibbutzim. (That's plural for kibbutz.) I guess you know what other kids do already because you make everyone tell you. If you get any good ideas from someone this year about what they did I'd like to know so I can have some ideas for next year. Celeste is talking about going to a spiritual retreat. Do you know anything about that? I'm a little worried because it sounds like a Celeste thing and not an Angel thing to do.

For the rest of the summer I had to improve my mind so I had to join Celeste's discussion group. Harmony was supposed to do it too but she just danced in and out of the room and Celeste didn't say anything to her at all. Boy she would have said something to me if I'd have done that. Celeste says it's important that I hang around with grown women. She says that's how young girls used to learn to be women by imitating adults and that we have lost that connection between the generations. Maybe young girls didn't mind doing that in the days before television and books and toys. Maybe it was all they had for entertainment. I am happy to say that I could find something else to do with my time. All the women do is talk and talk about anything at all but mostly about men and how men oppress women. They talked a lot about sex too. Celeste says sex is natural and that maybe we shouldn't try to be MONOGOMOUS. That means staying FAITHFUL TO ONE PERSON FOREVER.

One time they talked about their vaginas. I already knew about those body parts. But they had to see theirs like it was some kind of miracle so they all stood in a circle and looked up their dresses with mirrors. Celeste said it was something that women should do to RECLAIM THEIR SEXUALITY. Whatever that is it sounds pretty kooky. She made it sound really important but she didn't make me look which was a good thing. Those women looked really silly. Stephanie fell over because she is chubby and doesn't have great balance. Celeste says I should say chubby and not fat because fat is insulting but if it's the same thing then how come one is okay and the other is bad? I don't understand that at all.

The ladies talk about MENSTRATION which they call their periods and how it is a wonderful part of being a woman and how it reminds us that we are part of the CYCLE OF LIFE. They talked to me about getting my period and how I should be ready because it could happen ANY TIME. I already knew about periods but I didn't know it could happen anytime. I thought I had a few years to go. Now I'm nervous. What if I'm doing gymnastics? What if I'm out somewhere? What if I'm swimming? What do I do then? This doesn't sound too terrific to me.

They say that it's a special part of life and will mean that I can have babies. I don't want babies. I've already seen what Harmony is like and I could not stand having a kid like her.

The ladies say they should have a ceremony for me when IT happens because I will be a woman. I tried to tell them that I'm only nine and have a lot of time to be a grown-up. I don't think there should be any rush. They told me about RITES OF PASSAGE that help us to celebrate growing into an important part of our lives. I said "Thank you but I'll stick to having parties on my birthdays." They all laughed like it was really funny. I wonder why adults think kids are so funny all the time. I didn't think I was being funny at all.

I hope they don't plan anything for me like I read about in National Geographic. I don't mean to scare you but some people cut out parts of girls' vaginas and some tribes send girls away for a month. The night I read that I had a terrible nightmare and Celeste told me not to worry the ladies' group would not hurt me they were thinking more along the lines of having a party for me maybe at night during a full moon. Celeste says that women are very connected to the moon and to water. I am not sure about this. I don't see how that can be. A party at night does sound like fun but I think if I get my period I'll just keep it quiet.
What do you think?
I hope you had a good summer.

Sincerely,
Angel Simone

I laughed out loud at my mother's little self. She was wonderful. Articulate and observant. She had been the kind of kid I would have loved being friends with when I was that age. The kind of kid I'd love to have around even today. What a unique individual she'd been. What happened? I wanted to wail at my sense of loss for not having met this girl in the body of my mother. I read the story again, my head swirling with questions and thoughts about who Mother had been back when she was just herself, her sweet little self. What had happened to her to cause her to change so much?

I had to pause before the next page, my heart was pounding and my face felt flush. Like a peeping tom or like someone accessing porn and not wanting to be caught, I was prying into my mother's past without her knowledge trying to find answers to mine.

I shook my head. It couldn't matter if I was invading her privacy. There were things I needed to know if I was to make any sense of myself, my life.

# CHAPTER FIFTEEN

**What I Did on My Summer Vacation**
**or**
**Why Parents Shouldn't Plan Holidays**
**by Angel Simone, Grade Five**

This summer was definitely not the best summer ever. Celeste and Denham said they were having a trial separation. This is not a trial like with lawyers and a judge. It's a trial like when you try something new to see how you like it. Celeste says she is trying to find herself. Denham says she's nuts and that she just needs to grow up.

Harmony and I spent half the summer with Denham at Gram and Gramps' house and the other half at home with Celeste. We have another set of grandparents we call Grandma and Grandpa so we don't get confused about who we're talking about. Celeste says we should call them Roy and Mildred, and Isabelle and Allan because she says that we are all equal. Gram and Gramps put their foot down (feet down?) and said, "No. We've waited a long time to be grandparents and we're damn well going to be called Gram and Gramps." So that was that.

I like Gram and Gramps better than Grandma and Grandpa who are Celeste's parents although I know that isn't very nice to say. I don't want to hurt anyone's feelings, but Grandma and Grandpa are really, really strict. We can't eat in the living room even though all of the furniture has plastic on it and would be easy to clean if there was a spill. We have to eat in the dining room and use real napkins and not put our elbows on the table. We have to speak like little ladies even though I'm not sure what that means and we are definitely not to run down the stairs. There are too many rules to remember and I always get into trouble when we go there. It's even worse for Harmony who can hardly follow the rules we have at our house and there aren't that many of those.

Grandma calls Harmony a wild child. I can't argue with her about that.

One time they visited us and took us to a fancy restaurant where the waiters wore black ties and white shirts and there were stiff white table cloths on the tables. There was tinkly music playing and there was a tall fountain in the middle of the room! It was for their anniversary and we were supposed to be celebrating.

The maître d' give us big menus with pages filled with gold writing inside. It was really impressive. I looked for the kid's menu but couldn't find one. Grandpa said that we had to pick something from the entrées to start. Harmony wanted hotdogs. That was when she was going through her wiener-eating phase. Before that she was in a macaroni-and-cheese phase and now she's in a nachos-only phase. Breakfast, lunch, and dinner it's just nachos, nachos, nachos. But back when we were at the restaurant it was hotdogs.

Celeste didn't say too much. I think she was laughing that laugh that people do when they aren't supposed to think something is funny. You know the one when you try to hold it in and get all red in the face and your lips get all crooked and your shoulders shake? That's what she was doing. Denham asked the waiter if there were any hotdogs in the restaurant. The waiter had a funny look on his face like something smelled bad. He said no. Harmony got mad. She started talking louder and louder about wanting stupid wieners and finally she stood up and knocked over her chair. It was an accident, but did Grandma ever blow her top! She said THIS IS THE LAST STRAW! and WHY CAN'T WE EVER HAVE A CIVILIZED EVENING OUT LIKE A DECENT FAMILY?

We left the restaurant before we got to order. Grandma and Grandpa drove to their hotel, but the rest of us stopped at a chip stand on the way home and we had hotdogs and fries. Harmony was pretty happy. I was too. It turned out to be a fun night after all. I guess Harmony's not always as stupid as she acts, but she is most definitely a wild child.

I'm glad that Gram and Gramps aren't like Grandma and Grandpa at all. Gram and Gramps are Denham's parents and have a pool at their house and a man comes to clean it so we can swim in clean water. We even get to swim before breakfast! I'm a pretty good swimmer now because Gramps took me to swimming lessons while Denham went to work. I got my red beginner badge. Harmony didn't go to swimming lessons so she has to wear floaties which I think is pretty babyish but she doesn't seem to mind. She got pink ones to match her bathing suit. Celeste says that Harmony has a natural feel for accessorizing. Big deal!

Sometimes I think about my family and I think it's funny that Grandma and Grandpa had Celeste, and Gram and Gramps had Denham. You would think it would be the opposite. Celeste says sometimes kids turn out opposite from their parents as an act of rebellion. I asked her what rebellion was and she told me it's when you break the rules that your parents give you. She said that some kids don't go into professions that their parents want them to or they do things their parents don't like. Stuff like that.

I guess it's like when I wear my tangerine top with my red plaid shorts to Grandma and Grandpa's house even though I know Grandma hates it. She says she could get a headache just from looking at me the "colours clash so" and Celeste smiles and says I'm showing my originality. There must be some red-and-orange rule that nobody ever told me about. But Celeste thinks it's okay. I think that's because it bugs her mother. She has a really hard time holding back, and sometimes she has to leave the room when Grandma gets upset. She thinks we can't hear her laughing from the next room.

I asked Celeste if she thinks I'll rebel. I asked if someone could rebel against someone else who thinks everything is normal and natural. She said I'm not the rebellious type. Then she looked at Harmony and got two deep wrinkles between her eyebrows and her lips puckered in that way they do whenever she's thinking about something really hard. I think she thinks we might be in for some problems from my sister's corner. If I had it, I'd bet a million dollars that she's right.

Anyway when we were at Gramps and Gram's I had to share a room with Harmony which wasn't too bad except that there is only one bed so we had to sleep together and everything has to be just so with her. Like the top sheet has to be folded down and smoothed out so it doesn't have any wrinkles. She thinks it feels nicer. Then she had to sleep with her two dolls. Not one, but two. Susie on the right and Janine on the left. At first I kept getting jabbed by one of Janine's pointy, plastic fingers. I learned soon enough that after Harmony falls asleep, I could move the dolls out of bed as long as I got them back there before she woke up. It's a good thing I mostly wake up before her. She says she needs her beauty sleep. What kind of a thing is that for a kid to say? I mean who does she think she is Brigitte Bardot? Cross my heart, I think she's loony. Celeste says I shouldn't let Harmony bug me so much, that we have different souls. Sometimes when she really gets on my nerves, Denham takes me for a drive and buys me some ice cream and says he understands me completely and that sometimes we just need a break from the creative types in the family. I guess that means he doesn't figure I'm creative even if I do mix orange and red. I don't think I like that.

While we were staying at Gramps and Gram's, Denham said he would prefer if we called him Dad, but he's been Denham for so long it's hard to remember. He says he understands this and wishes he wouldn't have let Celeste have her way in this matter. That's what he called it... this matter... like it was really, really serious. He looked at little sad, and I was afraid he was going to start crying so I told him I'd try.

Maybe he was lonely. A person could be lonely being married to someone who thinks that being an individual is important, like Celeste. She says that's why she has to keep looking for her inner truth. I notice lately that Denham's lips go into a thin, white line when she says that. He says Celeste could find her inner truth on weekends and help contribute financially during the week. He says he's tired of trying to pay for Celeste's indulgences. (I had to look that word up. It's a good word for Celeste: taking pleasure freely. One good thing about my parents is that they use really interesting words. They got me my very own dictionary and it's not one of those kid's ones that have the pictures in it, it's a real Oxford dictionary and it's my favourite book.)

Denham says someone has to pay for these indulgences and that it was okay when they were kids but they're not kids anymore.

I asked him if that was why he and Celeste were having a trial separation. He didn't answer me for a while and then he said: "No. Celeste wants to see what it's like to be free of all responsibilities. It's another experiment that we all get to pay for."

I felt really bad. I wanted to ask him if that meant she wanted to get rid of us, but figured I better not. Instead, I asked him what it was like when they first met.

He said that Celeste was lots of fun and different from other girls. He loved that she worried about the world and wanted to do something to make things better for other people. But then they got married and bought a house and had children and her quest to do good in the world twisted into wanting to do good for Celeste. And he was just tired and wanted to come home to a clean house and dinner for a change.

When half the summer was over, we moved back to our house with Celeste. She was still looking for herself which I still don't really understand. I mean, you only have to look into a mirror for that. When I said that it got her laughing and she explained that she meant her spiritual self. I got worried that she might want to go away to another ashram so I didn't ask any more questions.

One weekend, Celeste took us to visit Grandma and Grandpa. It took us almost a whole day to get there because they moved to their retirement home in Cape Breton. Celeste said that "at a time like this a girl needs her mother." I think she meant the trial separation but she must have forgotten that she and Grandma don't see eye-to-eye although I don't know how a person could forget something like that. I don't understand why Celeste does some of the things she does like going to see her mother when she knows they usually fight.

Denham calls Grandma the Ice Queen which sounds beautiful, but isn't and says he can't figure out how Celeste was born. I told him he was just being silly. He knows as well as I do where babies come from.

Grandma didn't seem very happy to see us. She and Celeste had a private talk in the parlour while Harmony and I ate dill pickle chips and drank Fresca outside on the patio. I guess the talk didn't go well. We watched t.v. and went to bed, then drove all the way home the next day. It was tiring and Harmony and I fell asleep in the backseat.

After that, Celeste started to write poetry and thought that she might have finally found her true calling. She changed her weekly discussion group to a writer's group and now the women have all started writing. Some of them are writing books, some just keep a diary and some write poetry. Oh, and one lady writes articles for the newspaper but she used to do that anyway. Every week they have to write something to share with the group. I don't know how you are supposed to find your true calling when everyone has to do the same thing.

One week, Celeste's poem was about not knowing who you are and talking with your mind and being alone with yourself. The ladies went crazy over that one. They said it was profound and was about how none of us know ourselves. I thought it was dumb, but I didn't say anything.

Two weeks after the trip to Grandma's house, Denham moved back home. I guess the trial separation didn't work after all and I'm glad even if they were all kissy and huggy for the rest of the summer. Yuck. Yuck. Yuck.

For the time being things are back to normal or as normal as they get for us. Celeste is still writing poetry though. Denham says he hopes it's a phase. He says most things with Celeste are, but at least she keeps life interesting.

So that's what I did on my summer vacation. I hope you like my story not like Miss Clarke last year who called child services and caused a big fuss over vaginas.

I stood, straightening my stiffened knees. "Jane!" I hobbled to the top of the stairs.

"What is it?" she sounded miffed at being disturbed. "Miss Marple's just about to identify the murderer."

Hopping down the stairs, I waved the loose sheets of paper in the air above my head. "Why didn't anyone ever show me these before? I love her. I just love her. She's wonderful."

Jane waved her hand in my face. "As usual, you're bellowing at the wrong person. I don't think your mother even knows these pages exist. I didn't till recently and Celeste wanted to be the one to tell you. You don't think I'd take that away from her, do you?" She gave me a hug. "I'm happy that you've discovered something new. Might open up your mind a bit. It was starting to get a bit musty in there."

I opened my mouth to rebut then realized it was useless. She had already gone back to her movie.

Musty indeed. Maybe she would pretend she meant the chest, but we both knew what she was talking about. I wasn't forgiving enough to be able to laugh it off. A few stories couldn't change the fact that my mother had caused me a lot of pain and I wasn't about to take the blame for any of her actions.

I huffed my way back to my room and stretched out on the bed, glancing out the window. The sun was setting and had cast a delicious rosy glow around the room. Without sunlight beaming in, the temperature had dropped and I drew a blanket over me before continuing my reading. I turned on a lamp, and straightened the mess of pages, organizing them into read and unread piles.

Grade six was represented by an essay.

# CHAPTER SIXTEEN

### How I Got Expelled From Camp

This summer I was sent away to camp for two weeks. Celeste thought it was time for me to spread my wings and get away from my parents for a while. Other parents complain that they don't spend enough time with their children, mine send theirs away. Harmony stayed at home though. Celeste said this was something just for me. I tried to explain to her that Harmony could go, and I would stay at home, but she just smiled that smile of hers that means I have to do what she wants anyway so I might as well stop arguing.

I went to Camp Julien. It was on a lake in the Laurentians. It was a camp just for girls and six of us stayed in each cabin with a counsellor. After the first few days I made friends with the girls in my cabin (Cabin Six) and settled in and it was okay.

The food was sort-of gross though. The spaghetti stuck together and the meat was always overcooked and dry. I wrote a letter to the camp coordinator to complain about it and all the girls in my cabin signed it, but it didn't do any good. I think that if they want you to spend a lot of time outside doing lots of activities then the least they could do would be to hire a decent cook because being outdoors makes you really, really hungry. I ate lots of cereal at breakfast and mostly filled up on bread or sandwiches, fruit and granola for the rest of the day.

The good part about camp was that there was something new to learn everyday. I guess they think that kids can't entertain themselves so they have to keep us busy every minute. At first, I wasn't very happy about this. I mean, what's summer for if you can't get away from classes, right? But they taught us some pretty interesting stuff.

I learned how to navigate with a compass although I'm not very good at it and came in last in the navigation competition. My partner was a girl named Bonnie who had freckles and worried about getting a sunburn. She had to wear a big floppy hat and loads of lotion that she reapplied all day long because "she was so fair." She kept saying that over and over. I think she thought it made her sound like a lady from Robin Hood or something like that. The fair Maid Marion. It got to be annoying after a while.

After about two hours of listening to her brag or complain, depending on how you looked at it, about her delicacy, I guess I sort of snapped and yelled at her: "Shut up about your stupid skin already! Nobody cares about how quickly you burn."

She ratted me out and I got into trouble for being rude and saying shut up. Geez. I had to work in the kitchen that night washing dishes. That was triple-times gross but not as bad as when I was done and they made me apologize to her. I wanted to smack her pink, turned-up, pig nose.

I got my revenge though because she did get a burn and her face kept peeling for the rest of the week and everyone kept telling her she had leprosy and her nose was going to fall off. Now that was funny! I guess she'd learned not to tell because no one got into trouble for that.

We all learned how to canoe. That was terrific. At first, it was scary because the canoes wobble whenever somebody moves and it feels like they're going to tip over so easily.

Before we could go out on the lake, we had to listen to some safety stuff and pretend like we were paddling. I looked around at all these girls standing side-by-side on the dock and pretending to paddle in the air and felt as silly as we looked. My only hope was that the camp counsellors knew what they were doing. When we finally got out onto the lake, there were two girls to a canoe. One instructor stayed on the dock and another one was out on the water in a motorboat so she could get around quickly if one of us got into trouble. This made me feel better.

We pushed the boats into the shallow water and got into them as gently as we could. My canoe rocked when I sat and I grabbed on to the sides to try and not fall into the water.

Once we got settled we were told to paddle out a little way from shore. There, Sylvia, the instructor on the dock yelled at us to make the boats tip. All that work to stay dry and she was yelling at us to go overboard! We rocked back and forth, screaming like the devil was after us as we got closer and closer to falling into the water. When we finally flipped and landed in the lake, we flailed around knowing we were perfectly safe. Candice, who was my partner, swam up underneath the canoe and discovered there was an air-pocket where we could tread water and carry on a conversation in privacy under our canoe-tent.

"It echoes," I said.

"Kind of, but it's more hollow-y than echo-y."

She was right. It felt like we were in another world. A wet, dripping cave. It was dark, but not so dark we couldn't see, and the water rippled as we swayed our arms across its surface to stay afloat. Water dripped from the bottom of the canoe which was now our ceiling and it felt like we could say things that would be secret, things that would never leave the underside of that canoe.

"Tell me one thing nobody at camp knows," I said.

She looked at me for seconds that stretched to infinity. "My parents are getting a divorce." And then she told me her father was going to have a baby with his secretary.

"Wow!" The sound of my voice hit my ears hard in that tiny space and I wished I could have taken it back. I'd never met anyone whose parents were getting an actual divorce. Not a trial separation like Celeste and Denham, but a real divorce. She said it so calmly that I wondered if she was lying. Making things up to look cool. But when I looked at her, she was staring at me hard, like she was daring me to say something childish and stupid, and I knew she was telling me the truth.

"Your turn. Tell me your biggest secret."

I didn't know what to say. "I hate my sister."

"That's a cheat. Everyone hates their sister. Say something else."

"I let a boy kiss me." It wasn't true, but I was stuck.

"A regular kiss or a French kiss?"

"A French kiss?"

"Kissing with tongues."

With tongues? Do people kiss with tongues? Geez, that's disgusting. "Oh, is that what that's called?" I tried to sound as grown up as she did and hoped my lie didn't show.

"Who?"

"Who what?" I had to think of a name quick. "Sean Gallagher?" My voice squeaked. "I met him one time when I went to visit my grandparents."

She looked at me, knowing I was lying, I was sure. If she found out I made it up, I'd spend the rest of the summer with no one to hang out with except whiny Bonnie. My cheeks felt hot and I was glad it was dark under the canoe so she couldn't see me turning red.

"How was it?"

"Boring." I dove into the water and out from under the canoe, my feet hitting the port side of the boat.

Good thing I got out when I did, Sylvia was hollering at us to get moving.

We had to figure out how to turn the canoe over and climb back in. It wasn't so hard. After a few tries we flipped it with a synchronized shove then I held on to one side from my place in the water while Candice crawled over the other side. Once she was seated, she leaned to port while I crawled over the starboard edge.

After that experience, I wasn't afraid of tipping any more which was, of course, the whole point of the exercise. We went out on the water everyday after breakfast and by the end of two weeks, I was a pretty good paddler. I loved the rocking motion of the flimsy boats. Getting wet was fun too, and all the girls worked as hard at tipping them as we did learning to steer so we could fall in the water and have an excuse to scream.

After canoeing, there were swimming lessons and then we

had free time till lunch. I would usually try to find a quiet spot so I could read without being disturbed. You'd think that would be easy out in the middle of nowhere, but believe me, with over seventy girls around, it was a challenge.

Every night we had a campfire. Sometimes the counsellors would tell us stories, sometimes we'd sing and sometimes we'd just goof around. It was the best time of day.

I read some of the classics this summer. Not all of them just Tom Sawyer, Treasure Island, and Jane Eyre. Treasure Island was my favourite although the others were good too.

When I got home, Celeste said that if I was going to read a bunch of "Victorian nonsense that gives women dreadful ideas about what's expected of them" then I should try to balance it with something a little more forward-thinking so I had to read On the Road by Jack Kerouac. I started it, but didn't finish. I didn't understand what he was writing about. His book may have been meaningful to some people, but it wasn't to me.

Celeste has a list of books that she says I should read. The list isn't very long but it has feminist books like The Second Sex, A Room of One's Own and The Female Eunuch and a bunch on spirituality like Markings by Dag somebody-or-other. I guess I should be happy that my mother cares about my intellectual growth, but I don't know any other mother who gets so involved. I'm saved from her list for now because she thinks I need to be older to read them, "to gain a full appreciation of the conditioning of Western society." I don't look forward to my teen years.

But that was when I got home.

While I was at camp I decided that maybe I should give Celeste's point-of-view some serious consideration. You know the whole idea about women and moons and tides and our special connection to nature. I wondered what I could do that would put me in touch with this special side of being a girl. There was a full moon during the second week at camp and I thought about what Celeste said about rituals and rites of passage and I thought that my cabin-mates and I should do something to mark our time together at camp.

The problem was that I didn't figure Sylvia would sanction an unauthorized activity in the middle of the night and she slept in the bed right next to the door. We'd have to figure out a way to get by her. The one thing we had on our side was that we could tell when she was asleep. She had a loud snore. (Ramona, one of the other Cabin Six girls, said that it sounded just like her dad so she never got homesick.) We figured that once Sylvia was asleep, if we were quiet enough, we just might be able to sneak by her.

I grabbed a margarine container from the dining hall at lunchtime and used some of its contents to lubricate the cabin door so it wouldn't squeak. After supper, I sneaked a lighter from one of the councillors during campfire time. I had already squirreled away a bunch of granola and cookies and Candice had a few cans of pop. We were as prepared as we could be.

Lights out was set at ten and I lay in my bunk waiting to hear Sylvia's snore. I was so excited about our getaway that I knew I wouldn't fall asleep. Our adventure was going to be a celebration of our pending womanhood.

It seemed like forever before Sylvia's breathing became louder although according to my watch it was only twelve minutes from lights out. I waited another five before flipping my flashlight on and off. A murmur ran through the cabin like a soft breeze. I dropped to the floor, my backpack filled with our provisions in hand. One by one the others followed me until we were safely out the door.

Mathilde started to giggle, but caught herself in time and we moved as quickly as we dared down the path, around the dining hall and to the fire pit at the water's edge. We waited silently, like does testing the wind for the scent of danger.

We were out of sight of the other cabins and we hoped far enough away that if we kept our voices low we wouldn't wake anyone up.

My heart was pounding with the exhilaration of adventure. I bent to the fire pit and lit the kindling. Soon we had a small fire going and were huddled around the flames.

I picked up a piece of charcoal and began to speak. "This is a special summer for all of us. Soon we will pass into womanhood and leave childhood behind." The words flowed magically without me having to think about them. I admit it felt pretty good speaking like that.

Mathilde started to giggle again, but Candice jabbed her in the ribs as a warning to be quiet.

"Tonight we are gathered as a testament to this moment and as recognition of the threshold we are approaching. We are moon's magic and as girls the night belongs to us. To give us guidance along our journey to womanhood we must each say one thing that is true about ourselves, one true thing that we will hold onto forever that nothing, not even growing older can diminish."

The girls looked at me waiting. I hadn't exactly planned what we were going to do, but it sure sounded good when I said it.

"I am words," I said. "I celebrate their meanings and create wonders with them." Then I marked my forehead with a charcoal star and passed the stick to Candice.

"I am colour. I create beauty with the colours of nature." She marked her forehead.

Each of the girls shared one thing that identified them and when we were finished we joined hands and stayed like that for a few minutes feeling the importance of this ceremony.

Then we walked to the water's edge and took off all our clothes and waded into the water. The edge of the lake was covered with algae-layered rocks and it was hard to find safe footing in the dark. We slipped and twisted ankles as we tried to keep our balance. Like I should have known would happen, we'd barely gone five feet out when Mathilde fell into the water, shrieking as she went.

As she yelped, the magic evaporated, and, afraid of being caught, we scrambled back to the beach to get our clothes on.

But it was no good. We were found out in seconds—and in the most humiliating way possible—counsellors and their bright flashlights caught us half-dressed and groping about trying to find the rest of our clothes in the dark.

They told us off and sent us back to our cabin with a command to meet in the administration office after breakfast.

It was a brief and uncomfortable meeting. As the ringleader, I got sent home ending my camp experience three days early. I suppose I should have been mortified, but I discovered I wasn't. For the first time in my life, I was a heroine. Those other girls thought I was the coolest of the cool and it felt terrific especially since I am known as the nerdy girl at school. I think it's one of those things I'll remember forever and ever. Just like I'm going to hold on to my one true thing no matter what.

I wasn't worried that Celeste would be upset with me and she wasn't. She was proud of me for "discovering a sense of self." Even Denham seemed to understand. He just patted my head and asked me not to grow up too fast.

Candice and I are still writing to each other. Maybe we'll be able to see each other again some day.

All-in-all camp turned out to be a pretty good thing. I wonder if they'll let me go back next year.

# CHAPTER SEVENTEEN

My stomach growled so much, I put the pages down and went in search of food. When I got downstairs, I discovered that Jane had gone to bed without her usual "good night" and I was alone. Turning on only the stove light, I fixed myself some toast and cheese in the semi-dark. Loneliness, my enduring adversary, joined me, carving its familiar, hollow ache in my chest. It was the dark that invited it in and I accepted it. There is comfort, even if cold, in known commodities and buffering myself from its chill allowed me to re-establish emotional distance from thoughts of my mother and the feelings of compassion that were growing in me for her.

I sat at the kitchen table eating and staring, unfocused into the gloom.

There would be no more reading for me tonight. My enemy had me in its grip and the only way out was through distraction of a particular kind.

I changed into a dress and drove to the city, seeking a place filled with happy, laughing people.

Brunswick Street provided such a place and I navigated Jane's car into a parking spot that emptied just as I drove up.

Paying the ten dollar cover charge, I entered the loud hall and ordered a Sleeman Honey Brown from a very attractive bartender then looked around for a table. There were none to be found so I located what I thought would be an inconspicuous corner from which to absorb the atmosphere.

I tilted my head back and gulped my beer. It's frostiness cut through my dry insides and I felt instantly better.

My hips swayed to the music and I felt a delightful sense of wickedness come over me. I wanted to dance. Who would be my partner?

I finished my beer and sashayed around the room, catching the eyes of men and boys as I went, summing them up in a second, deciding who would be the one.

Nearing the dance floor, a hand reached for mine and I spun around.

It was my aunt.

Instantly, I regretted my decision to come.

"Hey, honey," she shouted over the din of music and other loud voices. "What are you doing here?"

Her eyes had the wild glint that only drunkenness brings and my good mood vanished.

"Thought I'd get out for a bit," I shouted back.

"Let's dance!" She dragged me onto the dance floor and I had no option but to do as she bid me. Despite her condition, she was an innate dancer and the beat of the music seemed to come from within her. She held a drink that sloshed over the edge of the glass as she gyrated. When she saw what she was spilling, she paused long enough to gulp it down by half.

I was barely moving, caught up in watching her create a puddle at her feet.

She emptied her glass. "C'mon. I want another." As she spun about, one of her four-inch high heels slid in the wet and she went down hard.

I grabbed her hands and helped her to her feet, knowing with certainty that my distraction for the rest of the night would not be the one I had hoped for.

I sighed and swiped at the large wet spot on my aunt's backside.

"We better head home. You're soaked."

She looked at me with dismay and, to my surprise, agreed. Perhaps she wasn't as far gone as I'd thought.

I stayed with her that night, sleeping on her couch and was up early the next morning, leaving her a note to call me if she needed company.

When I arrived at Jane's, she was already in the garden and I quickly changed into more appropriate attire before joining her.

"I saw Aunt Harmony last night," I offered as an explanation of my absence.

"Is that where you were?"

I nodded.

"How is she?"

I shrugged and she grimaced. No other explanation was needed.

"How's the reading going?"

"Half done. It's amazing. Confusing. So much of it isn't the way I pictured. I mean, some things are so funny, but sad too."

"That's life, eh?"

"Yeah, Janie. That's life."

We hung up our gardening forks and brushed the earth from our knees before entering the house. Jane hugged me and kissed my forehead as she walked past me, on her way to the shower. "I'm here if you need me."

Tears, inexplicably, jumped to my eyes and I turned quickly toward the counter so she wouldn't see. When she left the room, I raced upstairs to gather the rest of my mother's stories which I took outside along with a steaming mug of black coffee.

September 7, 1973

Dear Mrs. Chang:

I am trying to maintain a positive attitude as I sit down to write this assignment you gave the grade seven class. Every year, teachers tell us to write the same story and every year I try to share the honest truth about my summer even though one time I got into big trouble with children's services and most of the rest of the time, teachers just end up avoiding me. The truth, as you are about to discover if you haven't yet, is that my family isn't like everyone else's. What I do on my summer vacations usually seems kind of weird to most people. So when you read about my summer vacation I would appreciate it if you would keep an open mind and remember that my mother means well even if she isn't like everyone else's.

Thank you,
Angel

## A Summer of Bonding

I've been told that having a sister is a wonderful thing. That may be true for some people. It isn't for me. At least not until this summer, sort of. Let me tell you about it.

My mother, Celeste, decided it was time that my sister, Harmony, and I develop a stronger bond. I couldn't imagine a worse way to spend summer vacation. Picking cotton till my fingers bled would have been a better fate than this. And no,

I'm not exaggerating.

Let me tell you a bit about Harmony. She's three years younger than me and is really annoying. She spends way too much time brushing her hair and worrying about coordinating her socks with whatever silly outfit she's chosen to wear. It's only the third day of school and she's already in love with some kid named Blair who she is going to marry one day. It drives me nuts. She doesn't read like I do, but she likes to draw and paint which is okay. Most of all, she loves to dance, and spends most of her time pirouetting or leaping instead of walking. She is forgetful and dreamy and gets into trouble because she doesn't pay attention in class. Celeste says that, "Harmony is very artistic and she will mature in her own way." I wish Celeste would be stricter with her because I end up getting called to Harmony's class and getting lectured about reminding Harmony to finish her homework or to bring a textbook that she's forgotten. Like I have any say over Harmony or her schoolwork. I think teachers just get frustrated with trying to deal with Celeste so they zero in on me as the easiest target. (If I get called to the principal's office at least now you'll know why.)

Celeste says that sisters are "each other's greatest allies" and she "wishes she had a sister." That, in my opinion, is because she didn't have one. If she had, she wouldn't be so keen.

If only Celeste would realize that Harmony and I are two very different people and the less time we spend together the better it would be for everyone. Celeste says that's her point and that we "have to learn to respect and value each other's differences."

With that as her goal, she decided we had to spend the summer bonding. Celeste thought that we could try a variety of things to get to know each other better. She suggested that we write each other a letter telling about ourselves as if we were writing to a stranger. Now, when I say that Celeste suggested we write a letter what I mean is that she put it forward as a suggestion, but she didn't mean it like a suggestion. There was no way we were going to get out of doing what she wanted.

When I gave it some thought, I figured that maybe writing

and reading might not be a bad idea because then I could read Harmony's words without having her dance all around me which drives me nuts.

This is what I wrote to her:

Dear Harmony:

As you know I am 12 years old, but everyone says I'm old for my age. Although we are sisters we've had very different life experiences, and I'd like to tell you about some of mine.

I've protested against the poor treatment of migrant workers and probably other things that I was too little to even remember. I've been to an ashram to learn to meditate and about cosmic connectedness. I've worked on a kibbutz and survived my parents almost getting a divorce. That last thing we did together.

I love books and read at a senior high school level already. I try to read different kinds of books to learn different things. One of my teachers said I have the gifts of keen observation and articulation. Another teacher told me that sometimes it would be better if I didn't articulate every observation I make, but I try to not let that bother me too much. "You can't be appreciated by everyone," Celeste tells me.

When I grow up, I'm going to be a reporter and travel around the world writing articles for magazines and newspapers.

If you don't mind me saying so, one thing that really bugs me about you is how irresponsible you are. Not everything is an opportunity to dance. Sometimes you have to pay attention to what's going on and you can't do what you want to do.

Well, that's the best I can do for now.

Your sister,
Angel Simone

The next day Harmony gave me her letter. She curtsied when she handed it to me then tapped out of the room waving jazz hands behind her as she went. I could have smacked her.

She had drawn pictures of pink and purple butterflies up

one side of her letter and down the other. She glued pictures of lambs and baby chicks across the top and bottom. In the middle she wrote: "I am a fairy princess. I am magical and can do spells. I live in the forest. I am beautiful and dance the dance of the woodland fairies."

That was it.

That was her attempt to tell me about herself.

I was so mad. That's just Harmony all over. She never does anything right.

Celeste says that Harmony's letter tells me a lot about her and I just have to look harder. Well, all it told me was that she's either crazy or lazy or both. Why can't she just do what she's supposed to do? Just once.

Maybe there is something seriously wrong with her. I called our doctor, Dr. Schuster, but she told me that there is nothing wrong with Harmony and that maybe I should speak with my mother about it if something is bothering me. I said: "Are you kidding? You've met my mom, right?" Then Dr. Schuster laughed and said she understood my dilemma.

Of course, Celeste wasn't going to stop at letter writing. Her next big idea was to get us to spend some time together. First, we had to do one thing Harmony liked and then we had to do something that I liked. We had to try and appreciate what we were doing from the other's perspective.

It sounded a lot like therapy. My friend's parents went to marriage counselling, but it didn't work. They got a divorce anyway. Maybe Celeste was a frustrated marriage counsellor. I told her that and she smiled and said: "Well maybe I am. I'll give it some thought." Then I thought maybe Harmony and I could get a divorce from each other. This time Celeste didn't smile. I guess I had taken my idea one step too far.

I was a little worried about what Harmony was going to choose for us to do together. I didn't want to have to pretend I was a fairy or put on a tutu and dance around town or anything embarrassing like that.

It turned out that Harmony wanted to show me one of her dances. I was lucky I didn't have to do anything except be her audience. She put on a fancy dress and some classical music and spent the next fifteen minutes running, swaying, leaping, and twirling around the living room. It was boring, but it could have been worse. When she was done, she curtsied and smiled as if she was Isabelle Duncan. All I had to do was clap. I haven't thought this all the way through yet, but something tells me that this is significant.

When it was time to do my choice of activity, I decided that we should go to the library and pick out a book. Harmony wanted to wear one of her dance leotards. Like usual, this really got on my nerves ("on my last nerve" as my Gram would say). Why does my sister have to draw attention to herself all the time? Celeste said it was okay though so there wasn't much I could do about it. When we got to the library, Harmony grabbed a book off the shelf without even looking at the title. Then she danced around the community room like it was her dance floor. The librarians all smiled at her. I was mad. This kid is so irritating. Can't she ever take anything seriously?

"I give up," I said to Celeste. "You can bond with her. I'm through."

I left the library feeling mad, but kind of proud too like I had proven something to Celeste. I should have known better. By suppertime, Celeste had another idea.

Did I tell you that Celeste doesn't cook? Supper is usually a hodgepodge of stuff that can be cut into bite-sized pieces and eaten with our fingers or slopped from a can onto a plate. For all of that it's pretty nutritious. Vegetables, fruit, yoghurt, sandwich meat, nuts, fresh bread. Celeste says it's how Europeans eat dinner and everyone knows they're healthier than North Americans. She neglects to mention that Europeans also have their big meal at noon. There is no big meal at our house unless it's bought pre-made or Gram takes pity on us and brings something over.

That night over dinner Celeste dropped her latest bomb.

"We girls need to get away together."

Denham closed his eyes and exhaled like he was deflating. "Where to?"

Celeste had heard about a retreat for mothers and daughters to help us reconnect with each other and with the great cosmic sisterhood that she had been going on about for years.

I could see the dollar signs in Denham's eyes.

"It's sponsored by the provincial government. Can you believe it? It's only $50 for a week and we'll do all sorts of outdoor activities."

Denham relaxed considerably at this, but I was worried like crazy.

She told us that we'd be doing archery and navigation and team-building games. We'd learn to rely on and trust each other.

Trust Harmony? I'd trust Harmony to be completely undependable. How's that for trust?

But I already knew as soon as Celeste started talking that she'd already booked us. "When do we leave?"

Beaming, she replied: "On Friday."

Two days away. I tried to maintain a brave front. Two days plus one week meant that in nine days we'd be back at home and hopefully Celeste would have run out of ideas to make best friends out of Harmony and me.

On Friday, Denham came home from work at noon to wave goodbye as we pulled out of the driveway. He didn't look anywhere near sad enough for my liking.

By supper, we had arrived at the lodge, were checked in, had unpacked, and were milling around the dining hall with a bunch of other mother-and-daughter teams waiting for instructions. There must have been about a hundred or maybe more people there. A whole bunch of moms with their daughters ranging in age from about eight to about eighteen. I wondered what we'd be doing and how painful it might be.

The people-watching was fun though.

There was the hippy crowd lead by women with long, naturally-greying hair and Birkenstocks. There was the rich crowd made up of women with styled hair, perfect makeup, and manicured nails. These women managed to look as if they owned the place even though they'd probably never been here before. Of all of us, I wondered why they were here. It wasn't the Hilton. There was also the crowd of regular people with slightly-overweight mothers in tracksuits and sneakers who came prepared with colouring books and crayons and snacks to keep their kids entertained during the wait. Finally, there was artsy crowd where we seemed to fit in best. These moms had the most flair that's for sure. Their clothing was the most colourful and their kids were happily engaged in solitary pursuits like reading or writing (I was taking notes. You never know what you'll be able to use for a good story.) or sketching. Harmony danced as usual and for once didn't seem like an odd-ball.

Eventually, two women entered the hall and marched over to the front of the room. The older one wearing a cowgirl outfit grabbed a microphone. Her round bosom seemed to be tied top and bottom with a drawstring at neck and waist. An equally round face began at the upper drawstring as though no neck separated her body from her head. Her hips spread out below in another rounded mound and I found myself thinking of a snow-woman—a western snow-woman. I couldn't figure out why she was dressed that way and felt panicky as I worried there might be square dancing. I hated square dancing. We had to do it in gym every spring and it was really lame.

"Good evening ladies. Welcome to your very own Journey of Discovery! (I wonder why women have to give cute names to things. It made it sound like a trip to Disney World. Or a Mary Kay convention.) My name is Daphne and this is Yvonne. We will be your guides during this week."

Everyone applauded like this was really outstanding news.

Yvonne was similar to Daphne only in hair style. Both wore elaborate do's piled high on their heads. Yvonne's was mouse brown; Daphne went in for electric red. Under her beehive, Yvonne was pencil thin. She wore a yellow mini-dress that was gripped at the waist by a three-inch wide, white plastic belt. The dress ended far too high up her scrawny thighs which only highlighted the chicken skin that hung around her knees. Ancient Go-Go boots flapped against her too-skinny calves as she strode across the room to a pile of papers on one of the far tables.

The screech of feedback from the microphone brought me to attention, and Harmony and I covered our ears against the sound.

"I hope that you've all had a chance to register and to find your cabins. If you haven't, please do so immediately following dinner which will begin when Yvonne and I have finished. (A couple of the kids cheered at this followed by shushing from their mothers.) We've divided you into groups of ten. Yvonne will be handing out a schedule of events while I continue. This week everyone will have the opportunity to learn outdoor skills. Learning new things together is a great way to bond. There will also be sessions set up for moms and daughters to share ideas and thoughts in more intimate settings."

A murmur went around the room. Anticipation filled the air. You could feel the giddiness grow. I had to hand it to Celeste, she didn't give up on an idea easily, and it sounded like she'd found the just what she'd been looking for.

"If you have any questions or concerns, Yvonne and I will be here to help you. Ladies please have a look at your schedules. There is a map of the compound attached."

Like Hyannis Port? I felt like a Kennedy all of a sudden.

Dinner was served after that. It was better than at kids' camp that's for sure. We had linguini with grilled vegetables and salad and garlic bread. I would have been a lot more willing to listen to Daphne after a meal like that. Being used to Celeste's suppers, this was pretty special to me.

I checked out the activities they had scheduled for us. After dinner there was a Getting to Know You game then singing around the campfire. Over the course of the week we'd learn archery, fly fishing, rifle shooting, how to cook over a campfire, navigation by the stars, how to recognize edible plants and a bunch of other things. It didn't sound too bad. I could survive this. Unless Harmony shot me or something. I watched her as she spun around the room, and I started getting nervous again.

When I flipped to the next page I swear the title Learning To Trust Each Other nearly stopped my heart. I hoped the moan I felt rising inside me hadn't slipped out by accident. I closed my eyes then opened them slowly, hoping I'd read the title wrong.

Nope. It was still there. I read on.

"One of the biggest challenges faced by mothers and daughters today is the difficulty we have in trusting each other. Trusting each other with our feelings, our secrets, our dreams, and our fears. During this week, we will use a variety of exercises to help us learn to trust each other thereby enhancing the single most important relationship in our lives."

If my relationships with Celeste and Harmony were to be the most important relationships in my life, I had a feeling I was in for a tough go of things.

I scanned the page and shivered at what was planned. Letter writing, sitting face-to-face and sharing information about ourselves, writing out our life goals and discussing them in "an atmosphere of openness and caring," leading each other blindfolded… One exercise a day. This was going to be harder to get through than the outdoors stuff. (I also had a feeling there was stuff about Celeste that I'd rather not know.)

After dinner we were each handed a piece of paper with a bingo square on it and in each box was a statement like "She loves the colour purple" or "She's been to every province." Our mission was to go around the room talking to people to find out who fit each square. Whoever got a bingo first would win a prize. You are never—not even in a million years—going to guess who won. Harmony! As soon as she realized a prize was involved, she was driven with an urgency I'd never seen before. She whipped around from person-to-person like she was on a mission from god.

She won a T-shirt that read: "I am my mother's daughter."

I laughed every time I thought about it.

Then we had a campfire and sang camp songs from booklets they'd made for us. Songs like Down by the Bay, Michael Row the Boat a Shore and Land of the Silver Birch.

Then we went to bed.

In the morning, our group did archery. I really liked it. I kept at it till my arm got so sore I could barely lift it. In the afternoon, we had our first mother-daughter exercise. We had to sit on the ground cross-legged and tell each other one thing that we really liked about the other person. I had another panic attack as I racked my brain to come up with something that I could say about Harmony. Was there anything that I appreciated about her? What could I say?

Celeste went first. "Harmony there are many, many things that I love about you. Since I have to pick only one, I will say that I really like your ability to be yourself no matter what anybody else thinks."

At that Harmony looked at me and scrunched up her nose like she was saying: "So there."

"Angel I love many things about you too, but if I had to pick one thing I would have to say that I really like your level-headedness."

That was a surprise. Most days, she made fun of me for being too serious. And then it hit me like a dart, Celeste knew me. She knew both of us.

I have known almost forever that my mom isn't standard issue. I've heard some things that people say about her. That she's flaky, weird, and other even less complimentary things. I'll admit that sometimes I've thought those things myself. I've been impatient with her constant search for something that means the rest of us have to go along whether we want to or not. She seems so oblivious sometimes, but here was proof that she wasn't. That was a really big surprise discovering that she knew us as individuals and who we were was okay with her. That was pretty cool. The coolest thing of the whole summer.

The rest of our vacation pales next to that, and knowing we could be different from her, and that what made us different was not only fine, but she liked it.

It may sound strange. That I would be so excited about my mother accepting me. But when you live with someone like her, someone who is her own force of nature (yes, like a hurricane) you can feel awfully insignificant beside her.

I loved her so much when she said that, I thought my heart would explode. For a few minutes, I even thought that Harmony was not that bad either.

That was what I did on my summer vacation. I learned something new about my mother. That despite her obvious flaws (like being messy and getting carried away with everything) she wasn't so self-absorbed that she didn't see us.

For the rest of the week, we did all of the stuff that had been scheduled for us and when we got back home Denham was happy to see us, and we took swimming lessons and Harmony and I started arguing with each other again. (Actually Harmony doesn't argue, she just ignores me and that makes me mad and I yell at her.) The rest of the summer went by like whatever happened at that women's camp didn't happen. But I remember that for one minute I learned something new and it filled me with something that felt powerful. I'm not really sure what this might mean to me someday, but for today it's a good feeling. I'm glad I'm writing this down so I don't forget it.

THE END

By the time I was finished, I could have wept. I don't think I've been as touched by anything I've ever read as I was by my those stories. Discovering a piece of Mother's history and, by extension, mine, made for gripping reading.

Awe wrestled with pain. Couldn't she find a way to love me for who I was? Frustration and hurt lodged in my chest like I'd swallowed something bitter and whole. I fought them down, hoping to find some answers.

The pages that followed had been ripped from a journal. My mother's personal observations. No "Dear Diary" for her, not for the next few summers. Perhaps her teachers hadn't requested the summer vacation treatise. This was intriguing. Mother had wanted to document what had happened. A budding journalist. Even without the school assignment, she'd wanted to get it all down. Funny, little girl.

It crossed my mind to wonder where the rest of the journal had gone to.

# CHAPTER EIGHTEEN

**Journal entry: July 30, 1974**
**Colorado, USA**

As July approached, I could tell that Celeste had something up her sleeve even though things were carrying on as usual.

School had ended and we began the summer by celebrating Dominion Day with a canoe trip around a lake. We have to do something that Celeste considers to be an aboriginal kind of thing so that we learn to revere "the Indians of Canada." I had learned how to canoe at camp a couple of years ago and I liked it, but my sister, Harmony, got nervous when we almost tipped over. She spent half the trip sitting on the floor of the canoe gripping onto the sides in total fear. Denham kept telling her that even if we fell in we could all swim and we had life jackets, but she was still afraid. After lunch, he forced her to paddle and, once she got the hang of it, she wasn't afraid anymore. We had packed a picnic lunch and had a really nice day.

Except for one thing. All day, Celeste seemed distracted which was unusual for her. My mother is nothing if not focused on whatever it is she wants. I watched her very closely all day, waiting to see if she'd say or do something that would give me a hint of what was on her mind. She didn't and, by the time we were ready to pack up for home, I figured it was nothing.

I should have known better. Of course it was something. It's always something. This is my mother we're talking about.

She let her bomb drop during supper.

Denham was using all of his built-up vacation time and taking the summer off and we were going to live in a commune.

That's right. A commune. As in hippies and farming and free love and drugs. okay, well, not the last two things.

When she made her announcement, I spewed my milk all over the table while she looked just as pleased as could be. Up till then, I'd figured that after our experience on a kibbutz, Celeste would never have gone back to anything like that, but she said that we had to learn different ways of living so that we knew that people could make different choices and we didn't all have to grow up and work nine-to-five in some corporate office somewhere. That made Denham grimace, he being the person who most definitely had to work nine-to-five in a government office. Celeste carried on without notice saying that we needed to see life from different points of view. As if having Celeste as a mother hadn't already shown us everything we needed to know about being different. I stopped listening after that.

I had thought our summers had been getting to be almost run-of-the-mill. I'd let my guard down. I should have known that normal and Celeste didn't walk hand-in-hand very often. It had been too good to last.

We had a couple of days to get ready and then we'd be driving out to someplace called Living Spirit in Colorado. Denham said we had about a week to get there.

"I'm looking forward to getting away from the office." He sounded strangely happy. Celeste must have done a brainwashing number on him. This just didn't sound like the Denham I knew.

I marvelled at my parents' capacity for deceit. We'd had no clue at what they'd been planning and this must have taken some organizing.

Celeste gave us each a brochure describing the facility.

"Located in the beautiful mountains of Colorado, Living Spirit Commune welcomes guests to escape today's artificial, modern lifestyle by experiencing a holistic and natural way of living.

"In our unique village, visitors participate in a way of life that has given profound new meaning to local residents. Existing slightly outside the mainstream consumerist society, we are able to work together to create a calm and nurturing environment …"

I groaned. Another summer spent on one of Celeste's hare-brained ideas. Arguing would get me nowhere. It never did. I packed some music, my tape recorder, clothes, books, notebooks, and was ready to go. At least I could retreat into music and writing during the trip out there.

Harmony didn't seem to be bothered by this trip at all. She shrugged and said maybe we'd meet new friends. "How optimistic of her," I remember thinking.

I look forward to the day when I'll be old enough to move out and escape my mother. It can't come soon enough for me. I dream of summers spent at beaches and reading in parks, maybe touring a museum or two, things I imagine other people do during vacations.

I had a lot of time to think about this on the drive west.

The trip took us six whole days, an excruciating amount of time to spend sitting in a car. Celeste and Denham shared the driving; Harmony and I wilted in the backseat and played tic-tac-toe and licence-plate cribbage, that is whenever she wasn't being totally annoying. We stopped regularly to stretch, but after a couple of days of staring at a strip of asphalt that went on forever, even a saint would have gotten irritable. I sure did.

Knowing my sister, I'd expect that she'd be her usual exasperating self and she was. She either talked incessantly, reading off every sign we drove by or sang out loud and off-key to music playing on the car radio. She just couldn't sit still and bounced up and down on the seat. To stop me from killing her, Celeste let me sit in the front now and again. That one small kindness is why I'm here and not in some high-security prison for murder.

We pulled into Living Spirit just before suppertime on the sixth day and were greeted by a woman about Gram's age. She was wearing denim shorts and a shirt with rolled-up sleeves. Muddy rubber boots were on her feet. She had just come in from weeding and watering the garden. She told us there would be fresh lettuce and green onions for the supper salad.

Her name was Naomi and after Denham parked the car, she

showed us to our cottage. There were a dozen two- and three-bedroom cabins for paying visitors like us. Money from tourism was one of the ways the commune paid for extra things like a new snowplough or college for the older kids.

We were staying in a two-bedroom with one bathroom and a sitting area. We would eat our meals in a large dining room close to the community centre, the hub of the commune. It held an administrative office, a small school, a medical clinic, a vet's office, a library, a gymnasium with a stage, and a corner store. There were other buildings out back.

Naomi told us that everybody contributed so many hours a week to the commune by teaching, gardening, doctoring, or whatever they could. The rest of the time they got to do whatever they wanted. There were craftspeople there who sold their stuff through a catalogue or in town at various shops. One woman made lotions and soap from goat's milk, there were artists, and one guy had a log-home business. They were really self-sufficient.

From the minute we got out of the car, I noticed how peaceful it was. There was a different kind of quietness here. Not just an absence of noise. It was kind of like a town out of an old movie, slow-paced and still. It took me a while to realize the stillness was a result of the few vehicles being driven around. The sound of motors was mostly absent. If someone had to get somewhere, they walked. It didn't only cut down on noise, but contributed to things moving a whole lot slower than I was used to.

As paying guests, we weren't forced to work which I was very happy to hear. I spent a lot of time walking around and studying what was going on. It was a pretty spot. I'd never seen mountains before. We'd see deer in the mornings and could hear owls and wolves at night. There were a lot of birds that I'd never seen before either. I loved watching the hawks swooping overhead.

I met some local kids who were really friendly. They were on summer break like us and said "hi" whenever they saw us. They played basketball or baseball, just like kids at home, but they helped their parents at whatever their parents were doing:

weeding the vegetable gardens, repairing torn fence, working in the barns, knitting or making crafts, that kind of thing.

Harmony followed me almost everywhere which drove me mad, but if I was just sitting and writing or reading, she'd get bored and take off soon enough.

After a while, I started feeling like being the only ones with nothing to do was weird. Even here in a commune, the one place you'd figure maybe we'd fit in, we stood out. Of course it was for different reasons than back home. I started feeling uncomfortable being the only one my age without responsibilities. It started like an itch and grew to full-blown attack of conscience. I asked Celeste and Denham if there was anything for me to do. I could tell that they were delighted I'd asked. I tried not to feel like I had been tricked into something, but did anyway. The bonus for me was that Harmony was still pretty happy being lazy so I was one up on her.

The next day, my parents arranged for me to meet up with some kids who were running a day camp for the little ones. I spent the day helping out and had so much fun. It was crafts and games in the morning and swimming and nap-time in the afternoon. All-in-all not a bad way to spend a day.

Things changed on the morning of the second day just as we were clearing up from snack time. That was when Harmony arrived.

She just floated right in, like she belonged there, wearing one of her pink, poufy dresses and carrying a case of cassettes in a lime-green corduroy bag. The little kids practically fell at her feet, spellbound by this glamorous new arrival. You could tell they thought she was some kind of princess. Oh, she makes me so mad sometimes. It was my idea to contribute and here she was horning in and getting all the attention—without having done any work, I'd like to add.

She asked the kids if they wanted to dance and of course they said yes so she put her music on and started doing some kind of ballet thing with scarves. I don't know how she managed it, but she pulled a bunch out of her bag and handed them out to each kid as she flitted by. The kids started twirling and jumping and scampering about. They were having a great time. They danced for most of the rest of the morning, stopping only to refuel with some juice or to catch their breaths before resuming their activity.

I couldn't believe it. Harmony was being useful in her own unusual way.

By lunch time, the kids were beat and Harmony left them to us for the rest of the day. She returned the next morning and the one after that staying for an hour to dance with the kids then leaving. She swanned in and out every day and the kids adored her. I hated to admit that she made our jobs easier.

At night after dinner, Harmony and I started to hang out with the kids our age at the community centre. We learned how to play pool and ping pong and darts. Sometimes we went swimming although at least one adult or a couple of the older kids had to come whenever we swam after dark. Sometimes there was a community bonfire and we roasted marshmallows and sang camp songs. There was one guy who could play a guitar and when he sang old songs all the adults joined in.

That brings me up-to-date for our travels this summer. More later.

## Journal entry: August 5, 1974
### 4 p.m.

Up until this morning, this had been one of our best summers. Everybody is really nice and they make us feel like we're at home. We're finally somewhere where Celeste and Harmony aren't considered peculiar and I'm not being treated like a drag. Things are really casual.

Over the past couple of weeks, we haven't spent much time with our parents. This is unusual for our family. Celeste normally plans something for us to do together every minute over the summer. This year, however, we only see them at mealtimes and in the evening if there's a neighbourhood event. Other than that, we do our thing and they do theirs.

It's been heaven.

I admit that I was pretty curious about how they were spending their time. They're not working and, after a couple of weeks, I've started thinking that it's weird that we never see them around.

This morning, I found out why.

I forgot my water canteen in our cabin so I returned from the day camp to get it. As I got closer to our lodging, I could hear angry voices.

I opened the door and I heard Denham say, "It just isn't working."

"C'mon Denny. Remember how we wanted this to be? Remember how we said we wouldn't get caught up in the nine-to-five, uptight world of suburbia? What's happened to you?"

"What's happened to me? What's happened to me? Are you blind? Who is the one who has to support this family while you—"

Denham looked up and saw me and stopped talking, his words hanging awkwardly in the air.

I mumbled something about having to hurry to get back to work and bolted outdoors.

I must have looked upset when I got back because even Harmony noticed and she never ever notices anything. She asked me what was wrong, but there was no way I could talk to her in front of everyone.

As a matter of record, I had never talked to her about anything important before. It was strange that at that moment—to my total amazement—she was the only one I could, or wanted, to talk to. But it would have to wait till later, when we'd have some privacy.

When I could finally tell her what I'd heard, she nodded, as calmly as could be.

"Yeah, I know."

I couldn't believe it. "You know?"

"Yeah. That's why we're here. So they can try to get it together. They're doing a lot of counselling at the centre."

I shook my head in disbelief. Harmony the Oblivious knew

about Celeste and Denham before me? "How did you know?"

"I've heard them arguing sometimes after we go to bed."

"How come I've never heard them?"

She held her palms up as if to say "I don't know" and I felt foolish. In a snap, she had become a sophisticated stranger.

"You sleep down the hall. I guess you can't hear them with your door closed."

"What do they fight about?"

"Celeste not working. The bills. Denham wanting some Denham-time. I don't know. He just seems to be really angry with her all the time. Haven't you noticed?"

I suppose I had, but I didn't think it mattered much. Celeste was just Celeste. I mean, when wasn't she adopting some cause or other and wanting to live a life that was, as she put it, "free from convention?" I knew Denham grumbled, but I thought he accepted it. She's always been that way since before they got married. At least that's what they tell us. So, what was the big deal now?

Complete amazement filled my brain. Did I actually have this conversation with my sister? It seems so unreal. We'd barely ever spoken. Actually, if I stopped to think about it, I'd been angry with her forever. We'd never had any common ground. Yet here we were not only talking, but talking about something that meant something.

I wonder if our family is going to come apart. I've never seriously considered that before. Even when Celeste and Denham split up for that summer I never felt like they'd stay that way. It was more like an experiment than anything serious.

This doesn't feel that way. I've never heard them argue. Sure Denham gets aggravated with her sometimes, but it doesn't last.

It's hard to describe my parents. Denham is pretty ordinary. He has a regular job in a regular office where he wears suits. He mows the lawn and washes the car and reads the paper. He does regular dad stuff. Celeste, on the other hand, is a woman of ideals. Yes, that's what she is. She believes in things and then tries to live what she believes no matter how short-lived those beliefs might be.

Or maybe it's that she tries to believe in the things she wants to believe. I wonder …

Everything Celeste wants to do is supposed to be really great and give us some terrific insight into how to live or why we're here or who we are. Everything is really great until it isn't anymore and we move on to the next great thing that's going to change our lives forever.

I can see how that would wear a person like Denham down. He's the guy who has to go to work and pay the bills for all these experiments of hers, and he's the guy who waits for her to come back home when she leaves or to let him come back home when she doesn't want to be alone anymore. Waiting can be exhausting.

This summer was supposed to teach us about community. At least I thought it was until Harmony told me about the counselling.

I can't see them not being Celeste and Denham. What if they aren't going to be together any more? Who's going to be there to balance Celeste?

I feel awful and I hate the idea of having to sit through supper with them tonight. Are they going to say something to me? I don't know which would be worse, talking about it or pretending nothing is wrong.


### Journal entry: August 5, 1974
### 10 p.m.

They must have come to some agreement during the day because when we joined them at dinner they were smiling. Celeste spoke first. Not that that was a surprise.

"Girls, Denham and I don't want you to worry about anything you may have heard. It's normal for married couples to have differences. We simply sort them out and go on. We have some work to do that will help us gain a richer understanding and appreciation of each other."

I was glued to Denham the whole time she was talking. He

had that tight-lipped look he has when he's angry about something even though he was nodding like he agreed with her.

"This is a very healthy thing for us to do. I know that it can be scary to realize that your parents aren't perfect, but you really don't have to worry."

And that's where she lost me. Scary to realize your parents aren't perfect? Okay. Earth to Celeste. We have grown up with a mother who's kind of nuts. For Pete's sake. With all her existing flaws, I hope being delusional isn't going to be added to the list.

But then I realized something else and I got mad. When she was speaking, she was confident and something I can only describe as joyful. That's when I understood that this whole summer is just one more Celeste-fest. I wonder if she went as far as creating some conflict with Denham so they could try this counselling thing. I wonder if this isn't just one more crazy, let's-turn-our-lives-upside-down kind of thing because she was bored. I wonder if coming here is to give her some sort of thrill from the excitement of maybe, nearly losing her husband.

Oh, I could throttle her!

I've never thought about her like this before. Sure she's wacky and usually embarrassing, but not manipulative, not cruel.

I ate my meal in silence. Celeste chatted about the day and Harmony saved me by answering whatever questions came our way.

Denham was quiet too. I wondered what he was thinking about all of this. I wondered what he thought of his life and his marriage. It was probably the first time that I had given him much thought at all.

He's told me about how they met. He always starts it with: Once upon a time, when I was a young man ... I get a kick out of that.

The way he tells me it, I can picture him as a studious guy working toward his degree in business. I can picture him pouring over books in the campus library, when one night, needing a break, he decides to go to a pub, but on his way there he comes to a crowd listening to a young woman with long hair. She is standing on a platform and speaking into a bull horn, telling students that they have to care about human and civil rights. They have to vote for the political candidate who will care for all people equally.

He said he had never heard someone speak with such conviction. He said it was like she cast a spell on him and he fell in love with that outspoken, gutsy girl.

The rest, as they say, is history.

Now, I wonder if he regrets his choice, if he would have been happier with Margaret Chilton, his previous girlfriend. She has become a society matron. I know because one day Celeste was reading the newspaper and saw an announcement about the mayor honouring Margaret for her charity work. Celeste teased Denham about his old flame. Would Denham have been happier with Margaret? Without us? It's so sad to think he might have been.

I should have paid more attention to him. Having Celeste as a mother doesn't leave a lot of time to think about much else. She is a full-time concern.

Here I am stuck in the middle of Hippy-ville with a mother who might not be as harmless as I always thought, with parents involved in marital negotiations, and with a sister who has turned into a capable, aware person.

It is a confusing time. Yes, I am definitely bewildered, befuddled, perplexed. (I just love a good thesaurus.)


### Journal entry: August 6, 1974

Well, just when you think things can't get any worse, they do.

First, this commune experience has turned out to be fine, better than fine. The other kids are nice, and it's great to have so much freedom to come and go as we please. It's also astounding that, by some miracle, Harmony and I are getting along well.

Naturally, this was too good to last.

Now that Denham and Celeste's problems are out in the

open, Harmony and I have been sucked into them. At breakfast this morning, Celeste announced that we are expected to participate in family counselling sessions in the interests of "family unity and equality" because "everyone's point of view is important and should be heard."

We just had the first session.

We had to sit on the floor in a circle and commit to listening to each other with respect and love.

I hate sitting on the floor. My back gets stiff and it's uncomfortable. Maybe that's why I was a little crankier than usual when it got to be my turn to speak.

The counsellor asked me how I was feeling.

I fumed for a moment and then threw my shoulders back, stuck my nose into the air, and said, with as imperious a tone as I could muster: "I don't want to be here. I don't belong here. This is an issue between my parents and I don't want to be involved. It's uncomfortable to listen to them talk about each other. And, since everyone's perspective is equally important, I'm sure you will respect the fact that I must leave."

And I did just that. It was so dramatic. Or it would have been if my knees weren't so stiff that I limped rather than marched out the door. It detracted from my defiance, but I was going to make a statement if it killed me.

Aching knees aside, when I left the community centre, I felt triumphant. Thrilled too. Thrilled that I had spoken up and done what I wanted instead of what was expected of me for a change. I'd done what I wanted. It was powerful.

After a time, Harmony followed me from the room and told me that the adults had agreed that neither of us have to attend sessions again. I won!

Yea!


### Journal entry: August 23, 1974

Just a quick note before we head back home. We're leaving in a few minutes.

I'm actually going to miss this place. The summer has been great with the exception of you-know-what. After that stupid counselling session, Harmony and I spent the rest of our vacation helping at the day camp and hanging out with the other kids and pretty much avoiding our parents which, in an odd way, felt like a totally normal, teen-aged thing to do.

Now we're going home and the therapy must have worked because everything seems to be back to the way it was—a mixed blessing for sure.

What is it that group sings in that song? "What a long, strange trip it's been." No kidding. No frigging kidding.

What had Gran been thinking, to drag kids to marriage counselling? One thing was certain, Mother's notes gave me a new view of my grandmother.

Jane called. It was time to us to leave and I hadn't even showered. We had decided to drive to the Valley. To Wolfville for a trip to the art galleries and a bit of lunch. If we were ambitious afterward, we might travel along the Bay of Fundy and dip down along the rim of Kejimkujik Park to land in Liverpool for supper.

"Give me ten minutes." I yelled, running upstairs.

I debated bringing the rest of mother's stories with me. In the end, I couldn't leave them behind and stuck them into my oversized purse before heading out the door.

Jane drove, and I meant to be good company, truly I did. My hands were itching to hold my mother's words, my eyes darting back and forth from the scenery to my purse nestled on the floor by my feet. I wedged my fingers between my thighs and the seat to stop them from rummaging through my bag. My right leg jiggled up and down on the ball of my foot.

After trying to get my attention for the third time, Jane said, "Oh, go on. Read. We'll talk over lunch."

I leaned over the console and kissed her cheek. "You're the best."

"Don't I know it?"

I dove for the pile of papers.

# CHAPTER NINETEEN

**Journal entry: July 2, 1975**

It's been another interesting start to summer at our house.

Denham has put an end to Celeste's strange summer ventures by renting a cottage! I use an exclamation mark because this is a very exciting shift toward the conservative for our family. A cottage on a lake with a canoe and a barbeque. What could be more ordinary than that?

We started as usual with our annual "Praise the Indians" tribute on July 1. This year was a contrived naming ceremony. I couldn't imagine why we needed names more descriptive than the ones we already have. It's not like we don't get teased already. Celeste must be running out of things to torment us with.

She lit a bonfire in our back yard. Yes, it is illegal. At least I figured it was pretty quickly once the fire department arrived, but that came later. Celeste was really excited about finding sweet grass. It's a sacred plant used by native people for healing and ceremonial purposes. She wove the strands together then lit the braided stalk over the fire and waved it in the air in front of Denham. I think he must have agreed to participate in the ceremony in exchange for the cottage.

So, the fire was going, and the sweet grass was burning, and Harmony was twirling and jumping around the yard to the sound of beating drums that came from a tape of aboriginal music purchased at the friendship centre downtown. Celeste was seated in a lawn chair while swaying from side to side with her eyes closed. Denham looked like he had a toothache, and I fortified myself with the knowledge that I had only had to get through this night and then we'd be going to a cottage on a lake with a canoe and I could pretend we were an average family for four whole weeks.

There are days when I can't help but wonder if I'm the only rational one in my family. Yet every time that thought crosses my mind, I begin to worry that maybe they're the sane ones and I'm crazy. As Gram says, "Wouldn't that be a kick in the behind?"

The music faded and Harmony sank to the ground as Celeste rose to her feet. I bet she was disappointed not to have had full native dress. Her hair was loose and she had wrapped a large blue shawl around her shoulders despite the summer heat. It fell to her knees. It took me a moment to realize it was the cloth from our kitchen table. A mustard stain from yesterday's ham sandwiches bloomed at Celeste's right shoulder.

She walked around the fire to Harmony and then to me and smudged ashes on our cheeks. I almost started laughing at my sister's dirty face till I realized that mine probably looked the same.

Celeste returned to her place and held her arms out in front of her.

Then she spoke.

"Mother Earth you have blessed us with sweet grass to purify the air and quiet our spirits to help us dispel negative thoughts."

I wondered if she had found this somewhere or was making it up on the fly. Whichever the case, she was putting her whole heart into it

"We are gathered together under the moon to welcome the souls of my daughters to the mystical world. Their childhood names have been given to them, but their spiritual names, they have earned.

"My daughter Harmony, your spirit is so evident that to deny it would be to deny you. I give you the name Satinka or Magic Dancer, one that I hope you will take with pride."

She pulled a necklace out of her pocket and put it over Harmony/Magic Dancer's head. Then she moved on to me. I admit that my nerves had kicked in imagining which of my many faults she might choose to recognize. Stick-in-the-Mud, Grumpy Bear, Smirk-Behind-Hand.

"My daughter Angel, you are my first child and have done so much to cause us pride. I give you the name Delsin or Truthful One because you take in everything around you and turn your experiences into wonderful tales that show us elements of life."

That was pretty cool and later when I went to bed I felt good, special even.

Celeste sure could surprise me. Once in a while—a very long while—this could even be a good thing.

Even the fire warden's visit to tell us to douse the flames didn't dampen my mood.

In the morning, we left for the cottage. Denham rented a small trailer to pull all the stuff we brought. He whistled as we backed out of the driveway. This would be one summer vacation he'd actually be able to share with the guys back at the office. A Simone first.

The drive took about two hours, not that anyone was complaining. We were all looking forward to a month of swimming and lounging around. I had a stack of books to read and my favourite music. I could handle sloth. We headed into the Gatineaus, to the northern tip of Lake Herrington, not far beyond Old Chelsea. The road zigzagged over hilly terrain and our journey into Quebec was punctuated by our staccato yelps of delight mixed with terror as Denham laboured up summits then plunged us downward into steep valleys, angling the car perilously in one direction and then the other. He drove with caution to ease our outbursts, irritating the locals who tailgated, waiting for an opportunity to zoom by—to their imminent doom, we thought.

Despite this, Denham caught my eye in the rear-view mirror and winked. Man, he was so happy. Like a kid with a new toy. Celeste chatted as she did during trips. Harmony bopped her head to whatever was playing on the radio, as usual. I was just sitting back and enjoying the scenery as carefree as I could ever remember being at the start of vacation.

And then it happened. I started feeling sick. Not throw-up sick, but my stomach felt really weird. Burbly. Like I had gas. Crampy. I felt like I was peeing. I tried to stop it, but it trickled out. And then it stopped. At least I thought it did. And then the light bulb went on.

My first period. Wahoo. And yes, that is a touch of sarcasm.

I figured I'd be okay for the drive. The books say that not much is supposed to happen the first time. I hoped the experts were right. I tried to ignore the pains in my stomach and the achy feeling that had begun to spread to my legs.

As though guided by some magical mom-radar, Celeste turned around and gave me a funny look.

"Are you feeling all right?"

Peachy.

"Yeah, I'm fine. Maybe a little car sick."

"Open the window wider." Reassured, she continued chatting with Denham and flipping through a magazine, some of her trash reading that she said was part of the cottage experience.

I knew I'd have to tell her and knew that she'd have to make a big deal out of it and knew she'd tell everyone. This was going to be so embarrassing. Yet again.

We got to the cottage just after noon. We travelled down a long, pockmarked laneway. It curved to the right as we got closer to the lake. Trees arched over the drive softening the strong sun. Birds flitted through the branches. Denham drove with painstaking care as the trailer bounced behind us, threatening to come loose from the bolt that held it in place. When the cottage came in sight, I breathed a sigh of relief. It was perfect.

Deep brown clapboard siding was topped by a Quebecois-orange roof. The windows were trimmed in forest green. The doors were painted sea-foam and had been decorated with hand-painted flowers. I could see the lake ahead with a dock and a canoe tied to the side.

I had little time to linger, however. Once the car came to a stop, I raced into the bathroom. I was safe. Nothing more than a smallish, red spot. I steeled myself to make my announcement to Celeste so she could get the appropriate supplies for me when they drove into town to do groceries.

Gritting my teeth and balling my fists, I spit the news out. Her reaction was worse that I had predicted. Way worse than when I made my debut in the lingerie department and she prattled on to the shop clerk about how I was shopping for my "very first bra." That was yet another lesson in humiliation, but at least it was done at a reasonable volume.

"OH MY GOD!" she shrieked. "DENHAM, HARMONY COME OVER HERE. YOU'LL NEVER GUESS WHAT HAPPENED. ANGEL HAS BECOME A WOMAN!"

Birds took to the air, no doubt terrified at the sound of the howling banshee beneath them. I hugged my shoulders wishing that I could join them and wishing she'd shut up.

Denham turned red to the tips of his ears and gave my elbow a sympathetic squeeze. Harmony gave me a look of commiseration. Hang in there, she seemed to say.

Celeste noticed my mortification and, with a cheery command to stop being so provincial, announced that we had something to celebrate.

I didn't bother to try to mask my groan. "What now?"

As we unloaded the trailer, she yakked on and on about the "threshold to womanhood" and "patriarchal society's invalidation of the feminine mystique."

I was about to be made an example of. It wasn't enough that I had begun years of pain and inconvenience, I was to become an example for the women's movement and Celeste would create an event as a symbolic reparation for every wrong cast on oppressed women everywhere. It was an awful lot for a thirteen-year-old to shoulder. An awful lot to expect of one, tiny, menstrual period.

I felt doomed, totally helpless to stop Celeste and whatever she would plan. The one bit of good news in all this was that it had happened in a remote village in the middle of western Quebec. I could reasonably count on the fact that the news of whatever Celeste would plan for me would not reach anyone back home. That, at least, provided immeasurable relief.

After Denham left with Celeste, Harmony and I changed into our bathing suits and sat on a couple of chairs on the dock. As I read, the summer sun made me sleepy. In no time, I was dozing and awoke only when Harmony touched my leg.

"They're home."

The moment I had been dreading had arrived and I steeled myself to whatever might happen. The suspense was to last a while longer as Celeste surprised me yet again by saying and doing nothing. We put the groceries away without a single comment about the big festivities and I began to hope that maybe, just maybe, she had thought better of it.

I couldn't completely relax though. Celeste seemed too bubbly-under-the-surface like she had just discovered the world's biggest secret and was dying to share it, but couldn't. But wanted to. But couldn't.

And yes, that did make me worried.

I couldn't tell if my stomach was feeling sick because of nerves or because of my "big event." I had decided that's how I'd refer to my coming of age. It seemed appropriate under the circumstances.

The rest of the afternoon was spent quietly enough on the water, paddling the canoe or reading. Celeste had hidden away in her bedroom and I found myself watching the cottage with growing anxiety as the day wore on.

The big bang hit at dusk.

We had finished clearing away supper dishes when Celeste called me to her room and closed the door behind me.

"Surprise!" she exclaimed.

As she moved away from her bed, I saw the most hideous dress laid out for me to wear. It was a pale blue, sleeveless, cotton dress and would have been nice enough had Celeste not turned it into a jungle oasis. Plastic flowers and leaves had been sewn all over it. It looked like a dime-store rainforest. All that was missing was a stuffed parrot or screeching monkey.

"It represents Mother Nature," she said looking at me with

a strange cast in her eyes.

"Mother Nature." My voice dropped.

"Yes, silly. We're going to celebrate your new connection with nature, the feminine earth, the cycle of life."

I must have groaned because she snapped, "Just put it on. I'll meet you at the fire pit."

When she left the room, I sank onto the bed and covered my face with my hands. It was no use. I was going to have to play along and get it over with—whatever it was. Celeste was as pig-headed as anyone so it would be easier to comply, no matter how painful submission was going to be, rather than to make a fuss. That would only prolong the inevitable.

I pulled the dress on over my head, then looked at myself in the mirror.

"Oh, my god." I was a freak. I looked like the Michelin Man except instead of a white, marshmallow body, mine was bloated by petals and leaves. Plastic and wired purple, pink, yellow, and red petals surrounded by moss-green leaves of all shapes and sizes. Brown stems trailed across and around my body. I half expected them to raise, writhing snakelike from my shoulders.

I heard my name being called and knew I could put it off no longer. Slumping, I made my way toward the blazing flames rising by the shore. Thankfully, it was dark.

Denham was sitting in a plastic lawn chair nursing a beer. Celeste stood expectantly with arms outstretched toward me. Was I supposed to run into them? If so, I didn't cooperate. It was all I could do to drag my feet across the sand. Leaping was out of the question.

When Harmony saw me, she began one of her dances, her arms and legs moving together with a grace I could never match. Usually, this would have irritated me and I would have made some smart remark, but, that night, I appreciated her attempt to draw attention away from me. It was her show of sisterly support and I understood it as such. Isn't it funny how you can spend years fighting with a person and then, every once in a while, really connect with them? I tried to smile to let her know

I appreciated her effort. My lips were frozen, the skin too taut to spread.

"Come, young woman, toward the fire," Celeste began.

She placed the palms of her hands against my forehead then ran them to the top of my skull and down along my shoulders. She was humming a tune I didn't know. It sounded like something from one of those big movies, Ben Hur or Cleopatra. I squinted at the colours of the fire and let my mind drift away, thinking about going to university and becoming a really famous writer. Harmony zoomed in and out of focus and Celeste began an incantation to Diana, the moon goddess. I watched her though my eyelashes making everything look hazy. With her arms raised high above her head, she was like an ancient Roman priestess.

I focused harder on thinking about the future and getting away from my mother.

And then there was silence and Celeste stared at me expectantly.

What was I supposed to do?

Taking a gamble, I hugged her which was exactly the right thing. She sent Denham to fetch the cake and I raced inside to change into something I could actually sit in.

All-in-all, I guess it wasn't so bad. I have to think she meant well. It is either that or realize that I am headed into years of therapy. I prefer thinking that the evening was her way of showing me she cared. Though I would have preferred a new pair of roller skates. The cake at least was good.

The summer is off to its usual weird start. Apparently, we Simones can make even going to a cottage a strange adventure.

Please celestial powers, let today be the last embarrassing day ever.


### Journal entry: July 30, 1975

I can't believe it's time to head home already. While the month hasn't exactly flown by, now that school is just around the corner, the time here hasn't lasted nearly long enough.

Not that I hate school or haven't missed things like television or the library, it's just that I'm going to miss the flow of our days here.

After the mortification of the first day, things settled down and we haven't had any Celeste-fests since then.

She's been quite tame. Really. Oh sure, she woke us up during the full moon to dance around the fire which was actually fun. And, yes, she did insist we go skinny-dipping together. Denham, thankfully, declined. Swimming nude with your female relatives is one thing, with your father it would be something else entirely. Call the shrink now.

Other than that, summer was really laid back. We floated from one day to the next "doing a whole lot of nothing" as Gram would say.

If I can brag for a sec, let me say that I have the best tan ever! I even sat out topless a couple of times when Denham drove into town for supplies so my bathing suit lines are hardly visible. Pretty neat, eh?

Okay, so I've got a confession to make. There is one thing about our vacation that's got me worried. Worried enough that I'm not even sure if I should be writing it down. What if somebody reads this? Somebody who shouldn't? (Harmony: If you're reading this, you better hope I don't find out.)

Hmmm.

This is supposed to be private and Celeste and Denham are committed to respecting our privacy. They claim to understand the boundaries of closed doors or personal notes. (Bodily functions, apparently, don't fall under the same guidelines.)

Well, here goes.

I think Denham is an alcoholic.

There, I've written it down.

I tried to talk about it with Celeste, but she said it was just a cottage thing and nothing to worry about. That lots of people cut loose when they are away from the constraints of the city and the office and drink a bit more than they usually do.

That might be true. I wouldn't know what other people do

since this is my first experience at one. It seems to me, though, that Denham is depressed. He's become our own Prince Hamlet, moping about all alone and gazing at something the rest of us can't see.

Our kinship—the silent partnership he and I have against the energies named Celeste and Harmony—has petered out. He isn't present. Here but not here. I've tried to speak to him and he doesn't hear me unless I call his name or touch him. And then, he puts on a fake smile and says: "You caught me thinking, trying to solve all the problems of the world."

I'd smile back and say: "That's okay. It wasn't important." Then I'd take off for a swim or something else, anything so I wouldn't draw attention to his state of mind.

He couldn't fool me at all. Saving the world just isn't his thing. I'm pretty sure he agreed with me that we couldn't afford to have two radicals in the house.

He had been so happy at the start of vacation. What happened to him?

Whatever it was, after a few days here, he started each day with a drink at breakfast—a shot of Bailey's Irish Cream or brandy in his coffee. Then beer with lunch and on into the afternoon. Sometimes he'd have wine with supper followed by scotch later on.

He returned a ton of empties to the nearby dépanneur yesterday.

And he seems so sad.

Why? Why? Why?

It's been such a great summer! What changed?

I'll never understand adults. Even when things are going well, they have to mess it up.

I miss him so much. Celeste has overshadowed him forever and I guess I took him for granted most of the time, but knowing he was there somewhere in the background and being his solidly reliable self helped me deal with all the craziness.

I've been trying to call Denham, "Dad" like he asked us to a long time ago, but he's been Denham to me forever and calling a person by one thing your whole life is a tough thing to change.

I'm going to make a real effort though. Maybe that'll make him feel better.

I've got to run. I hear Celeste calling for me. I've got to help get things packed up. We're leaving for home tomorrow. School doesn't start for another five weeks. That's time enough to figure things out.

If the great cosmos gets my vibes, maybe you could lob a prayer out there for me.

Grandfather was an alcoholic? This was the first mention of that I'd ever heard. It seemed that things in my mother's world had begun to get a lot more complicated than I'd ever imagined. To me, her childhood seemed filled with so much fun. Gran and Aunt Harmony's stories of the family had painted images of such hilarious escapades that I'd fantasized about experiencing such adventures my whole life. I'd imagined my uptight mother had turned her back on these frivolities for reasons stemming from her own character defects: her narrow-mindedness, her outdated sense of decorum, her priggishness.

What I was discovering was something else, someone else. And I was falling in love with her. And worrying about her.

"How's it going?" Jane asked, rolling her head from side to side, working out the kinks from driving.

"Want me to drive?"

"I'm fine. You go on. What you're doing is important."

I was glad not to drive. I didn't want anything to take me away from my task. I was in a hurry to know everything about my mother these pages contained and couldn't tear myself away from them. Like a dying woman on a quest for water who's found a fountain to sustain me, I'd rather drown in it than be torn away.

# CHAPTER TWENTY

**Journal entry: July 2, 1976**

Yesterday was another Simone disaster. This time it took the form of an inter-cultural incident.

For our Dominion Day festivities this year, Celeste decided we'd do a sweat and, as usual, Denham refused to participate, so it was just us girls. Oh, goody.

It's not that a sweat is a horrible idea, and it might have been a good learning experience unless you take into account two facts. One, that yesterday was one of the hottest days on record, and two, no one in my family has any idea about how to participate in such a thing without collapsing from heat stroke.

We drove to Akwesasne, a Mohawk community on the border of Canada and the U.S., and were led to a low-lying lodge that had been specifically constructed for this sacred purpose. A fire was built inside, and while Harmony and I lay on the cool ground barely tolerating the intense temperature, Celeste sat immediately in front of the hot stones to get the full impact of the experience. She was certainly successful and, after absorbing more heat than she could tolerate, passed out and had to be hauled outside.

This disrupted what is supposed to be a holy purification ceremony that people prepare for in advance. The lodge represents a womb and as we sweat, we are supposed to be cleansed and are reborn as we exit the lodge and re-enter the light of the world.

While we waited for Denham to come and get us, the elder

leading the sweat had to pray to get rid of our negative energy. At least, I think that's what he was doing.

And while Celeste's collapse provided a welcome break for Harmony and me, she was quite sick afterward and had to be taken to the hospital for rehydration.

Was I concerned? Well, sure. No one wants to see their mother suffer. On the other hand, what kind of a nut takes their kids to something that can be dangerous without finding out anything about it beforehand? I mean, geez. Does it ever occur to her that just because the Mohawk do something it's benign? That maybe she needs to be looking out for our welfare? That maybe we needed to drink a lot of water beforehand or wait till a cooler day so we weren't already overheated when the ceremony began?

As we drove to the hospital, I could see Denham's lips moving in the rear-view mirror, but there was no sound coming out. He kept looking at Celeste who was slumped over on the passenger side and shaking his head.

With any luck, this will be our very last Dominion Day commemoration.

The bad news we discovered only after Celeste was examined by a doctor. She was to be admitted at least overnight and our escape to the cottage would be postponed for a day or two.

As it turned out, she was fine by this morning, but we still have to hang around till tomorrow to make sure she doesn't suffer a relapse.

I hope we can leave tomorrow. Our cottage rental starts today and it's not like we get to add days on at the end if we're not there on time. Damn! She always, always finds a way to ruin everything!

Does that sound callous of me?

I guess it does.

I'm turning into a horrible person, aren't I?

Sigh.

Angel

And there it began. The self-hatred I had seen in her forever without having recognized it as such. I'd been so blind and my heart ached to think we shared the same self-loathing. What a legacy! Who would have thought it, that we'd be so much alike?

I stared into space, the pages of my mother's early life held limply on my lap. I wanted so much to see her then, to talk with her, and to have her respond. To have our souls connect in a way that couldn't have been possible before.

And yet, could we? I shook my head and as sorrow overtook me a tear slipped down my cheek, unnoticed till it dropped onto my arm.

I clutched the papers to my chest just as Jane turned off the highway toward Wolfville.

"Have you finished?"

I shook my head and held out the few unread pages for her to see.

"There is not much more to come."

"I know."

"Are you frightened?"

"No. Yes. A little. I can see her as she was. You know? And I feel so bad for all the terrible things I've said to her, all the awful things I've thought about her. She was so … pure. And now, well now she's just sad, isn't she?"

"Perhaps."

"She's coming tomorrow. What will I say to her?"

"Finish your reading. It might help you decide."

"Oh, Jane! Just help me. This isn't the time for Native maxims."

She cuffed me lightly on the side of my knee. "Maybe you should do what you need to do and stop expecting everyone else to have the answers. Life isn't that easy."

We found a place to park and strolled along Main Street stopping in at two galleries. The collections ranged from felting, to sculpture, to naïve and high-concept art. I loved the variety and the whimsy of many of the pieces there. Eventually, hunger got the best of us and we ducked into a coffee shop for sandwiches made on artisanal breads.

As difficult as it was to focus on anything but the last story that awaited me, I made a serious effort to be a reasonably sensitive lunch guest. "You haven't talked to me about Gran since the funeral."

"You have other things going on."

"That shouldn't stop you from talking to me."

"I know." She looked into the distance. "I never knew I could feel like this. It's an empty shadow inside me. Like when my mother died. I'm glad you're with me. It's good to have someone in the house."

"Will you go back to teaching in September?"

"Definitely. Give me something to do."

"How was she with you? I always thought you were happy, but now that I'm reading things about Gran that aren't very complimentary, I wonder about you."

"Your grandmother was very sad when I met her. We met at a class on Mi'kmaq spirituality and became friends. I don't think she was the same woman she was when she was married to your grandfather. Still boisterous, but she could be introspective too. I think that's why she gathered those pages for you. Regretting some of the things she'd done."

"I wish she'd given them to me years ago."

"Maybe she was afraid."

I nodded. I could understand that. I slid my hand over to cover Jane's. "How are you? Really?"

"My heart is broken." She faltered, her voice shaking with emotion. "I get up some days without knowing why I bother. But then I think of you, and know I have to get up."

I walked behind her chair, bent over, and hugged her to me. "I love you, Janie."

She patted my arms crossed around her neck. "Let's go. Get on with our journey."

We walked to the car, Jane insisting on driving. "Go ahead with your business. You're almost done and your mom will be here tomorrow."

I picked the papers off the seat, wondering about Gran's choice of keepsake items. If my mother didn't know these stories of hers still existed, Gran must have come across them on her own, maybe after Mother left for Toronto, maybe when Gran packed to move back to Nova Scotia. However she had found them, she had obviously chosen them with care. There was no journal, for example, only pages ripped from one. Celeste had left me a strong message about my mother by selecting only these to save. She had also left me quite an indictment of herself. It was brave of her, although I was challenged not to feel angry with her for waiting so long.

I began reading where I'd left off.

# CHAPTER TWENTY-ONE

### Grade Eleven Assignment
### Background

Each September I approach the new school year with a sense of trepidation. (*Please note use of last year's vocabulary words as per course instructions—an element of this assignment I would like to protest as juvenile. Words are marked by *v.w.) My apprehension comes not from what you might think—meeting a new teacher and new classmates. It stems from the fear of having to write this annual paper.

Why, oh why do you teachers force us to recount tales of our adventures over the summer months? Every year? Year after year?

Maybe we've done nothing worth remarking. Maybe our summer has been an endless torment of babysitting, lawn mowing, and car washing that we'd rather not relive. Maybe our parents lost their jobs and we couldn't afford to do anything. Maybe the very fact that our exploits, in comparison to those of our peers, have been dull and meaningless will force one of us to break, to stand up and say: "I can't take it anymore and I'm not going to do the assignment." Maybe what happened on our summer vacations was so emotionally-charged that we couldn't possibly do it justice with the printed word. Maybe to attempt to do so will drive one of us to emotional collapse.

I wonder, Ms. Krugman, what you did on your summer vacation. I think it would demonstrate a unique approach to teaching that would really get us excited about school. What do you say? Care to turn the world on its ear?

I am imagining that you are giving me that withering stare for which you are so famous. I take your meaning. I am to quit procrastinating and get on with sharing the foibles (*v.w.) of my family. Here I go…

### The All-New Adventures of the
### Family Simone
### 1977

Let me introduce you to my immediate family. There are four of us. My parents, Denham and Celeste, are two later-day hippies, at least Celeste is, which is why I'm stuck with being called Angel and my sister is named Harmony. If you knew either of us, you'd get the irony.

This summer began as per usual.

We got our report cards at the end of June. I did well, four A's, the rest were B's. Harmony got D's. In everything. How is that possible? Did she bother to do any work at all?

Denham wasn't very happy, but Celeste insisted that we all grow at different rates and we shouldn't judge Harmony harshly. She was simply marching to the beat of her own drummer. A very slow drummer, apparently.

I shake my head in stupefaction (*v.w.).

Anyway… the summer.

We started off July by indulging in a little anarchy. We completely ignore Dominion Day. Celeste says it's a day that commemorates white oppression of Canada's aboriginal peoples so she refuses to participate. The idea itself is cool. It's the execution that is sometimes lacking.

Although I had figured after last year's fiasco (*v.w.), which I won't detail here, Celeste would finally let go of her notions about colonialism, I was wrong. This year, fortunately, she was happy to have us visit the local friendship centre on Wellington. It seemed simple enough. The women at the centre politely answered our questions about Mohawk history and traditions. When Celeste started lecturing us about how "arrogant and cruel our forefathers were" (Yes, I am quoting.) that the staff started smirking. I could almost read their minds, "Stupid, white person."

I'm not saying she was inaccurate. But going on like some over-the-top nut was embarrassing. I know I use that word too often, but with Celeste it's appropriate. Most things are embarrassing with her around.

She didn't stop at that either. She regaled us with horror stories of genocide right in front of the people whose families had been the victims of this government policy, showing no concern for their obvious discomfort. Even I had nightmares for a week.

That's how summer kicked off. Just once, I'd like to see some fireworks. Watch a concert on the Hill. Maybe eat a beaver tail.

However, that was not to be this summer.

Once we got through that part of our yearly tradition, we packed up the car and fled for the cottage—the same one we've been staying at for the past couple of years. Now that Denham has enough seniority with the federal government to allow him a ton of vacation, we get to stay for the whole summer.

So, the day after Dominion Day we went shopping for cottage supplies. As usual, Harmony wants a couple of new bathing suits and I try to squeeze into my old one from the previous summer or insist that I can get by with shorts and a T-shirt. Celeste is firm on this point. Shorts and tees are not to be worn swimming. They don't dry fast enough and they mildew. She swears this causes skin irritations or worse. She's never explained to me what "worse" could be although I have a great imagination and picture my skin becoming infested with microscopic parasites and turning green.

Her concern about mildewed skin is kind of funny because she isn't known for being terribly hygienic. I mean to say that she is personally clean, but our house is a disaster. "Organization destroys the creative mind," is a commonly heard Celeste-ism.

While we shopped for clothes, Harmony was as happy as a pig in you-know-what. She wanted new shorts and sun dresses.

Tiny tank tops in terrific tones. (Get the alliteration (*v.w.) there.) I hate shopping. I can never find anything that fits. Celeste says I should be happy I've "bloomed." That's really what she says. Bloomed. I think it's gross.

Then we hit Canadian Tire and loaded up on replacement water gear. I admit to liking this part of the excursion (*v.w.). Floating in a rubber raft on the lake with a cold drink is my idea of a good time. I used to try and read while I floated, but since losing my copy of The Drifters to the murky depths of Lake Herrington, reading has remained a land-based activity.

Because of the annual expenditure of the Celeste- and Harmony-led shopping expedition and the cost of the cottage, Denham decided that we had to cut back on other expenses. We didn't rent a trailer and we bought groceries before leaving the city where food is less expensive than in the village. To make matters worse, Harmony invited her friend, Brianna, to come to the cottage. So, for the two-hour trip, the three of us were squashed in the back of the car with about 500 pounds of food piled on top of us.

Harmony and I grumbled. Brianna was polite enough to stay quiet.

I could tell we were getting on Denham's nerves. From my vantage point in the rear, I could see his jaw clenching and unclenching faster and faster as our complaining continued. Celeste seemed blissfully unaware of the growing volume of our discontent. She read a magazine and chatted brightly while Denham drove, hands in a death grip around the steering wheel.

By the time we arrived at our destination, the ice cream and chocolate frosting on the cake had melted, leaving a nasty stain on the back seat and Brianna's jeans. It's still there—a memento of Denham's financial savvy. It'll cost $50 to have the seats cleaned and $15 for a new pair of pants for Brianna. Celeste figures we saved about $20 on food.

After we unloaded the car, Denham sulked down on the dock. While we swam, he kept company with a bottle of scotch and a plastic glass. He scowled when we sprayed him. I hoped he'd be happier the next morning. His petulance (*v.w.) could put a real damper on the festivities.

The cottage is really nice: rustic, but with all the amenities of home. There's a loft that has a large bedroom with its own half bathroom. The main floor is made up of an open living space of kitchen and living room. Two other bedrooms and a full bathroom take up the rest of the main floor. There's a second shower jerry-rigged outside for hosing off sand and dirt before coming inside. Smart idea, I think.

The loft is made for kids. It has four single beds and low shelves filled with ancient, dog-eared books. There is no television reception on Herrington Lake, but we spend most of our time out-of-doors coming inside only on rainy days to play board games and cards, or to read or nap. Our musical concerns are taken care of with my portable tape player and the battery-operated radio that comes with the cottage. We usually took one or the other with us when we went swimming or lounging.

Brianna and Harmony claimed the loft. I could have slept up there with them, but figured they'd drive me nuts. Plus they needed the extra room for their clothes. I brought books; they brought outfits. I don't know who they were trying to impress. We were in the middle of nowhere.

The one cool thing about Celeste was that she really gets into the spirit of things. Meaning that she thinks cottage-time is for relaxing and doing our own thing. We get up when we feel like it, sleep when we felt like it, and do as little work as humanly possible.

I arose early on our first morning there, and noticed Denham sitting in a lounge chair on the dock, his head tilted to the side at what looked like an uncomfortable angle. I crept toward him, not wanting to startle him or let him know I was there.

His clothes were damp with dew and goose bumps stood the hair on his arms into a dark halo over his skin. His mouth hung open, the air roaring in and out. The bottle of scotch was half empty. He had spent the night there.

What was I to do in this awkward situation? Wake him and

let him know that his drinking was scaring me? Or creep away and pretend nothing was unusual? It seemed wrong to let him continue to sit in the cool morning air, shivering in his sleep. I argued with myself and then shook him awake which he did with a start, grabbing his neck in pain.

He looked at me, his eyes not quite focused.

"Harrumph," I think I heard. "Must have fallen asleep."

He got up with difficulty rubbing his lower back and made his way into the cottage.

I looked at the bottle of scotch and back at his disappearing frame and knew that something was wrong. Surely, it couldn't be over the grumbling we had done in the car, could it?

Over the next two hours, everyone arose except Denham who we didn't see till mid-afternoon. When he finally joined us under the awning of the back porch, he was wearing sunglasses and sipping a glass of tomato juice. As usual, Celeste was unruffled.

Harmony and Brianna changed clothes for the third time that day and announced that they were going for a walk into the village for ice cream. Could they have some money?

"Money's in my wallet on the nightstand." Denham's voice was a croak. I noticed he had switched back to scotch. Maybe if he finished the bottle today things could return to normal tomorrow or the next day.

Celeste grabbed a towel and some paper. She was working on another poem for the book she had been working on for years. An Ode to the Clitoris (definitely not a vocabulary word) or some such thing.

I grabbed a book and followed her to the dock. No way was I staying with Denham.

"What's up with him?" I asked tipping my head in his direction.

She looked up from her chair with a slightly bewildered expression. "What do you mean, dear?"

"He slept out here last night."

"Oh, Goose. That's nothing. He's just relaxing. Getting away from his accounting head space."

She waved her hand as if to dispel (*v.w.) my misgivings.

Over the next couple of days, things stayed pretty much the same. Denham didn't speak unless he was spoken to, the girls tittered and changed outfits, I read, and Celeste wrote and went for long walks in the woods.

When his bottle was empty, Denham travelled into the village and bought more. Celeste asked him to get her a bottle of Bailey's for her evening coffee. He was the one to use it first thing in the morning.

"Don't you have to wait till noon?" I asked.

He kissed the top of my head. "Not anymore."

Something was definitely wrong, I didn't care what Celeste said. It was like he was sleepwalking and I wanted to shake him with all my strength to wake him up.

I was desperate and had no idea what to do. In absence of a better idea, I did what millions of people around the world do in such situations, I prayed. I did it everyday. I figured if there was a God, this would be a good opportunity for him/her to intervene (*v.w.). I wasn't sure how to go about it, we hadn't been formally introduced. In the end, I talked to the sky and hoped help would come.

It didn't. Maybe you have to be one of the flock for God to hear you.

Celeste must have figured I was upset about something because she got out a deck of tarot cards. "Come, let me tell you your fortune."

This was Celeste's latest kick. Fortune-telling. She insisted that she was empathic and with some practice would be able to overcome her conditioning that had led her—that leads all of us Euro-whatevers—away from our psychic paths.

She was convinced that everyone was born with these abilities, but that our Western, science-oriented culture forced us to disbelieve our own instincts. Over time, we stopped having intuitive moments. We no longer connected to the natural world.

It was an interesting premise. I'd love to be able to see into the future. I just didn't see how reading from a pack of cards was a measure of psychic ability. They were just cards.

Still, it was harmless enough and if it made her happy, I could oblige.

She had me shuffle so my aura would suffuse the deck. Again, I was sceptical. Then she told me to concentrate on one question that I wanted answered. Just one? That was tougher than trying to hold a straight face while she went through her oh-so-serious explanations of what she was doing.

I told her I was ready, hoping that something would come to me if she asked me to share my question. She spread the cards.

She explained that she was just learning and I tried to pay attention and take it seriously. It was hard to do because she had to look up the meanings of each card as she came to it.

While she flipped cards over and murmured their portents, she told me that she was looking into Wicca.

"Like witches?"

She smiled at her dim-witted and not-in-touch-with-her-natural-self daughter and explained paganism.

Celeste now worships trees, especially oaks and mistletoe, and let's not forget groves. Whatever they are.

It seems that her group of writer gals is keen to give this Wicca thing a try. I can't believe how they follow every whim of hers. Baaaaaa.

Over the years, Celeste has dabbled in most of the –isms you can think of. I say dabbled because, after a while, I got the idea that jumping from one –ism to the next was nothing more than Celeste just being Celeste. She sticks to nothing. She's one of those people who instantly fall in love with anything new and all we can do is hold on for dear life as she dives into one new escapade after another, insisting with each that she's "finally discovered her true path."

So now her true path is tarot and Wicca. I wonder how long it'll last and what Denham thinks of it. It must be like being in some sort of accountant hell.

I feel badly for him. He's not the dad I remember anymore. It's like I don't know him and he acts like he doesn't know me.

He used to be more fun and more understanding. Nerdy, in a friendly-rather-than-off-putting kind of way. He has played along gamely with Celeste's flights of fancy, but she's worn him out over the years. Between her new idea of the month and her really bad, unmarketable poetry, and her gaggle of girls, he's gotten tired. You can see it in his eyes and in the tightness around his mouth. Celeste doesn't notice or if she does, she gives a good impression of being obtuse (*v.w.)

Like with the drinking.

Anyway, back to the tarot deck.

As Celeste laid the cards in the Celtic cross position, I found my question. I wanted to know if I was going to be the next Barbara Walters.

She set the eight of staffs in my present position telling me that I was ready to achieve my goals. This sounded promising so I settled more comfortably into the chair.

She placed the king of chalices in position two indicating that love was about to enter my life though I couldn't imagine who this might be. There wasn't a single guy at school who was even a little interested in me, and the feeling was mutual. They were all brainless. Not that Harmony thought so. She'd already been asked out at least a dozen times although she was too young to be allowed to date.

The third card was the knight of swords, giving me direction to let go of whatever might be impeding my progress. I watched Celeste's expression as she read this to me, but saw no acknowledgement that she might see herself as the cross I carried.

The eight of vesicas—two intersecting circles—filled the fourth spot. The card of patience. Not one of my strongest traits I had to admit, but Celeste said it was telling me that I had to be patient with the creative process.

The card that represented my past was the maid of chalices. I grimaced when she told me that I was no longer the open, trusting soul I had been.

Then came my spiritual guide. The hermit.

"Great," I muttered.

"Shush. It's not a bad card. It just means that you need your space and must pick those around you with care."

Like two furry caterpillars, I felt my eyebrows creep up my forehead in surprise. I grabbed them and pulled them back into place. How did the card know? If only I had some choice in picking my family. Here was proof they were eating away at my soul. The cosmos had spoken. I tried not to laugh and Celeste looked annoyed.

"Go on," I said. "I'm listening."

The star card promised inner peace and a change in my future.

"Like the calm that follows a great storm," she said.

"A storm named Celeste?"

"Tsk. Pay attention."

I was intrigued. Just as I knew it was impossible, I also knew those cards could read me.

The next was the lovers, signifying a powerful energy about to enter my life. My hopes were represented by the ten of staffs—the responsibility card.

I groaned.

"Well, that answers that."

"What?" I asked.

"You consider responsibility to be a burden."

"Who doesn't?"

"Not everyone. Some of us like to learn from our lessons."

"Like you?" She had to be joking.

"What do you mean by that?"

"Geez. You're kidding." But she wasn't. Not at all. Celeste didn't see herself as odd or laughable. "Never mind. What's the last card?"

"Five of swords. Time to recover from wounds, let go of the past and end the struggle in your life."

There it was, my past, present, and future laid out in ten little cards. I wished I could trust their meanings as true portents, but I'd never tell Celeste that.

She looked at me with a sly grin. "Well, what do you think about that?"

"It's pretty interesting, I guess. When did you start reading?"

"Last week."

"I see and now you want to be a witch?" I sighed and excused myself to go for a swim. There were only three others for her to test this on. She'd get bored with it soon enough.

But still. It was amazing how the cards could tell about my life. Maybe my aura had entered them.

If they're right, I might be a reporter after all.

Wouldn't that be something?

The End

How could she have been anything else? She'd been born to record life. In the same way Aunt Harmony was born to dance. The two of them were destined for their vocations at birth.

My heart was in my mouth as I looked at the last diary entry in my hand. It was for 1978, Mother's final year of high school.

"Last year," I told Jane.

"How are you holding up?"

"Fine. But there's so much here."

"Too much?"

Maybe. It's a lot to take in." I considered my next words carefully, not wanting to offend or hurt Jane's feelings. "You know I loved Celeste, and I still do. It's just that, from Mother's perspective, Celeste was so incredibly thoughtless. Is that really how she was?"

"It's your mother's truth, obviously. How she felt about things."

"But was it like that? Denham's life was so sad and Celeste didn't seem to care."

I can't say what their relationship was like. Remember, I met her some years after your grandfather died. She's never been that way with me, but I know she's regretted things she's done. Keep in mind that she picked these pieces to tell you something. That's what's important."

"But what?"

"I can't figure that out for you."

"Damn it, damn it, damn it! Can't anything be black and white? Does every answer have to also ask a question?"

"Read. We'll talk more over dinner."

# CHAPTER TWENTY-TWO

**Journal entry: September 9, 1978**

The grinding bitterness of despair and disgust has left a twisted hole where my heart used to be. I have avoided writing, talking, even thinking over the past weeks, trying to make the knife edge of pain go away. But, as I try to fight the urge, my fingers find a pen, its ink finds paper, and words cascade from the space in my chest. There is no flow to this today, my thoughts are awkward, jumbled, cart wheeling about without order. There is so much to write about. I don't know if I have the capacity to document it honestly. My life has changed entirely and yet, even as I write these words, I cringe inside. So artificial and dramatic they sound. Sadly, it is the best I can manage and I absolutely must manage it so there is no forgetting, no softening of focus or rewriting of history.

This summer was to have been our last at the cottage, at least the last one we could rely upon to be shared by the four of us together. September would launch my final year in high school and this would likely be my last full summer at home before I would leave for Toronto and university, the alma mater of Simone women. As for the summers that would follow, who could tell where fate might take me?

With this knowledge, a mood of nostalgia surrounded us as we readied for our annual exodus, understanding that we were coming to the end of something known and approaching something strange and new.

Perhaps my imagination got the better of me for it seemed that during the first weeks at the old cottage we were gentler with each other as we fought against time passing too quickly instead of with each other.

I was astonished to find how little I knew myself. I'd chomped at the parental bit for the past few years, dying to get away to the anonymity of the big city, far from Celeste and the judgements my peers had about her and, because of those, of me. What I discovered instead was a growing anxiety, like I was ascending the high arc of a roller coaster with fear of the looming descent growing in my belly. I could, like Columbus, discover the earth wasn't flat, but I would have to brave the horizon to find it out. And that, I was learning, was a scary thing.

My last year at home.

Harmony was proving to be less annoying than usual. We frequently stayed up late chatting at the fire pit or, on particularly warm nights, swimming after our parents had gone to bed, laughing about everything and dipping into Denham's beer. We were finally becoming friends. Who'd have guessed?

Though Denham continued his slide into introspective alcoholism, we had learned to disregard it and him. It was too sad to think about. If I did, it tore me apart. I missed my old dad. He had become increasingly muted and had, without any fuss, ebbed into the background of our lives. He went to work, paid the bills, and continued to appear at such family activities as Christmas and birthdays and on the first Saturday in July to drive us to the cottage. We left a place for him at the table at mealtimes, a place he either occupied or didn't. Either option was of equal, limited consequence.

The biggest difference this summer was with Celeste who was particularly quiet. Uncharacteristically, even disturbingly, so. There were no off-beat religious activities. No rants about women's subjugation. No forced family outings.

For my part, once I settled into the knowledge that she wasn't about to explode, I was delighted with this development. For the first time ever, she was ignorable, and I jumped at the opportunity to do so.

It proved to be a mistake.

On Friday, August 2, as we were clearing the dinner dishes, Geneva arrived.

Geneva was the newest addition to Celeste's women's group. Recently, divorced, she'd moved to our neighbourhood only months before and, within weeks, became a fixture around our house. Attending weekly meetings was one thing, but it was soon unremarkable to find her sitting in the living room with a cocktail in hand when we returned home from school, or for her to join us for dinner on weekends.

Geneva isn't even her real name. She changed it from Susan, selecting something that would underscore her impartiality, her "non-judgemental nature." If you knew Geneva, you'd see the irony in this name choice. She is about as judgemental as you can get. I think she gets away with it because she's really funny. At least the other women in the group think so.

Me, she made uncomfortable. Her French cigarettes and bleached hair, her miniskirts and see-through shirts over black push-up bras were a sharp contrast to Celeste's denim skirts and embroidered peasant blouses.

Like a wolf honing in on the scent of some animal frailty, my ongoing single status was her favourite topic, and she smiled with wicked pleasure at my discomfort each time she would bring it up. Her knowing glances told me she considered my plain features to be the reason for my state, something she chose to highlight whenever Harmony's beauty and obvious appeal for the male half of our species was discussed, as it often was in my presence.

My sister is not only beautiful, she is a world-class flirt and can get guys to do almost anything for her.

"She's just discovering her femininity," Celeste says.

I suspect that most mothers wouldn't be too happy about their fifteen-year-old daughters exploring their budding sexuality, but I could be wrong.

Until Geneva came along, I'd never considered myself ugly. My looks were unremarkable, certainly, but that woman made me feel like I was absolutely repulsive. I was ill- at-ease whenever she was around, my conversation became stilted, my gait, lumbering. Oh! How I hated the sight of her.

Celeste, as in other times, remained unaware of my discomfort, and the hatefulness of her new friend toward me.

Harmony became my champion though and treated Geneva with open distain. The more spiteful her remarks, the more Geneva tried to win her over. I wished I could mimic my sister's approach, but I couldn't and so I suffered.

Geneva's arrival then on that Friday evening, was ill-timed and unwelcome, at least by me.

Celeste, however, was thrilled and ran to greet her friend as soon as we heard the crunch of car tires roll down the driveway.

Geneva leaped from her red Fiat Spider and flew into Celeste's open arms.

"Oh, Celeste! How I've missed you! Steve is such a bastard. I just couldn't get through this without you!"

Steve was Geneva's latest conquest. He was about a hundred years younger than she. Between tears and curses, I gathered that he had found another companion to support him.

Denham joined Harmony and me as we stood at the front door watching the scene before us. He rolled his eyes. I couldn't blame him. Whatever else was going on with him, I figured he didn't need the drama that was Geneva "rubbing his last nerve raw" as Gram would put it.

The women hugged and Celeste called Denham to get the bags from the car. Funny for two feminists to so easily revert to old gender roles when it suited them.

"Wonder how long she's staying?" I heard Denham mutter as he unloaded a massive red suitcase and matching make-up bag from the trunk.

Celeste told him to place it in my room, and announced that I'd have to move in with Harmony.

Denham gave me a look of what I hoped was sympathy. Either that or he was thinking about his next drink and I got in the way.

I gathered my things and moved them to the loft.

"Great," I growled to Harmony. "It looks like The Bitch is here for a while."

"I don't know why you let her bother you so much. You're a million times smarter than she is."

I grimaced.

"C'mon. Let's take off," Harmony urged, then banged down the wooden stairway, throwing a tea towel she'd been holding onto the kitchen counter. She tossed me the car keys and we raced passed Celeste and The Bitch, yelling that we were heading into the village to play some pool.

"I wonder if Celeste knew she was coming," I mused as I backed the car onto the dirt road that traveled the distance into town.

"She won't be here for long. Denham despises her."

"Lot he'll do. He's barely conscious most of the time."

"He still pays the bills, sister-o-mine. Don't let his demeanour fool you into thinking he's already dead."

"Might as well be."

How I hate myself for saying those words about him. Honest, decent Denham.

The next day, the women chattered and drank wine and Geneva smoked her smelly cigarettes. I heard the name Steve mentioned more than once. Geneva cried or laughed hysterically, depending upon her mood that shifted like the wind.

Harmony and I stayed out of their way while Denham paid a visit to one of the local taverns to steer clear of the "weenie roast," Geneva's term for getting a guy out of her system. Denham called it man-bashing. Whichever it was, I wanted no part of it, and although, I suspect, Harmony would have loved to eavesdrop, she stayed with me roasting marshmallows instead of men, and listening to scratchy music pouring from the battery-powered radio.

When we figured it was late enough, we tiptoed into the house, hoping to pass unnoticed. Denham was passed out on the couch and we could hear whispering coming from Geneva's room. It appeared we were safe.

We were mistaken.

Later that night, I heard a deep yelp, then Celeste's voice. I looked over at Harmony. The moonlight caught her still-sleeping face. I threw off my sheet and ran down the stairs.

What a scene awaited me.

Denham was weaving, standing in his underwear outside what had been my bedroom door. In the low lamp light, I saw a picture that will remain with me forever: Celeste in bed with Geneva, completely, undeniably naked. Celeste's heavy breasts drooped to the side as she rose from the bed. Geneva's were equally bare, but small and firm, her nipples erect.

"Denham, really. You're being silly." Apparently, Celeste feels that everyone except she and her friends over-react. "Geneva's upset. She's needs comfort. Don't be so conventional."

Denham was blinking rapidly, and rubbing his face, possibly trying to wake himself from a bad dream. I could tell he was smashed. He must have woken from the couch and gone looking for Celeste when he found their bed empty.

You had to hand it to Celeste for her aplomb. Her husband had just found her in bed with her best friend, and she was as cool as could be.

"Let me make some herbal tea. It'll make us all feel better." Celeste rose from the bed and put on her robe. No one had taken the slightest notice of me till now.

She ruffled my hair as she breezed by. "Did we wake you, pumpkin?"

My answer got caught up in my throat. All I could do was squeak in response.

How does one handle a situation like this? Denham and I chose the easy way out. We returned to our beds. I didn't sleep. Given his blood-alcohol content, he may have fared better.

When he awoke, later that morning, Denham packed his bag. Ever the sensible person, he asked Geneva for her keys to leave us the larger car. We'd never all fit into a sports model for the ride home.

I suppose there was some comedy in that, albeit black. If I weren't so closely involved I might have been able to find some amusement in dear Denham finally taking a stand in full control of himself. No tantrums or outbursts of rage. Accountants are so practical. Poor Denham.

"Don't leave us here." I couldn't stand the thought of staying behind.

He patted my head and said, "Sorry, honey. I need some space."

He drove off, leaving Harmony and me with Celeste and Geneva.

"Dad!" I ran after him. But it was too late. He wouldn't respond to that name anymore.

Celeste and The Bitch were dressed and making coffee when I returned inside. I passed them without comment and strode to the loft to wake Harmony. We were still talking about what to do when the Sûreté du Québec arrived.

Denham… Dad was dead.

He'd been driving too fast and had lost control on one of the many hairpin turns along the road home. An open bottle of booze was still clamped between his legs when the police found him, his head bashed in from the impact with the steering wheel when the car flew over an embankment. A local had seen the car take flight and called the police. The Spider's engine was still warm when they got there.

Celeste burst into tears, pushing me over the edge. I marched over to her and smacked her face just as hard as I could. I heard a crack as her neck snapped to the side and, for a second, was afraid I'd broken her spine. When she looked at me, the imprint of my hand clearly outlined on her cheek, all she could do was to sputter in disbelief. We stared each other down until she opened her mouth to speak. I started to scream.

"It wasn't enough to make him miserable. You had to kill him. Is widowhood your next big experiment? I hate you. I hate you. You're a selfish, pathetic fraud and I hate you."

I don't remember what came next. Harmony said that I pushed Geneva aside and ran out to the lake. When she caught up to me I was in the canoe untying it from the dock.

"Wait," she yelled. "Just wait there. I'm coming with you."

She ran back to the house, re-emerging many minutes later with two backpacks, sleeping bags, and a lantern which she threw into the canoe before taking her spot in the front.

"Where to?" She was panting, a sheen of sweat glistened on her face.

"Anywhere but here."

We swung out into the lake, paddling hard in a hurry to get out of sight of Mother and her lover. Her lover. Jesus. That, I do remember.

The lake wasn't huge, but large enough that it would be hard for them to find us, if they bothered to try. As the sun began to ease from its apex, we found an uninhabited spot on a small island and made for land.

Throwing ourselves onto the spongy floor of the pine forest, we remained silent as our breathing calmed.

"What are we going to do without Dad?" In death, he finally got the name he wanted. It was awkward to roll it off my tongue, but he'd never be Denham to me again. Nor would I ever refer to Celeste as anything other than Mother. She would get nothing she wanted from me ever again.

Harmony was oddly collected. "You will finish high school, go to university, get a great job as a journalist, and forget about today. Push it far from your mind and get on with building the life you want. I've got my plans. This time next year, we'll both be out of that house."

"Both of us? What are you doing?"

"School is a total waste of time for me. I know what I want to do. I've always known. As soon as I'm sixteen, I'm heading to Montreal. I'm going to be a dancer."

"But you're too young to leave home." I burst into tears. Everything was happening too fast.

"Don't worry about me. I know just exactly what I'm going to do."

"Who are you?"

Harmony didn't answer at first. She opened the first backpack and emptied the contents. Thermoses of water, four bottles of beer and a quart of orange juice, a loaf of bread, a jar of peanut butter, two bags of chips, a block of Cheddar cheese and crackers, a bottle opener, a sharp knife, a butter knife, a flashlight and matches.

"I'm not the ditz you think I am."

"What's in the other bag?"

"Warm clothes for overnight, two tarps, toilet paper and the folding hatchet."

"What? No pillows?"

We laughed. It was a joyless sound born of loss, but it had notes of the desire to survive as well. It was then I knew we'd get beyond the tragedy of that day.

Harmony had come to my rescue once again.

We stayed away overnight, and built a fire near the shore where we slept in the sleeping bags wrapped in tarps to stay dry in the heavy evening dew.

When we returned the next day, Geneva was gone. Mother had driven her back to Ottawa then returned to the cottage to wait for us. Harmony and I packed our things and travelled home without a word. We went through the requisite motions of the standard Catholic funeral that had been arranged by Gram and Gramps, and shunned Mother in a way, I imagine, that only daughters can.

For her part, Mother moved around the house without speaking, the dark circles under her eyes told of sleepless nights and a troubled conscience. She had even disbanded her group or maybe the group had abandoned her. She deserved it. I was bothered by not telling Gram and Gramps the truth. They ought to have known how and why their son died. He wasn't just a guy with a drinking problem. He was a worn-out, unhappy man who had given up and had a wife who didn't want to acknowledge his pain. Convenient, since she was the cause of it.

The three of us pretended Mother and Geneva had never happened. Predictably, that bit of make-believe was shattered the first day we returned to school.

Geneva, it appeared, hadn't been as quick to get over Mother as Mother had been to get over her. Two rejections in forty-eight hours were more than she had been able to tolerate. She'd told members of the women's group about the affair, who were overheard gossiping by their children, who took the juicy information about the first two lesbians they'd ever heard about to school.

On the first day back, there were the snickers as I walked down the hall.

On the second day, DYKE was painted on my locker and the whispers I heard as I walked the halls became not-so-whispered.

By the third day, a wanna-be cheerleader had been persuaded by the team captain to ask me out in front of the squad. Such hilarity.

Fortunately for Harmony, she hasn't been teased as badly as I. It seems she's too pretty to be anything other than heterosexual—at least that's what the boys want to believe. Cretins.

So, I grit my teeth, knowing this can't last forever. The razzing has already died down a bit and it's only been a week. Who knows, by mid-terms, they might have forgotten about my mother altogether.

In any event, I have only the year to get through. That's not so bad. Anyone can handle one crappy year. Right? It's not like I don't have practice dealing with kids who think I'm weird. Still, it's going to be a tough couple of semesters.

I wish I was more like Harmony. Whoever would have guessed I'd ever say that? She doesn't care one iota about what anyone thinks and, therefore, has the entire student body begging for her attention.

The countdown for Toronto has begun.

Angel

P.S. If there are any cosmic forces at work, please tell Dad I love him and miss him, that I wish I'd been a better daughter. I wish I had paid more attention to him. Please tell him I'm sorry. And that I'm keeping his watch. I hope that's okay. ♥

I finished the last page and tears streamed down my face. The man's watch she had worn forever had been her father's. She never mentioned it and I never asked. To me, it had been part of her. Over the years, the leather strap had been replaced as needed, new leather softening with use then wearing out. I had thought nothing of it. One year, I purchased a new watch for her birthday, thinking it was time to retire the old one. She may have worn it once before returning to her favourite. Now I knew why.

I thought of Mother and all her anger, all that resentment that had gathered and grown year after year. I'd never understood it till now.

I could even understand—though I didn't like it—what Jane represented to her and why Mother treated her so coldly.

But something still rankled. Why had she turned her hatred on me? I could understand her anger toward Gran, but why me? What had I ever done?

Jane pulled to the side of the road, turned off the engine, and hugged me as tightly as she could in the cramped confines of her little car.

I sobbed uncontrollably without fully understanding why. After some minutes, my tears abated and I searched for tissue in the glove box to blow my over-stuffed nose.

"I feel so badly for her. To lose her father like that… But she and Aunt Harmony were so close, and now Mother hates her. She seems to hate me too. Why? Do you know?"

"She doesn't hate Harmony and she doesn't hate you. Never. You're her child. She loves you."

"Really? Because it sure as hell doesn't feel like it."

"Talk to her. You know so much more now. Use it to build a bridge."

Could I? I didn't know where to begin. "Can we go home now? I need to be alone for a bit."

Jane zipped south to the highway and we pulled into the driveway less than two hour later. I hugged her again, then fled to the backyard, and beyond to the water's edge where I sat thinking and re-reading random passages from Mother's pages until a cold wind forced me indoors.

Jane was watching television; she'd been doing a lot of that lately. I guess she needed something to occupy her mind too.

As I had before, I curled up next to her and fell asleep with my head on her lap.

# CHAPTER TWENTY-THREE

"How was your flight?" It was Saturday and, as promised, Mother had arrived to help with anything that needed doing.

"It was fine. I hope the delay didn't put you out."

"I barely noticed. I had a book to read," I lied. It had been impossible to focus while I waited for the flight to arrive and for her to deplane. As was often the case, the flight had been held-up on the runway in Ottawa and arrived twenty minutes behind schedule.

While we waited for her luggage, I was on edge, wanting to blurt out my newly discovered information.

"I know you," I wanted to say. "We can be friends now." Instead, we stepped gingerly around each other, trying, maybe for the first time, to avoid an argument. There were so many topics that could start one.

But it's different now. Surely she could she see in my eyes my change in attitude. That I knew of her life and if she could just tell me why she disliked me so, I'd listen and somehow it would be all right, and we'd be fine together. I now knew there would be a reason. A good reason. Something that had nothing to do with me being unlovable. A reason that would give me some hope that happiness could be a part of my future.

I'd played this meeting over and over in my head.

In my imagined scenario, I had given her a hug when I said hello and she had been pleased at my affection. She had held me in front of her, her hands gripping my shoulders as she scrutinized my imperfect face to see what change had taken over me. She smiled, laughed even. Her joy, like the ripple of chimes.

Then I'd tell her what Gran had left me and why she'd left it. I'd be speaking very quickly so she wouldn't be able to interrupt and her mouth would have dropped open in disbelief, happy disbelief, that her mother had done such a brave and generous thing to make amends for a difficult past.

Then we'd race to get back to the house to see Jane, and we'd call Aunt

Harmony over and they would become part of this major reconciliation.

Only nothing was turning out the way I'd planned. Rather than tears of joy, the only thing showing on her face was the strain of a stilted and polite exchange.

My shoulders drooped and I slipped my sunglasses over my eyes so she couldn't see the disappointment there.

During the trip to Jane's, she fiddled with the radio and wrote notes in her agenda book.

"You should get a smart phone."

She snorted. "This is just fine."

Mother considered the purchase of a cellular phone to be her biggest concession to the twenty-first century. Like Aunt Harmony, Mother didn't like knowing that people could reach her anywhere. "There are no boundaries anymore," she was known to lament. But her work often required that interviews be conducted from a distance, or that sources be able to contact her around the clock. A cell phone was an evil necessity. That was as far as she was willing to go; her paper agenda was quite acceptable.

The balance of our trip was made in silence. I heard her sigh and saw her square her shoulders as we turned into the driveway.

She was expecting a confrontation. My eyes shot heavenward. Please not today.

And then Aunt Harmony pulled in behind us.

"Did you know she was coming?" Mother glared at me.

I shook my head then looked toward the house in time to see Jane coming down the front walk.

"Hello," she called out as though we were long-lost friends rather than the dysfunctional relations we were. "I'm so glad you've arrived together. Lunch is ready."

She took Aunt Harmony by the arm and waved Mother and me inside. "Would you look at this weather. Isn't it a wonderful day?"

She's finally cracked, I thought. Finally cracked. The challenge of having to deal with us so frequently in the past two months had proven more than her faculties could bear.

The aroma of Jane's barbequed ribs met us at the door and hunger goaded previously reluctant feet to hurry and lazy hands to throw luggage aside so we could dive into the marvellous meal.

But my Jane was a devious thing. Far from falling over her mental edge, she knew just what she was doing. The grin she flashed and sly wink told me so. No one spoke, we were too busy smacking our lips and groaning in pleasure. Our faces and fingers were coated in Jane's special sauce in seconds.

Only when Jane began to talk, did I grasp her plan. With our mouths full, she'd have the floor. Crafty, crafty woman.

"While you've been away, I've made a few decisions," she announced, her gaze lighting on each of us in turn.

I was here. You didn't tell me anything. I wanted to run from her betrayal. I didn't want to hear whatever she had to say. I knew I wouldn't like it. Was she about to send me away?

Mother's back straightened and she swiped at the sauce around her mouth with her napkin. Aunt Harmony's eyes met mine. I had nothing for her.

"There has been a cloud hanging over all of us for far too long. Out of respect for Celeste's wishes, I have remained silent, knowing she wanted to fix things with you. But she left before she could complete her task so it's up to me to do what I think is best."

The tick-tocking of the clock on the wall behind me grew louder; a fly buzzed past.

"I want the bitterness to end." Her voice faltered ever so slightly. She inhaled to steady her course. "I want you to decide what to do with Celeste's belongings."

Mother rose to wash her hands at the kitchen sink. "Mother left a will?"

"She did."

"Then what is there to sort out? It's already been done."

"Your mother left everything to me so whatever I decide to do is what will be done. My wish is for the three of you to work this out among you. I don't want to be on the receiving end of your resentment anymore."

"What about you? It's all yours. It should be." I was worried. What if Mother decided Jane should have nothing? Could she do that? Did she have that much spite in her?

"I am fine. I have my own job, savings, a pension when I retire. I have family. I will be just fine as long as things are sorted out in a way that you agree is fair." She retrieved some papers from a drawer. "Here is everything you need. Information about Celeste's investments, an updated appraisal of the house. Half of that, of course, is mine. There's some property that your father's family left him and a copy of Celeste's will, if you want to see that."

Mother grabbed the latter from the stack of papers now laying on the table between an almost-empty platter of meat and half-filled bowl of potato salad and scanned the pages. Her hand trembled and I saw that she wasn't really reading. She just needed a moment to absorb the meaning of Jane's decree. When she finished her cursory review, she flipped the pages back to the pile, a blue-tabbed corner landing in a pool of barbeque sauce.

"This is ridiculous. I've three days off work and came solely to help sort through any items you might want to get rid of. I'm not interested in having a family debate."

"Then don't have one. But you will decide. All of you together. There will be no more bad feelings because someone feels unfairly treated. My future, our futures, as they say, are in your hands."

Jane left the room, then popped her head around the corner. "I'm heading to see my family tonight. I'll be back in 24 hours. I hope you've got a plan of action in place by then."

I followed her to the door and kissed her goodbye. She picked up an overnight bag from the front closet.

"Why didn't you tell me what you were planning?"

"That wouldn't have been fair, would it? How could I ask you to keep a secret that I had failed to keep?" She patted my shoulder and left.

"Well," Mother looked at us. "What are we going to do?"`

"You're the brains," Aunt Harmony huffed. "Why don't you tell us?"

I held my palms up between them. "Let's not get this off on the wrong foot, okay? Maybe this is a good thing, you know? Making us act like adults."

Mother sighed. "Let's get the dishes washed. Maybe then we can have a look at this stuff and figure out where to go from there."

"You go ahead," Aunt Harmony intoned. "I'm going outside for a smoke."

The spray of water and clink of dishes were the only sounds as we cleared the mess from the room. As I dried the last dish, Mother turned to me. "This is because of me, isn't it? She thinks I can't stand her, doesn't she? That I'd cause a fuss over money?" Her chin quivered as she held back her tears. "I'm not like that. I'd never fight over something like that."

"Quite the opposite. She understands. Really, she does. Actually, I've been wanting to tell you—" I froze, unable to say the words that were caught within me, afraid that once spoken a course of action would be launched that I wouldn't be able to un-launch.

Aunt Harmony returned, looking at me quizzically. "Did I interrupt something?"

"Nothing important." I twisted away from her, thankful for the excuse to avoid what I'd been dying to talk about. I bumped my hip on the table. Divine retribution.

"Let's have a look at this stuff," Mother said, waving at the papers Jane had left us. "I can't think where else to begin."

Aunt Harmony rolled her eyes. "I can think of better ways to spend my time."

"She must have a reason for wanting us to do this together." Walking on eggshells made me tense.

"Like what?"

Mother moved between my aunt and me. "Does it matter? Maybe she doesn't want to deal with it all. I suppose we can do that much for her. Let's just get it done so we can go home."

We sat back at the table, each taking a document.

"Holy crap!" Aunt Harmony barked. "Did you know how much money our mother had? She was loaded. There's got to be over a million bucks here."

We leaned toward my aunt to read the document before her. It was a series of investment statements from a broker in the city.

"That represents a lot of death," Mother said.

"Life insurance policies, you mean?"

Mother nodded. "From her parents, Dad's parents and, of course, Dad."

"Still, I never thought she'd have all this."

We knew what Aunt Harmony meant. It would have been more in flighty Gran's character to have frittered the money away than to have invested it.

"Must have been Jane's influence," Aunt Harmony said.

"Looks like she's got a piece of land near Shelburne," Mother said. "It belonged to Gram and Gramps. I never knew they had it. You?"

Aunt Harmony shook her head. "This feels peculiar. Going through her finances like this. Like vultures."

"It does have that quality about it," Mother said.

Aunt Harmony threw the statements on the table. "Well. What are we going to do? There's half of this house, a stack of cash and ten acres of land on the South Shore."

"I think Jane should have it all," I ventured.

"Most of this is family money. Not money they earned together." Mother's lips were pinched as though she'd just bit into a lemon.

"What difference does that make? They were married. They were together for almost thirty years." Anger mixed with dread stirred in my chest.

"I know that, Kate," Mother said. "But even Jane knows that wouldn't be right. That's why she's giving it to us to divide."

"Really?" Sarcasm oozed into my voice. "And I thought it was because she didn't like you. Isn't that what you said?"

"Whoa, girls. Calm down," Aunt Harmony cautioned. "Let's not get carried away."

Mother examined the financials while I buried my face in photos of the ocean-front property. "This is really pretty. I wonder why they never built there."

"Hard to say since we never knew about it," Mother said.

"What if we just let Jane have the house and split the rest into thirds?" Aunt Harmony said.

"I'd like Kate to have the land. Mom would have wanted that."

"Then she would have put it in her will, but she didn't," Aunt Harmony snapped.

"There were lots of things she should have done, weren't there?" Mother jumped to her feet. "You of all people should know that. I can't believe you'd deny Katie something that should so obviously be kept in the family. If we divide it, it will have to be sold and then it's gone. None of us will ever be able to afford something like that again."

"Well, what about me? Why should I let it go?"

"What about you?" Mother's voice rose; her hands were clenched at her sides. "Yes, what about you? Dear Harmony. What about you? Let's worry about you. You who have never worried about another individual in your life. But by all means… LET'S FOCUS ON HOW THIS WILL AFFECT YOU!"

She threw the paper she'd been holding onto the table and fled to the bedroom we were once again sharing.

I watched my aunt's lips twitch, the veins at her temples bulge. She ran to the bottom of the stairs and yelled at my mother. "Just because I've done what I've wanted doesn't make me a bad person. You can go to hell."

She marched back to the kitchen and threw herself onto a chair.

"This is great. Just great," I said. "There's more to share than any of us would have thought and we're still fighting. I don't want the land. I don't care what we do with any of it. I just want us to stop this stupidity. God! I am so sick of it. You're both exhausting. No wonder Jane left."

"Kid, you have no idea what you're talking about."

"Actually, I do. Jane showed me some old stories my mother wrote and I do know what went on."

"Old stories?" Aunt Harmony turned pale. "What old stories? Where are they? When did she write them?"

I watched my aunt's odd behaviour with curiosity. "They were written almost every year till the end of high school. Why? What's the matter?"

Colour returned to her face and she regained her sense of nonchalance. "Nothing's wrong. I'd just like to see them, that's all."

"Well, they're in the bedroom, and I haven't even told Mother about them so I'd appreciate it if you'd stay quiet."

"I've had enough of this for one day anyway. I'm going out for a while. I'll see you in the morning."

"But you are coming back, right?"

She grinned and walked out the door.

# CHAPTER TWENTY-FOUR

Mother and I sat on the porch drinking coffee. Autumn was beaconing from around the corner and we could feel the early signs of the weather ahead.

I shivered, wishing I'd worn a jacket.

"Wait till the sun comes out. It'll be warm then."

I nodded and blew the steam from my mug.

Mother seemed relaxed as she rocked on the old Shaker rocker, sipping her coffee and staring out to the water. Seagulls called to each other and bobbed on the waves. In the distance, a loon called for its mate.

We sat quietly, mother watching the ocean, me watching my mother. It would have been enjoyable if I could have shut off the voices in my head telling me to talk to her, to tell her about her old stories.

I shouldn't have felt as frightened as I did and admonished myself for my foolishness. Yet my self-scolding advanced me no further. I played a dialogue to myself about how I'd begin.

Mother. Mom, Jane gave me... No, that wouldn't do. She'd get angry with Jane.

Mom, I came across some stories of yours from when you where young and I read them. Don't be angry. They were wonderful …

Even in my imagination, I faltered under what was sure to be her icy glare. I tried to go on.

They're wonderful, Mom. They made me realize so much about you that I never knew before, and I think I can understand why you've been so distant…

But then, I'd envision her anger. Distant? What do you mean, distant? You've been the one who's turned away.

It was no use. I'd never find the courage or the words to tell her. The epiphany I'd had was to be mine alone. So sad, really. It was meant to be shared, and I could feel it tug at me, wanting to be let out.

"When's Jane coming back?" Mother asked, her gaze still on the horizon.

"After supper, I think."

"I want you to have that land. It's worth a fortune now and will give you some security. It shouldn't go to strangers."

"Jane isn't a stranger."

She closed her eyes and breathed deeply to control herself before responding. When she did her voice was sharp. "I am aware she isn't a stranger. But she didn't buy that property either. My grandparents did. It isn't hers, it's yours."

"Why mine? Why not keep it yourself if it means that much to you?"

"Because I'm practical. Harmony won't ever have kids so it'll go to you eventually anyway. Might as well save paying the taxes for two transfers and do it once instead."

"I'm not comfortable taking anything from Jane. Thirty years is a long time to be with someone."

"Tell me about it," she responded. Her voice was thick with emotion and I knew she was thinking back to sometime in her past.

Silence returned and I shivered.

"Oh, for heaven's sake, get a coat on."

I bit my lip to stop the retort that was waiting there, and did as I was told, returning with the coffee pot to refill her cup.

Aunt Harmony joined us then, holding her own mug out for me to fill.

"Should we get started?" Mother asked.

"Give me time to wake up first. Take a shower."

"Hurry up then. We've got to have this done before Jane gets back. I don't want her to be involved."

"Yesterday, you didn't want to do this at all," I pointed out.

"I've changed my mind. There is too much here that came from Dad and I don't think it would be right for it to go to her."

I sighed. So many years and so much pain. How could divvying the proceeds of a death make amends? This was going to be one heck of a day. What had Jane thought she'd been masterminding? I couldn't see any good come from it and worried that we'd end up with an even bigger rift than had existed till now.

I went indoors to make another pot of coffee although more caffeine was likely the last thing we needed today. While we waited for my aunt, a sense of foreboding filled me and I shivered again though, this time, it wasn't from the cold.

Sitting at the table, I folded my arms in front of me and laid my head upon them. I closed my eyes and must have dozed off because I was startled by the sound of voices and someone scraping the legs of a chair away from the table.

"So," Mother began, taking her place at the head of the table. "How are we going to do this? It seems we all want something different."

"I don't want Jane to be hurt," I said.

"I want things to be equal," my aunt said.

"What's equal?" Mother asked.

"The same dollar value for each of us."

"Fine. I want Kate to have the land. I don't care about anything else. You can have my share of the money instead."

"How generous you are," Aunt Harmony hissed. "That land's probably worth a million and you want me to settle for a quarter of that from you?"

"You'll get your quarter plus mine. That's half a million. Jane can have the house, some of the money and Kate will get the land and her share of the investments. How is that not fair?"

"Because I need it the most. You have a house. What do I have? A bum knee and a lifetime of teaching brats how to dance."

"You've made your own choices in life. If you don't like them, well, you have no one to blame but yourself, do you?"

I wanted to throw up.

"It wasn't my choice to get injured. What if it was you? How would you feel?"

"Like life sucks. But that isn't the point."

"No? Then what is?"

Mother rubbed her temples then leaned close to her sister and dropped her voice to a whisper. "This is for Dad. He wouldn't have wanted the land to be divided."

"Dad's dead. He's never going to know what happened with it."

"Harmony. Look at me. You know what she did to him." Mother's voice was pleading. Her eyes darted to me then back to my aunt. "He worked so hard and got so little."

"That's water under the bridge. You've got to let it go already."

"I can't." Mother's eyes shone from the tears she was holding back.

I wanted to reach out to her, but couldn't. My heart was torn. I knew she was wrong about Jane, but knew too that Jane symbolized the event that had taken her father's life. Under her veneer of cool authority, Mother was just another hurt little kid who had never gotten over her father's death. If only we'd been closer. Maybe that would have allowed me to hug her and let her know everything would work out.

But we weren't. It came down to this: I had no idea how to give her comfort. She had spurned me for so long, I didn't have what it would take to love her, to put her concerns before my own, to know what she needed.

It wasn't my fault. She hurt me first.

"It was so long ago, Angel. He's not in heaven watching over us. He's part of the soil."

"Then let it go. If you don't care about it, let Kate have it."

"No."

"No? Just like that? No?" My mother shook with anger. She held her body rigid, her teeth clenched. Her lips were white and pulled tightly against her teeth. "Who are you to say 'no' to me? After everything I've done for you? Everything I gave up?" Her fist hit the table. "You don't have the right to say 'no'."

Aunt Harmony's eyes grew wide. She was afraid of something, but wasn't about to give up. "I am the other kid. Remember me? The one you and Denham ignored? That's who I am to say 'no'."

I stood and backed away from them till I collided with the pantry door. They seemed to have forgotten me.

"Ignored you? That's rich. You got your own way in everything. When did you ever care about us?"

"It doesn't matter anymore. Our parents are dead. Both of them and I'm going to get what's coming to me. I count for something too."

"You count for very little. After what you did. You would have abandoned her if it wasn't for me. I took care of her. I loved her and I lost my husband over it. And you. What did you ever do to deserve anything at all!"

"I was a kid."

"You were twenty-three. Not exactly a child."

"What was I supposed to do?"

"Be responsible. Take care of your own responsibilities."

What are they saying? My mind slowed until their voices turned into meaningless garble. I couldn't think. Couldn't think.

Think.

What you did.

Abandoned her?

Lost my husband.

Take care of your responsibilities.

194

"Stop!" I yelled, holding my hands out in front of me to ward off more words. "Right now. Stop."

When they swung their heads to face me, they looked like crazed animals. I blinked and saw fear replace their fury.

"What are you saying?" I demanded. "My father left when I was two months old. That's what you said. Who did you take care of?"

Mother was on her feet, caught between Aunt Harmony and me. She looked desperately from one to the other of us.

"You can't…" Aunt Harmony said.

"Mother, what is it?" And then I knew. "Oh, my god." My hand flew to my mouth trying to grab the thought before it could crystallize and become real. "Oh, my god. No way. Mother?"

Her eyes met mine and I saw my anguish reflected there. "It's not what you think, Kate." She looked back to Aunt Harmony. I heard her whisper "I'm sorry."

My knees began to shake, a tremor at first and then more violently. I slid to the floor. It was easier than standing. Mother's face had gone white. She dropped to her knees and crawled toward me. Grabbing my hands in hers, she held them to her chest. "Look at me."

I tugged at my hands, but she held them tight. "After Harmony went to New York, she met a man and got pregnant. What was she going to do? She was so young. Making her way as a dancer. Living in a hovel. How could she raise a child?" My mother's eyes beseeched me to understand. "We agreed that I would raise you and agreed you would never know."

Aunt Harmony, who had jumped to her feet, now slumped back to her chair. She covered her face. She may have been crying, I couldn't tell. My head was pounding, and my mother and aunt had became blurry.

"Listen to me," Mother demanded. Her words blunt and urgent, poured forth over her clenched jaw, trying to drown the fire that rose in me and blistered my cheeks. "Harmony called as soon as she knew. She was already four months along. I wanted you and I swear I loved you from the first day I saw you. Nothing else mattered to me as much as you from that first introduction. When my husband told me he didn't want to be a father, I chose you. He hung around for a couple of months and then he left. You were wanted. I wanted you."

She dropped my hands and cupped my face, forcing me to look at her. "I never thought you'd find out, especially like this. I'm so sorry."

Although it would be an overstatement to say the room went dark, for all I remember of what came next, it might just as well have. I have tried to recreate the day since then, but have failed. I recall that I crawled to the couch and listened to Mother and Aunt Harmony arguing until their voices became nothing more than white noise. Perhaps that is all it had ever been. Eventually, they became quiet and some time after that, Aunt Harmony left the house.

It wasn't until the next day that I discovered what they had decided about me, about the will, about Jane.

On that day, I knew nothing. It didn't matter. Nothing mattered.

# CHAPTER TWENTY-FIVE

The November wind whipped around us as we walked along the rugged beach at Rose Bay. Waves crashed against the shoreline shining, glinting in the autumn sun.

We hadn't seen each other in nearly four months, my mother and me, and we strolled over the hard-packed sand like two acquaintances, tentative and polite, wanting so badly to get to a place of comfort without knowing how.

We were dressed warmly. Although the day was mild for early January, a stiff breeze blew in from the Atlantic cutting through our winter coats. In minutes, my face felt raw, my fingers like ice.

We were there for a purpose. Two, actually. To reconnect, and so she could see the acreage her grandparents had purchased. After months of probate, Gran's will was settled and, as Mother wanted, I now owned the family land.

In the end, she and Aunt Harmony had managed to settle things. Everyone was taken care of financially, and because they'd had to come to mutual accommodation, they'd been able to, if not dissolve, at least lessen old hurts. Jane had been right to handle it as she had.

Mother had even begun to resolve her issues with Jane. It happened so much easier than I had ever dreamed it might. Once the thorny secret of my parentage was out, the walls between and among us crumbled. Oh, there was still rubble to be cleared, but there were no skeletons worth hiding anymore.

"It's really beautiful, isn't it?" Mother asked. Her blonde curls blew into her face as she turned toward me. It was the first time she'd been here. I wondered if she sensed her father walking along with us.

"I love it."

We left the beach for the warmth of Mother's car and travelled along the narrow dirt road that rounded the bay and would take us to my new property.

"I've decided to build here." I spoke to her profile noticing the fine lines that arched from her eyes to the corners of her mouth when she spoke or smiled as she did now.

"I'm glad. It's good to have a home. Something that's yours."

Silence descended upon us once more until we arrived at an overgrown driveway that had been put in place by my grandfather or his parents. I didn't know which.

"It's here." I motioned to the right side of the road where we stopped and got out.

We had to climb over a fallen tree, knocked down in some long-forgotten storm, and make our way through weeds and shrubs that, over nearly thirty years, had managed to grow through the thick gravel and stone of the driveway. I led my mother to the shore. If we looked to the right around the curve of the bay, we could see the beach we had just strolled along. With the trees at our backs, we looked out to open air beyond a boundary of ancient, rounded rocks that the waves rushed and tumbled over before spilling back to their ocean home.

"It's a beautiful spot," Mother repeated. Was she picturing her father standing where we now stood, gazing out to sea, and feeling the same sense of solace that I hoped she felt with me? It was too bad he'd never done anything with this land. Of course, his parents had outlived him. It could be that he'd not had time to make plans for the place.

"We'll never know," I said aloud.

Mother looked at me curiously.

I asked, "How did his parents find this place?"

She shook her head and turned to leave, but stopped instead and reached for my sleeve. "I'm sorry," she said, her eyes growing moist.

Unsure of my voice, I didn't speak.

"I didn't mean for you to find out that way."

Our eyes met. We both fought the urge to cry. My chin quivered and I clenched my lips together. Mother looked at the ground.

There were still unanswered questions that I longed to find the courage to ask. Could I? Could I?

"I love you," she said.

It was too much for me to hear; I burst into tears. Really crying. The snot-running, chest-heaving, can't-breathe kind of crying. I wailed the words that tumbled out between sobs. "Then why did you do what you did? Why did you ignore me? Treat me like I was a nuisance? Why didn't you ever make me feel like you wanted me?"

For the second time that day, she grabbed my arm. "What do you mean?"

My breathing calmed and I shook my head, fighting the heat of anger as it rose in me. "You aren't asking me that. You aren't."

"All I ever heard was Aunt Harmony this and Aunt Harmony that. It was like you knew." Her eyes were pleading, begging me to understand. "Like you knew she was your real mother. I was just the stand-in."

"She paid attention to me."

Mother shook her head. "No. There was a bond there. I could feel it and it didn't matter what I did, what I sacrificed or worked for. What I achieved."

"But I didn't care about any of that. How could I even know any of it? I just wanted you to be happy with me."

We stared at each other in disbelief. For so many years we'd completely misunderstood each other. Was it possible that nothing more profound than misperceptions and hurt feelings were what got us here?

She shifted her gaze away from me, staring at some distant spot on the horizon. "I loved you from the second I saw you. I know everyone says that about their child, but I've come to realize that they say it because it's true. It didn't matter to me that my husband left or that I had to work and raise a child on my own. It didn't matter because I had you. But you loved your aunt… your mother… so much more than me. I felt like I was only there to pick up the pieces of my messy family, like always." She paused. "That sounds so pathetic. I'm sorry. I'm so sorry."

She hid her face in her hands, breathing deeply. I was afraid for her though I couldn't say why.

"Mother." No, that's not right. "Mom. It wasn't like that. At least it wasn't like that for me. What I mean is that I never thought she was better." My lie floated, suspended in air. "Or at least, I didn't till she started to notice me. For those brief bits of time I had with her, she was so focused on me. She made me feel special. I thought she loved me. I thought you didn't. I never seemed to be able to be good enough for you."

And there it was. My truth. It was the first time I'd ever spoken it out loud, and I was terrified of it. I wanted to run away from my vulnerability, yet wanted so much for my mother to accept me, to reach for me and draw me in.

"I've messed things up so very badly." She walked toward the rocks and bent to pick up a stone that she hurled into the water.

Don't walk away from me. Don't stop talking to me. I flung my arms around myself, hugging my shoulders. Despair crept into my bones.

A blue-jay screamed overhead, pronouncing our solitude where we stood only yards, yet miles apart. The wind picked up and rustled the few dried birch leaves left on the trees. They mirrored the sound of water on the shore. The temperature was dropping though the sun had only begun its descent. Its weak rays weren't enough to heat the chill of a shaded forest floor. Cold seeped from the icy ground through my shoes to my feet, spreading beyond my legs and into my core. I was freezing yet unwilling to move, hoping that Mother would turn around and make everything better.

I wanted her reassurance so desperately, it hurt.

Suffering with waiting and the cold, I rubbed my arms and stuck my hands into my pockets, not sure how much longer I could tolerate standing there.

"Would you come over here?" She sounded tentative, her voice barely audible through the growing roar of wind and crash of sea.

I stepped beside her.

"Maybe we could start over?"

My chest expanded.

"It was me all along, wasn't it? Dragging my own childhood nonsense into our relationship? I can't believe the grief I've caused."

More tears caught in my throat. I could hardly bear the emotions threatening to burst through my chest. Cut it out. This is ridiculous. And then, thinking that being angry was easier.

Could I trust her?

Once again, I lost my words; they wouldn't form in my mouth. Emotions were such fickle entities. Here was the thing I'd wanted, thought I'd wanted, presented to me simply, but, as I was discovering, not-so-easily taken. Wasn't it what I wanted?

My mother didn't look at me, but continued to stare out to sea. She rocked back and forth on the soles of her feet, her hands tucked deeply into her pockets.

"I know I wasn't much fun. I never meant our lives to be like that. " Her pain hung in the air like the plaintive cry of notes plucked from a fiddle. "It crushed me that you would prefer her to me." She wiped tears that had fallen onto lips lined and dried from the wind, then folded her arms across her chest.

The spectre of our unresolved relationships with Harmony haunted us. I had spoken with my aunt, taking tentative first steps in forging a new relationship. After years of dreaming of her as my mother, now that I knew she was, I couldn't think of her as anything other than my aunt.

The mind is a strange place.

As I'd often done, I traced my mother's profile with my eyes, outlining her tangle of hair, the lined forehead, her long nose, and full lips. The faint, white scar along her chin, received in an ancient accident. Regal, she looked standing there with the wind whipping her skin. I could picture her as a Celtic warrior waiting for her next battle.

I saw too the sadness in the slope of her mouth and the softness that had begun to form under her jaw line. Age and hard work had left their marks on her.

In that second, I knew her. From the little girl who poured her life into words to the scarred adult who'd wanted so much for me. I felt proud of her and sorry too for the hurt I'd caused.

I slipped my icy hand into the folds of her arms and we stood there for a while, leaning against each other, the heat of her body warming mine. I felt a gentle tremor under my ribcage, the tightness in my bleak space shook itself loose, ever so slightly.

Mother stirred, hesitating from pulling away. Neither of us wanted to end the moment, frightened that our fragile accord would shatter with the gentlest shift. But the cold eventually forced us to move and we retraced our steps to the car, unspeaking.

As we tramped through the underbrush, I thought, as I had so many times in the past months, about the stories of my mother's that Gran had found and kept for me, little documentaries that allowed me to meet my mother in a way most children never can. I'd still not told her about them.

But that was okay.

We had time.

# ABOUT THE AUTHOR

COLLEEN GAREAU is the author of *My Mother's Summer Vacations* and *Sam(uel)*. She lives in Kingston, Ontario, Canada and has worked in public relations for 20 years. Colleen enjoys literary fiction, especially CanLit and the work of Southern authors. She periodically needs a nature-fix to keep her sane.

www.ingramcontent.com/pod-product-compliance
Lightning Source LLC
Chambersburg PA
CBHW060926120626
46557CB00003B/889